The ground shifted beneath Matt's feet and he deepened the kiss, needing to taste more of her.

Annalise made a small sound in the back of her throat. Before Matt could do more than register her reaction, she suddenly pulled away.

"No," she panted, color streaking her cheeks. "I don't want this."

That damn sure wasn't how it felt. Feeling as though he'd had the wind knocked out of him, Matt tried to collect his wits.

"You aren't going to hurt me again." She gathered up her skirts, grabbed her medical bag and ran.

* * *

Whirlwind Reunion
Harlequin® Historical #1023—January 2011

Author's Note

Does anyone remember the Western TV series set in the 1880s that introduced "newfangled" scientific techniques like we have today? I was immediately hooked on the idea and dubbed it *CSI: Bonanza.* But how to use it? It stayed in the back of my mind as I wrote my Whirlwind series.

Matt Baldwin, like his brother, has been part of the series from the beginning. Though introduced as Whirlwind's most infamous ladies' man, he is also the leader in the hunt for a gang of vicious rustlers. As such, he's been targeted.

When those rustlers catch up to him, so does his past, in the form of Dr. Annalise Fine. Ambushed and left for dead, Matt is Annalise's newest patient. No one has seen anything like his strange injuries or has any idea what could've caused them. Cue my *CSI: Bonanza* idea. What could be more perfect than giving my heroine the knowledge of a newfangled way to analyze and identify the unique wounds?

Matt wants nothing to do with the woman who rejected his marriage proposal and left him to become a doctor. She has no intention of mending fences with the sexy cowboy who broke her heart. But in order to find his attacker, they must join forces. I hope you enjoy their story.

Happy trails.

Debra Cowan

Whirlwind Reunion

DEBRA COWAN

HARLEQUIN®

TORONTO • NEW YORK • LONDON
AMSTERDAM • PARIS • SYDNEY • HAMBURG
STOCKHOLM • ATHENS • TOKYO • MILAN • MADRID
PRAGUE • WARSAW • BUDAPEST • AUCKLAND

Recycling programs
for this product may
not exist in your area.

ISBN-13: 978-0-373-29623-1

WHIRLWIND REUNION

**Did you know that some of these novels
are also available as ebooks?
Visit www.eHarlequin.com.**

To heroes, past and present.

Praise for
DEBRA COWAN

Chapter One

West Texas, 1886

Matt Baldwin could go straight to perdition. Dr. Annalise Fine couldn't stop the thought as she watched the dark, handsome, lowdown snake she had once loved. Who had once claimed to love her.

On a cool April night, she stood on the edge of the dance floor in the lobby of the Fontaine, the fancy hotel where his brother's wedding celebration was underway. The big, rugged rancher hadn't looked at her once. She couldn't seem to stop looking at him.

Even though she had been back in Whirlwind, Texas, for two months, this was the first time she had set eyes on him. His wavy black hair was longer than she remembered ever seeing. Slightly ragged, it brushed the stand-up collar of his white dress shirt. The crisp fabric stretched across shoulders that were more broad than the last time she'd seen him. Touched him.

His frame was solid, hard, from the strong line of

his sun-bronzed neck to the powerful thighs beneath his dark trousers. Trousers that fitted him so well they bordered on indecent. Her chest tightened painfully.

The notes of a waltz filled the air, swelling over the clink of glasses, conversation and dancers. She had known she would see Matt, and she had made herself come anyway. It was time to get it over and done with.

His brother, just as big and an inch taller, swept his dark-haired bride around the floor. Russ hadn't stopped smiling since before the wedding.

Like Annalise, Matt's father, J.T., wasn't dancing tonight. An accident he'd suffered several months ago had left him crippled.

Cora Wilkes, a lifelong friend and now a widow, thanks to an outlaw gang, stood talking to him. Tall, with perfect posture, the older woman walked over to Annalise. Her hazel eyes twinkled as she sipped her second glass of champagne.

Annalise glanced at the big man, still surprised each time she saw him in the wheelchair. He had been a good friend to her father and to her, especially during the year she had cared for Hardy Fine before he died.

"Is Mr. Baldwin expected to walk again?" Annalise asked when Cora paused beside her.

"Dr. Butler first had hope, but now he isn't sure. J.T. isn't recovering the way the doctor had anticipated." Cora's face softened. "Has J.T. asked you to look at his leg? He said he might."

"Not yet." Considering the way his youngest son felt about her, Mr. Baldwin probably wouldn't ask, regardless of their former friendship.

Try as she might, she couldn't ignore Matt, and that had frustration churning in her belly.

As he escorted a curvy redhead into the dining room,

Annalise noted with resentment that his rugged good looks hadn't faded in the last seven years. If anything, he was more compelling. With those smoldering blue eyes, his was a face that had a woman sighing. Annalise should know; she'd done her share.

But there was more to him than just his looks. Beneath the easy charm, the slow drawl often mistaken for laziness, was a razor-sharp intellect and a keen instinct about people.

"I think I'm finally getting used to seeing your name over the medical clinic instead of your daddy's," Cora said. "Hardy would be so proud of you."

She hoped so because Matt sure hadn't been. He reappeared in the dining-room doorway, this time with an unfamiliar blonde, and Annalise jerked her gaze away to scan the lobby. The polished wood of the oak floor matched the large registration desk positioned to greet people when they walked through the double doors.

Russ and his wife, Lydia, had done a wonderful job with the hotel that had been built in the years Annalise had been gone. Pewter wall sconces above the moss-green sofas on either side of the desk burned continuously on gas lighting. The high ceilings and the staircase opposite the registration desk were accentuated with oak molding.

Annalise had known many of the people here since childhood: Davis Lee and Riley Holt, Bram and Jake Ross. Now all except Bram were married.

"Did you finalize the purchase of Jed Doyle's house?" Cora asked.

"Yes." Annalise smiled, thinking how perfectly it had worked out that the gunsmith had wanted to sell his house just as she had returned.

The frame building was exactly what she needed.

She used the upstairs for her living quarters and the first floor for her medical clinic, the way Jed had used it for his gunsmithy.

"Have you seen any patients yet?"

"Several, and some people have dropped by to introduce themselves. Everyone has been welcoming."

Except Matt. Annalise didn't want a welcome from him. Which was good because she knew she could wait until hell froze over and she wouldn't get one.

"Russ's wife seems nice." She smiled as the groom tugged the bride into his arms and kissed her. The resulting burst of applause surprised Annalise.

"Lydia's very nice. Smart, too. She came here as Russ's business partner. They both owned half of the Fontaine." Cora chuckled, speaking loudly enough to be heard over the noise of the party. "She keeps him on his toes. I'm starting to wonder if Matt will ever settle down, and so is his pa. Especially now that Russ is married."

Annalise's stomach knotted. She didn't want to talk about Matt settling down. She didn't want to talk about him at all. She made a noncommittal noise.

Cora continued, "He's with someone different every time I see him."

Annalise could say the same. From the corner of her eye, she was well aware of Matt whirling a raven-haired beauty around the floor. Evidently the man who had once sworn to belong only to one woman—*to her*—no longer limited himself.

"Since J.T.'s accident, the running of the ranch has fallen mainly to Matt, and he's heavily involved with the Stockraisers' Association. A little too reckless in his quest to hunt down the rustlers that have been plaguing this area, but he won't stop until he finds them."

"I heard other ranches were losing cattle, too."

Frustratingly aware of the man who had broken her heart, she didn't think she could stand here much longer.

Cora nodded. "The Ross ranch and Riley's place. Between that and the women, Matt stays plenty busy, but he shows no signs of settling down."

Lucky for women everywhere, Annalise thought uncharitably.

Cora slid a sideways look at her. "Y'all were sweet on each other once. Any chance—"

"No." Annalise cut her off firmly, sharply. "None."

"That's a shame. I thought something might come of that."

Something had. Heartache and a baby. Annalise's throat closed up. And Matt had never responded to her letter about her miscarriage of their child. Not one word.

Her friend continued to talk about newcomers to the town, but Annalise's nerves were stretched taut. Despite the open front door, the air in the room was stifling, as were the reminders of the past. She couldn't take it any more.

She had stayed at least ten feet away from him all night and that was as close as she intended to get.

Having already given her congratulations to Russ and his wife, Annalise quietly said good night to Cora and threaded her way through the group gathered behind her at the foot of the oak-and-wrought-iron staircase. She reached the coat stands on the wall along the staircase and found her shawl.

Once outside, she took a deep welcome gulp of cool air. It felt good against her heated skin, bared by the square neckline of her jade-green silk bodice.

She swept the wrap around her shoulders and started off the hotel's porch, looking down to pull the edges together. She saw a man's boots at the same time she ran into a rock-hard chest. The momentum caused her to stumble.

Hard masculine hands shot out, cupped her shoulders. "Whoa, there."

At the deep familiar rumble, the apologetic smile on her face faded. Her gaze jerked up, clashing with a hot blue one. Matt.

Her pulse stopped then resumed, beating so fast that her chest felt too small for her heart. The warmth in his eyes died, replaced with a cold flatness as he practically pushed her away. He dropped his hold so quickly, so forcefully that she had to take a step back to keep her balance.

A woman stood beside him, the same pretty blonde Annalise had seen with him earlier.

The other woman looked from Annalise to Matt. She slid her hand from his arm and nodded at Annalise. "Good evening, ma'am."

"Good evening." She was surprised to hear the words. Her throat felt as if it were bolted shut and wouldn't work.

The blonde glanced at Matt. "I'll wait for you inside."

"No need," he said harshly. "I'm coming with you."

After another look at Annalise, the woman hurried around her. Who was she? She remembered Cora saying that a furious husband had confronted Matt last year and accused him of having an affair with his wife. Cora flat-out hadn't believed it. But as Annalise stared into the face of the man she had once loved, a face she had once known as well as her own, she wasn't so sure.

They stood there for a frozen moment, eyes locked. The world narrowed to her and him. The scent of man and sandalwood soap on the crisp winter air. The tiny lines of fatigue fanning out from his blue eyes, in the creases around his mouth.

When his lips tightened, she jerked her attention away from them. The stillness of the night and the muted music made it feel as though they were the only two people in the world. Thank goodness they weren't.

Annalise hadn't expected this feeling of suffocation. Of panic. The bone-squeezing pain in her chest.

His gaze slid indolently down her body, hungry and frankly sexual. A look that had been focused on her before. Just the memory made her shiver.

Then his expression changed to one of contempt. His eyes narrowed. He vibrated with anger. The realization had Annalise stiffening.

What did he have to be angry about? He was the one who had turned his back on her.

In the split second it took her to read his face, his eyes shuttered against her.

She was so furious she couldn't breathe for a second. Before she could say anything, do anything, Matt stepped around her and onto the Fontaine's porch. Pointedly, blatantly ignoring her. Turning his back on her again.

Enraged, she looked over her shoulder. "Ah, your back. The side of you I recognize so well."

He went stock-still for a long moment, shoulders rigid, muscles coiled with tension.

She shouldn't have said it, even though it was the truth. Breath suspended, she waited for his reaction.

He continued inside without a backward glance.

The blonde stood in the wide doorway of the hotel, flashing him a quick smile. "Who was that?"

"Nobody." His voice was flat, brittle.

Pain slashed at Annalise. Angry tears stinging her

eyes, she walked briskly toward her house at the opposite end of town.

Had she believed they could put the past behind them, even be civil? She knew better now. She made a sound low in her throat and walked faster. Just seeing him, being that close to him had caused her stomach to flutter. And her palms were sweating!

Even knowing she would eventually have to see Matt, she had left Philadelphia, come home to Whirlwind and reopened her father's medical practice. But the sheer depth and agony of coming face to face with him had been more than she anticipated. Still, she had done it, gotten it over with.

There would be other times—they both lived here, after all—but she wouldn't get that close to him ever again.

Annalise Fine had some damn nerve. Returning to Whirlwind. Showing her face at his brother's party. Black fury drove through Matt. He wanted to hit something. Or someone.

Once inside the Fontaine, he left Willow in the dining room with Ef Gerard, the blacksmith, and his new wife, Naomi, then slipped out the hotel's back door. His gaze settled blankly on the hotel's laundry house some yards away.

Seething, he clenched his fists, unclenched them. He was burning to get his gun and shoot at something. He didn't care what. Maybe the cool temperature would soothe his temper. His body was throbbing, nerves stretched taut, sensation skimming the surface of his skin in a way it hadn't in seven years. He could still feel her slender shoulders beneath his touch, the tease of her breath against his neck when she had run into him.

Her heart-shaped face was even more beautiful, the shock in her light-green eyes every bit as strong as the shock he had felt upon seeing her. She was still slim and delicate, but now her curves were more defined, womanly. Where they had once been more angular, her hips now flared slightly from her taut waist and her breasts were fuller. He'd felt that for himself when she had run into him. And her skin still looked as soft as down.

Immediately, he had wanted to put his hands on her, his mouth, which blistered him up good. He killed that thought real quick.

"Matt?"

He stiffened at the sound of his brother's voice. The last thing he wanted was to spoil Russ's wedding day.

"What's wrong? Is it Annalise?"

He gave a sharp nod. With little effort, Matt had stayed away from her all night, then his past had walked right smack into him. There was no point in denying why he was so angry, especially to his brother.

Dragging a hand down his face, he turned, battling to force the sound of her smoke-and-honey voice out of his head. "It happened outside. How did you know about it?"

"You were lathered up when you and Willow came back into the hotel." His brother, a year older, watched him steadily. "I knew it had to be because of her."

Matt wanted to rip into his brother and ask why she had been invited, but the whole town had been. It wasn't Russ's fault Annalise had shown up. Wasn't his fault the woman still affected Matt so strongly. Drawing in her light clean scent of primroses had tied his gut in nine kinds of knots. How could she still smell the same? Why did he have to remember it so well?

"I figured she might come," Russ said quietly.

Matt had tried not to give it any thought.

"Did you talk to her?"

"Oh, she did all the talking," he bit out. He felt as though he could explode any second. "Don't you have a bride waiting?"

"What did she say?"

"Leave off." Matt shoved a hand through his hair. "There's no reason to ruin your night. You've got a good woman. You should be in there enjoying her."

"Tell me." Moonlight slanted across Russ's face as he braced one shoulder against the hotel wall.

Matt knew that patient stance, the expectant tone. His brother wouldn't leave until he knew. "She made some smart-mouthed comment when I started walking away. Something about how she recognized my back since I was so good at turning away from her."

His brother cursed.

Matt gave a harsh laugh. "You and I both know who turned their back on whom. The minute her pa died, she planned to leave even though she—" He broke off as he wrestled with another savage urge to hit something. To ride the hell out of Whirlwind.

"Even though she had agreed to marry you," his brother finished quietly. "What else did she say?"

"That's it." Which was one reason Matt couldn't figure out why seeing her had hit him so hard. Had torn into the deep hole inside him he thought had healed. They had been inches apart for less than one minute. He'd seen the hurt in her eyes, but he didn't care. He wouldn't let himself. "It was no secret she had always wanted to be a doctor. I didn't like her decision to go back east by herself, but I understood. Not the other though."

"The miscarriage."

His eyes stung. "If she hadn't been so damn determined to go to medical school right then, our baby would be alive."

Even now, after all these years, Matt's throat closed up when he thought about his child.

"She swore she didn't know about the baby until after she arrived in Philadelphia," Russ reminded. "That she lost the baby before she could write to tell you she was expecting."

Matt had burned her letter, but it didn't matter. The words she'd written weeks after leaving him were carved into his brain forever. "How could she not be aware that there was a life growing inside her? Her pa was a doctor and she helped him with patients often. She had to have known she was expecting."

"Why would she lie?"

"She wanted what she wanted. She didn't need anything here." Even him, Matt thought.

"She'd been caring for Hardy for over a year."

"And we helped her." Them and Pa. That was when Matt had fallen in love with her. "So?"

"She left so soon after he died. Maybe she was grieving so hard she couldn't think clear. Remember how I was after Amy ran off with that married man she'd been seeing while engaged to me?"

When he had lost his first fiancée, Russ had been negligent, withdrawn and as cantankerous as a bear with a thorn in his paw. Maybe Annalise had been a couple of those things, too. And if she had stayed in Whirlwind, Matt thought angrily, he could have helped her through it.

His brother shifted, disrupting the shadows. "Maybe she made a mistake by leaving then."

"A mistake to go when she did, maybe, but claiming

not to know about the baby? That was no mistake. That was a flat-out lie."

It had been some years since he and Russ had talked about this in detail and his brother's calm suggestion still angered him. And solved nothing. She was back, but for how long?

At the thought, hope rose. She had left once; it was entirely possible she might leave again. He jerked a thumb toward the hotel door. "Get back in there. I don't want Lydia taking a strip off my hide because she can't find you. You're the groom, remember?"

There was an innate contentment about his brother these days, a sense of calm. Despite the somber expression on his face just now, Russ was happy. Settled. Matt had once thought he wanted that with Annalise. But he didn't. Not with her, not with any woman.

Seeing his first love had left him feeling raw, cornered.

"You'll be in for the toast?"

Matt nodded. "Get me a glass of champagne, okay?"

"If you'd rather, I can ask Pa to give it."

"I'll do it." Annalise Fine wasn't going to ruin this night more than she already had. Matt had moved on—many times—from her. He could do it again.

As his brother opened the door, he said, "I'll be clear-headed when I make the toast, Russ. I won't let you down."

The other man squeezed his shoulder. "I know that."

Matt stayed outside a few more minutes, trying to calm the fury pulsing through him.

After finally catching the band of rustlers who had been stealing cattle from the Triple B and surrounding ranches in several counties, he had anticipated things going back to normal, looked forward to a rest. The

Landis brothers, all seven of them, were awaiting trial in Abilene's jail because Taylor County was where they had done the majority of their rustling. Callahan and Nolan counties planned to extradite the gang to their respective counties once the Taylor County trial ended.

The capture of the seven bastards had been a long time coming and the result of more than just Matt's efforts. He had every right to feel victorious. And Annalise had leeched it right out of him.

He had a Stockraisers' Association meeting to attend in two days. Exhausted after months of spending intense effort on the rustlers, he didn't look forward to the trip, but he was glad to have it. Come tomorrow morning, he would be on his way to Graham and away from Dr. Annalise Fine. And when he returned to Whirlwind, he intended to stay away.

In the days after seeing Matt, Annalise stayed busy. She treated a case of pneumonia, several sore throats, an earache and accepted an invitation out to Riley Holt's for supper. She had known him and his brother, Davis Lee, her entire life and welcomed the chance to meet their wives, Susannah and Josie.

She had also examined J. T. Baldwin's injured leg. She wanted to examine him more thoroughly before saying she agreed with the doctor from Fort Greer that he would walk again. At the end of their visit, Matt's pa had mentioned—twice—that her former beau had been gone all week to Graham for a Stockraisers' Association meeting.

She had murmured some unintelligible comment. She didn't want to know where he was or what he was doing. She didn't want to think about him at all.

Five nights after Russ and Lydia's wedding celebration,

she responded to a frantic plea from Davis Lee Holt, Whirlwind's sheriff, to examine his pregnant wife, who had begun to bleed.

It was well after dark when Annalise stood at the foot of Davis Lee's and Josie's bed, asking questions. It was difficult enough to see her lifelong friend terrified, but the fear of miscarrying their baby on both his and his wife's faces wrapped around Annalise like a coil of barbed wire.

For a heartbeat, the pain of her own miscarriage was so sharp she couldn't breathe. She forced away the memories, struggling to keep all her focus on her patient.

Seven months along, Josie lay in the big bed. The lamp on a table beside her was turned as high as it would go and the soft amber light showed she was as pale as chalk. Annalise could see the sheen of sweat on both their faces.

"This has happened before," Davis Lee offered hoarsely.

Annalise frowned. "Miscarriage?"

"Two." The bleakness in his eyes cut her to the bone.

Two? Her heart twisted. Going through one had nearly destroyed her will to live. "You said the bleeding just started?"

"Yes." Josie pushed a strand of brown hair out of her eyes. "I realized it was happening about ten minutes ago and sent Davis Lee for you."

"That's good." Annalise was glad she lived only a hundred yards from the couple. She started to lift the sheets at Josie's feet, expecting the lawman to step out of the room as other men did. When he didn't, she glanced up.

Josie took her husband's hand. "Is it all right if he stays?"

Annalise was surprised. In her experience, men didn't want to be anywhere around female issues. "If that's what you want."

As Davis Lee eased down on the edge of the bed, Annalise raised the linens, noting the crimson stain was in only one spot.

Davis Lee spoke softly to his wife. "Just keep your eyes on me, honey. It's going to be okay."

Josie gave him a small smile.

The man's tenderness put a lump in Annalise's throat.

The blood didn't appear to be spreading and there were no clots. That was promising.

She lowered the sheet to cover Josie's feet. "The bleeding isn't heavy. That's a good sign. Have you had any cramping?"

"Only at the beginning tonight."

"Do you have any pain now?"

"Some, but it isn't sharp. It's the baby, isn't it?" Josie asked fearfully.

"Yes," Annalise said gently.

Tears welled in the woman's green eyes. Davis Lee stroked his wife's hair, his eyes closing briefly as agony streaked across his handsome features.

Annalise's chest ached. "You've done everything right so far—stayed in bed, sent Davis Lee for me."

"So now what?" he asked quietly.

"More of the same. Josie, I'm afraid you'll be confined to bed for the duration of the pregnancy." The other woman's history made the outlook even more grim, but Annalise had no intention of saying so. "You must take extra care. Especially considering your two previous losses. You have less than two months to go. Right now, complete bed rest is your best chance of keeping this baby."

"But—"

Davis Lee squeezed his wife's hand. "You heard the doc, Josie. You aren't going to lift so much as a needle."

She started to argue, but quieted when her husband gave her a look. "Yes, all right."

Annalise bit back a smile. "Davis Lee, if you'll pick her up, I'll change the sheets."

"Oh, no!" Josie protested. "You don't need to clean up!"

Annalise smiled. "Putting down clean sheets will allow me to judge better tomorrow if the bleeding has slowed."

He scooped up his wife. In short order, Annalise had the bed stripped and a clean sheet on the moss-stuffed mattress.

Once her patient was settled, she took her leave. Davis Lee walked out with her.

"You don't need to see me home," she said when they paused on his porch. "Not since I live so close to you."

He nodded, glancing over his shoulder then pulling the door shut quietly. He shoved a hand through his dark hair and she could see his hand was shaking. "This can't be any better for her than it is for the baby. Is she gonna be okay, Annalise? Even if she loses the baby?"

Annalise didn't need the wash of moonlight over his rugged features to see the man was terrified of losing his wife.

"I told her—" He broke off hoarsely. "It was too soon to try after the last one."

Annalise's throat tightened painfully. She laid a hand

on her friend's arm. "I'm going to do everything I can to make sure she is fine and I know you are, too. You're taking good care of her, Davis Lee."

He searched her face then a resolve came over him. "She won't be getting out of that bed. You can count on it."

She smiled. "Any more questions?"

"Not right now."

"If she has further pain or thinks she's bleeding more profusely, send for me right away."

"All right."

"Count on seeing me tomorrow."

He hugged her. "Thanks again. I'm glad you're back."

"Me, too." She stepped off his porch, angling toward her house. Josie was lucky to have a husband like Davis Lee. To have *anyone*. Except for a midwife she had only just met, Annalise had been alone when she'd suffered her miscarriage seven years ago.

Once inside her house, she removed her blood-streaked apron, unable to dodge the memories any longer. She had known she would have to relive them at some point and they flew at her like arrows. If her loss hadn't been raked up by a possible miscarriage, it would've been triggered by a troubled pregnancy or stillbirth.

Moving as though in a daze, she washed her hands, then the dishes she'd left in a hurry when Davis Lee had fetched her.

With tears blurring her vision, she changed into her night clothes, brushed out her hair and plaited it then lay down. The images wouldn't stop. Neither would the guilt. Memories of the pain, the blood, the resulting infection. She'd been lucky to survive.

She finally dozed off, waking with a start when someone pounded heavily on her front door.

Afraid it was Davis Lee again, she sprang out of bed. She grabbed her cotton wrapper from the back of her vanity chair and pulled it on, tying it snugly as she rushed down the stairs. She snatched up her medical bag then opened the door. And froze.

"Russ?"

The big man's back was to her and he was carrying someone. He looked over his shoulder, features taut. Urgent. "He needs help."

Ef Gerard, Whirlwind's blacksmith, stood in the darker shadows holding the man's feet.

She flung the door wide. "Bring him in. Follow me."

Hurrying, she led them to the back room and the patient cot in the near corner. After placing her bag on the floor, she lit an oil lamp while Russ and Ef carefully laid the man face-down on the mattress then stepped away.

"His back's the worst of it," Russ said.

Holding the light high, she walked over to the patient. She searched for injuries, her gaze skimming over sock feet and powerful thighs in denims filmed with red dust. Blood caked the back of his white shirt. It had splattered on the sleeves, too. His face was also bloody. Swollen and—

Her heart stopped. It was Matt!

Chapter Two

Annalise froze for a second. *Matt.* He needed help. Though stunned, she remembered her training and managed to gather her wits. Pushing the lamp into his brother's hand, she bent down to feel for her patient's carotid pulse. It was strong.

A closer look in the wavering light showed his ripped and bloodied shirt was stuck to his back. Rising, she pushed aside the curtain separating the clinic's two beds and went to the glass-fronted cabinet for a pair of scissors.

"What happened?" she asked Russ. "Who did this?"

"I don't know. Matt hasn't been conscious for us to ask." He shoved a hand through his hair. "I hope he can tell us when he wakes up. Why won't he wake up?"

"Maybe because he's lost a lot of blood." Annalise eased down onto the edge of the bed, snipping the hem of the shirt then ripping it up the middle. "Or maybe he was knocked out."

Russ shifted behind her, throwing shadows against the wall. "How bad is it?"

"The wounds need to be cleaned before I can tell." She carefully peeled back Matt's shirt and swallowed hard at the sight of his torn, mangled flesh.

Russ and Ef both made a sound of shock. Annalise folded the fabric out of her way, revealing the strong broad lines of his back, the fluid muscles of his shoulders and upper arms. His smooth bronze skin was now ripped and gaping. The wounds didn't extend past his lean waist, the worst of them on and between his shoulder blades. *Who* had done this?

Emotion surged inside her, a mix of compassion and regret. She realized her hands were shaking.

Steeling herself, she managed to control the tremor in her voice. "Where did you find him?"

"A couple of miles east of Whirlwind." Russ handed the lamp to Ef and moved to the foot of the cot. "His mare was nearby."

She returned to the cabinet which also held bandages, powders, instruments, various salves and antiseptic treatments, including carbolic acid. "Can one of you fetch me a bowl of water?"

While the blacksmith did that, Annalise took the carbolic acid and a couple of clean squares of linen from the cabinet. The rush of footsteps had her looking over her shoulder.

Lydia Baldwin hurried through the door. "Russ?"

"Sugar." He pulled his beautiful raven-haired wife into his side as her gaze went to the man on the cot.

"Oh no," she breathed. "How is he?"

"He's alive." In the smoky amber light, Russ looked pale, bleak. "Don't know much else yet."

The brunette placed a soothing hand on his chest. "I saw you and Ef ride in so I came on over."

He brushed a kiss across her hair.

Swallowing past a lump in her throat, Annalise moved back across the room. "What made you go look for him?" she asked Russ.

"He was late getting home from his trip to Graham. He made half the trip yesterday and stayed the night in Albany. He said he'd be back in Whirlwind by supper tonight. When he wasn't, and when there was no telegram saying he'd be delayed, I knew something had happened to him."

Ef returned with a basin of cool water and, at her direction, placed it on the small table beside the bed.

Russ said tightly, "I'm afraid I know who did it, too."

Annalise recalled part of the conversation she'd had with Cora the night of Russ's wedding celebration. "An angry husband?"

She felt Ef's gaze slice to her.

Russ glared at her. "An angry husband? Hell, no. You shouldn't listen to gossip."

His wife said quietly, "She's not accusing him, Russ."

"I don't care."

Annalise wasn't convinced, but it wasn't her business who had hurt him; it was her business to treat him. *Patch him up and send him on his way.* "Who do you think would've done something like this?"

"The rustlers he's been chasing for months, the Landis brothers. About two months ago, he caught up to them and they beat him up."

"We think they decided to try again," the blacksmith put in.

"And kill him this time."

Annalise had overheard some talk during her supper at the Pearl. "I thought they were in jail in Abilene."

"Five of them are," Russ said flatly. "Two escaped. Davis Lee told me late this afternoon."

She wet the cloth with carbolic acid and began gently cleaning the caked blood from Matt's back. For a long moment, there was only the sound of the combined breathing of those in the room, the occasional push of the wind outside. The scents of dried blood and dirt hid the clean, masculine smell she remembered from the other night. Tension pulsed in the quietness.

Russ stood to her left, looking down at his brother. "They stole his boots. That's gonna make him madder than hell."

After a few moments, Annalise was able to discern the actual wounds and she winced. His back was flayed by what at first looked like shallow cuts. She leaned closer, motioning for Ef to bring the lamp lower.

The lacerations were ragged, uneven, as though someone had dragged a jagged blade down his back. Bile rose in her throat.

Behind her, Russ cursed. "It looks like he's been whipped."

"No," the blacksmith said quietly. "I've been whipped and the marks are different than that."

"Well, what is it then?" Russ asked in frustration—the same frustration Annalise felt as she scrutinized Matt's back.

"The wounds are shallow, most of them no more than an eighth of an inch. A few, like these in the middle of his back, are almost a quarter-inch deep. And they're all long, three and four inches."

"Like someone bore down on the weapon as they slashed him?" Ef asked.

"Yes, exactly.

"Do you think a knife did this?" Russ asked with quiet anger.

"The gashes aren't clean like they would be from a knife blade. The edges of the wounds are ragged."

"Then what the hell did that to him?"

"I don't know yet." After further examination, she straightened.

"Can you tell how bad it is?"

"The bleeding seems to have stopped and that's good, but I don't know how much blood he lost before you got him here." She felt her way up his strong denim-covered calves, the backs of his powerful legs and then his sides. "I don't feel more injuries."

"So, we can take him to the hotel now?"

Her gaze caught his. "No. He shouldn't be moved. Not now anyway."

"Well, what are we supposed to do?"

"What do you mean? He can stay here, just like any other patient."

"He'll kill me if I leave him here."

Russ's wife started, pinching his arm.

Even though Annalise knew the man's words were said out of worry for his brother, she couldn't keep the sharpness from her voice. "Well, we certainly can't do something he might not like. You go ahead and move him. When he starts bleeding again, send for me. Or don't."

Russ frowned.

Lydia tugged her husband's head down to hers and said in a half whisper, "For goodness' sake, Russ, she isn't going to hurt him. Especially since he was the father of her baby."

Anger shot through her. How many people knew about that? She had foolishly believed—*hoped*—that his brother would be the only one privy to the information.

Matt stirred, his big hand clamping hard onto her knee. His heat reached through her skirts and skimmed along her nerve endings.

"Matt?" Russ stepped forward.

Blue eyes opened, clouded with pain as they focused on Annalise. "Angel?" he whispered.

At the endearment, an unexpected knot of longing tangled in her chest, but it was quickly gone. His calling her that surely meant he was out of his head with pain.

His brother leaned over the bed. "Matt?"

Matt's eyes closed and his hand slid from Annalise's leg.

Reading the look of concern on the other man's face, she said, "It may take him a while to come to."

Russ nodded. "I want to stay with him tonight so I can be here when he wakes up."

"All right."

After Ef was convinced he'd done all he could for now, he handed the lamp over to Russ and said goodnight. Russ assured the blacksmith he would send for him if anything changed and told Lydia the same when she offered to stay with him.

When he returned from walking his wife out, Annalise had retrieved a crock of honey from her cabinet and was carefully applying it to Matt's back.

"Why are you putting honey on him?" Russ asked sharply.

"It will form a barrier to keep the dirt from getting into his body. It may also help dull his pain."

"I've heard of that, but I didn't know if it really worked."

"I've had good results in the past."

Russ nodded, a brief glint of respect in his eyes.

She pointed to the second cot. "Feel free to sleep there if you want."

"Thanks, I might do that later." He pulled over a chair from beside the door and sat down at the foot of the bed.

She worked in silence for a few moments. As she finished treating the wounds, Russ spoke, "Sorry about what I said earlier."

"It's all right." She gave him a small smile. What had hurt more than that was what Matt had said. *Angel.*

Her throat closed up. Feeling suffocated, she rose and walked to the sink across the room to wash her hands.

Between this and Josie's threat of miscarriage, Annalise felt trapped. The best thing for her would be to send Matt to the hotel with his brother, get him out of her clinic. That was what she wanted. But seeing the extent of his injuries had changed her mind about getting him out of here. He could start bleeding again and he might get a fever.

She stared at the medical certificate hanging above the supply cabinet. It didn't matter how uncomfortable she found this situation, Annalise knew she couldn't, wouldn't turn her back on him the way he had on her.

Feeling as though he'd been beaten with a fence post, Matt forced his eyes open, squinting against the sunlight streaming through the window a few feet to his left. He sorted through his fuzzy brain, trying to get his bearings. Buttery-yellow light slanted in a wide band across a clean pine floor. He was on his belly in a narrow bed that smelled of fresh air and lye soap. And something sugary-sweet.

He wore trousers, socks, but no shirt. His bare back

burned like fire as his gaze tracked what he could see of the room. Another cot, also narrow, sat several feet away behind a half-drawn curtain. Between the two beds was a small table holding a lamp and a pint-sized brown crock. A glass-fronted cabinet filled with things he couldn't identify from this angle was against the far wall.

A vague memory of a woman's voice and gentle touch floated through his mind. He had thought it was Annalise. Real or a dream? He remembered the Stockraisers' Association meeting in Graham, recalled stopping overnight in Albany on his way home, then being close to Whirlwind when he'd been ambushed.

He tried to turn on his side and agony seared his back. Hissing out a breath, he went still.

"Matt?" Russ moved next to the bed, going to his haunches so Matt could see him.

The rattle of a wheelchair affirmed that Pa was there, too. The older man rolled to Russ's side. "Son?"

Matt's mouth was dry, his head throbbing. "Where am I?"

"In Whirlwind," his brother answered. "At Annalise's clinic."

Annalise? Hell. So, he hadn't dreamed her. She really was here. "Why didn't you take me to Catherine's?" he rasped.

"Annalise was closer."

A hell of a lot closer than he wanted her, that was for sure. He was surprised she hadn't turned him away. "What time is it?"

"Late afternoon," Russ answered. "You've been out since we brought you here about two this morning."

His back felt raw, torn. "What happened to me?"

"We're hoping you can tell us." J.T. angled his chair out of the way so Russ could help Matt sit up.

He bit off a curse at the pain arrowing through him. Sweat broke across his forehead as he braced his hands on his knees and panted with the effort to breathe through the misery. "Thanks."

His brother sat beside him in case he needed support, for which Matt was grateful.

"Ah, you're awake," said a smoky feminine voice. *Her* voice.

As Annalise walked into the room, his muscles tightened, sending a lash of agony through him. He looked up, taking in her practical gray day-dress and the thick mahogany braid hanging down her back.

Her skirts made a soft swishing noise against the wood floor. "I brought you some water and something to eat."

"No whiskey?"

"Water's better for you right now."

Maybe so, but it wouldn't take the edge off.

She eased around J.T. and his wheelchair then set a real glass and a china plate on the small bedside table. After she removed the lamp and the crock, Russ moved the table within easy reach for Matt.

He hoped he could manage to eat under his own steam because he didn't plan on staying here.

Annalise stepped to the head of the bed. "I sent Andrew Donnelly for Davis Lee."

Evidently, Annalise had renewed her acquaintance with Catherine Blue's kid brother in the two months she'd been here.

Russ glanced at Matt. "Are you up for some questions?"

"Yeah." He took another bite of the bread and ham Annalise had brought, realizing how hungry he was. And how weak. "I was ambushed."

"By Reuben and Pat Landis?" his brother asked.

"I don't know. Couldn't see their faces." Mindful of the pain in his back, he carefully lifted his glass for a drink. "Why'd you ask about those two?"

"Davis Lee got word yesterday that they had escaped from the jail in Abilene."

As Matt talked with his brother and father, Annalise moved behind him into the space between the bed and the wall. When she touched his shoulder, he flinched.

"Sorry. I want to make sure your back isn't bleeding again." Her voice was cool, detached. And close. Too close.

Matt tried not to tense up because it hurt like the devil when he did, but he couldn't help it. Trying to focus, he fixed his attention on his brother and father. "Who found me?"

"Russ and Ef." J.T. situated his chair a few feet away. "You were a couple of miles from here. Tony Santos sent his boy, Miguel, out to the Triple B before dawn this morning and I came on to town. Russ spent last night here with you."

Matt nodded, going still when Annalise slid a hand into the back of his hair and probed gently. Her breast grazed his shoulder.

Before he could ask what the hell she was doing, she said, "You have a knot on your head here. Do you know what you were hit with?"

"No." He cleared his throat, sensation stirring in his belly. If he weren't in pain, he knew he'd be feeling that same slow curl of heat below his belt.

Her hand moved from his head. "Are you hurt anywhere else?"

"No," he ground out. Did she have to touch him so much? Or stand so close? He wanted her to step away.

J.T.'s sharp blue gaze went from her to Matt and he smiled. "Annalise has been taking real good care of you."

Matt took a drink of water so he wouldn't have to respond. The clinic's front door opened and Sheriff Davis Lee Holt strode in with young Andrew Donnelly, their boots thudding against the pine floor.

Finished eating, Matt greeted the dark-haired lawman, a longtime friend, and the stocky teen who lived with his sister and her husband past the edge of town.

After asking if Matt was going to be all right, Davis Lee turned his attention to the ambush. "Did you happen to see who jumped you?"

"No."

A dark look crossed the sheriff's face. "I was hoping you had."

"Russ told me Reuben and Pat Landis escaped jail yesterday." Matt's back throbbed like blue blazes, the discomfort made more intense by the occasional soft stroke of Annalise's fingers on his skin.

"They still owe you for shooting off Reuben's earlobe, I reckon."

"Probably, though they've got more than that coming to them." The brothers and their five siblings had been thieving from here to the Panhandle for months. "How much longer are we gonna have to chase those SOBs? I thought we'd finally stopped them."

The lawman shook his head, looking as grim as Matt felt. "Tell me what happened."

"Someone came straight at me on his horse, knocked us both out of our saddles." He paused, feeling light-headed. "I punched him and another person hit me from behind with something. That's all I remember."

"So you don't know what they did to your back?" Annalise asked in a quiet distant voice.

Matt wished he could forget she was so close, but he couldn't. Her clean, light scent had stolen into his lungs and settled there. "No, I don't know what they did."

Davis Lee walked behind the cot to see Matt's back, and cursed. "What could've ripped you up so badly?"

"What does it look like?" Matt asked.

Russ shook his head, still propping his brother up. "Annalise, Ef and I tried to figure it out when I brought you in, but we couldn't."

"Is my back torn to shreds? That's what it feels like."

Davis Lee leaned closer. "These almost look like stab wounds, but they're not very deep. If they used a knife, why didn't they just stab you to death?"

"When we catch them, I'll be sure and ask," Matt said dryly, fighting the weakness and pain that was draining the energy from him. "Somebody tell me what it looks like back there."

"There are long lacerations," Annalise responded. "Uneven, like someone plowed furrows down your back."

She explained about the shallowness and pattern of the wounds. They didn't compare with the blade of any knife she'd ever seen.

"And you have no idea what they could've used, Matt?" Davis Lee moved around to the front of the bed.

"Everything's a blank after I got hit on the head."

Except for those shadowy images of Annalise. Her touch fluttered like a butterfly against his mangled flesh. He felt the occasional wash of her breath against his neck and back, and it put him on edge.

As Davis Lee, Russ and J.T. discussed going after the men who had attacked him, Matt realized he could be stuck here with her, completely at her mercy. Like hell.

"The men who jumped Matt could've gone in any direction afterwards," J.T. said.

"If it was the Landis brothers, maybe to Abilene?" Russ suggested. "To try and free the others?"

Davis Lee shook his head. "The guard over there has been tripled. They won't get within a hundred feet of the jail now."

Annalise came around to feel Matt's forehead, her hand cool and soft against his skin. "Good. No fever."

Says you. She still spoke in that detached emotionless voice and it bugged the hell out of him because he knew how she could burn beneath that prim exterior. How she could make *him* burn.

He cut off the thought. That was the last thing he wanted to remember.

The fatigue etching her fine-boned features didn't detract from her beauty or dull the peaches-and-cream skin that was so fine-grained it was almost translucent.

He'd known he would have to see her again, but why this soon? And why like this, when he was injured and hurting?

She again moved behind him, the warmth of her body flirting with his. Every muscle from his calves to his shoulders drew tight. Being this close to her put a knot in his chest. He had to get away from her.

"Are you dizzy?" she asked.

"A little." Growing weaker, his frustration mounted.

"Headache?"

"Yes, and my back hurts like hellfire." So why could

he even feel how close she was? Why was he even this aware of her? He sure as hell didn't want to be.

"Russ, Jericho and I can fan out from Whirlwind, each of us in a different direction, and see if we can find any tracks leading from the spot where Matt was found," Davis Lee was saying to J.T. and Russ. "I doubt I'll have trouble getting another volunteer to ride with us. Jake or Bram Ross would gladly help."

Matt was sure the Ross brothers would agree, but he wanted to go. He didn't care that he was as weak as a newborn kitten. "I can do it."

"It's not a good idea," Annalise said firmly.

Her touch was feather-light on his back, yet he felt it like a red-hot brand. Frustration and resentment had him snapping, "Leave me be!"

Conversation abruptly stopped and the three men in front of him stared warily at Annalise.

Matt thought about apologizing until she leaned in and whispered, "I can't. I'm the doctor, you're the patient. I need to check all your wounds."

The brush of her lips against his ear sent a shaft of heat through him and his muscles twitched in reaction, sending a wave of pain over him. Hell!

He looked at his brother. "Bring me a shirt and my horse. And my boots."

Russ grimaced. "Uh, well, they stole your boots."

A red haze of anger misted his vision. If there had been one ounce of energy in his body, he would have punched the wall. As it was, he could barely sit up.

J.T. frowned. "Son, Annalise is right. You're in no shape to ride out right now."

Davis Lee and Russ nodded in agreement.

Matt didn't want to admit it, but he was about to give out just sitting here. He would be worse than useless on a horse. It didn't help that Annalise was torturing him under the guise of doctoring him.

Andrew spoke up. "I could check that spot by the creek bed where the McDougal gang used to rendezvous. They might not be the only outlaws to use it and someone might've been there recently."

That outlaw gang had been wiped out a couple of years earlier. Thanks to Jericho, Jake, Davis Lee and Riley, the men who had murdered Cora Wilkes's husband as well as Josie Holt's parents and former fiancé were gone for good. Matt really wanted to make that happen for the Landis brothers and anyone else involved in the rustling.

Davis Lee squeezed the boy's shoulder. "That's a good idea, Andrew. Take my deputy with you. He's at the jail."

Andrew nodded, his young face earnest as he looked at the lone woman in their midst. "I won't go until we finish for the day, Dr. Annalise."

"You can go on, Andrew. It's important." There was a smile in her voice.

The answering smile on the boy's face was blinding and pure adoration. He looked to be *this close* to falling at her feet.

Hell, Matt thought. Andrew should watch out or she'd kick him in the teeth while he was down there.

It was an effort, but he said, "The longer we talk, the further they get."

Russ gave him a flat stare. "You're not going. We've got it handled. You need to heal up 'cuz we both know this is going to start all over now that two of them have escaped."

Matt knew Russ was right to insist he stay here and it blistered him up, but the only thing keeping him from passing out was sheer will and his pride. He refused to let Annalise see how right she was about his being shaky.

"How about moving me out of here?" he asked his brother in a low voice. "Maybe to the Fontaine?"

"I already talked to Annalise about that and she said it wasn't a good idea."

"She doesn't have the last say."

"Until you're stronger, she does," J.T. said. "I'll stay here with you."

She helped Russ situate Matt on his side. Her movements were brisk, impersonal. Still, he felt her touch all the way through his body.

Davis Lee turned for the door. "One of us will let you know what we find, Matt. I'm going to see who can ride with us."

He nodded.

"When Andrew gets back from checking the McDougal's old rendezvous spot, I'll wire the sheriff in Abilene and those in the surrounding counties to let them know what's happened so they can keep an eye out for anyone suspicious and for the Landis brothers, too."

"That's good." Though what little strength he had was slipping away, Matt still chafed at being left here. He called out to his brother as Russ reached the clinic door. "Bring me some boots before you leave Whirlwind."

Russ agreed and walked out. Annalise went to the door with Davis Lee and Matt caught her conversation with his friend.

"How's Josie doing?" she asked quietly.

"So far, she's following your orders."

"I'm glad to hear it. I'll be over in a bit to check on her."

"I appreciate it. Lydia offered to stay with her if Russ

and I needed to go after Matt's attackers so she won't be alone."

"That's good." She gave the lawman a warm smile as she closed the door behind him. A friendly smile.

A smile Matt hadn't seen in years.

She moved back into the room and gathered his dishes.

"What's wrong with Josie?" he asked. "Is it the baby?"

Surprise flashed across her face then she shook her head. "It's not for me to say."

"Is she going to be all right?" He hated the thought that pretty, vibrant Josie Holt might lose another child or otherwise be in a bad way. "Can you tell me that?"

She hesitated, then said, "She's taking every precaution."

Matt could tell by the stubborn slant to her jaw that he wouldn't get any more information. While he wanted to know more, he couldn't deny that he found Annalise's discretion admirable in this instance, although he sure hadn't found it admirable when she had kept information from *him* seven years ago. Dammit.

"You can roll to your stomach when you're tired of that position," she said, "but don't lie on your back."

He didn't think he would be able to anyway, not without screaming like a girl. He felt like hell, and she really had helped him. He doubted she had enjoyed it any more than he had.

As she walked out with his dishes, he said grudgingly, "I guess I should thank you for doctoring me."

"Wait until you see my fee," she said sweetly and stepped into the front room.

His pa chuckled and Matt clenched his teeth.

As he listened to her footsteps go up the stairs, his frustration returned in full force. So much for staying away from her.

For now, he was stuck here. He fully expected it to be pure-dee hell.

Chapter Three

Being irritated drained the last of Matt's energy. He drifted in and out of sleep, time moving in a slow murky haze.

When he finally came fully awake, he was on his stomach and lamplight filled the dark room. The spring night was cool, making the interior of the two-story house a comfortable temperature. He vaguely remembered Pa leaving to have supper with Cora Wilkes and promising to bring a meal back for Matt.

"Mr. Matt?" Andrew Donnelly appeared in front of him. "You want some water?"

Matt gingerly rolled to his side and propped himself up on one elbow, sharp pain ripping through him. The dark-haired boy offered him a full glass and hovered as he drank a little more than half of it.

When he returned the glass to Andrew, he became aware of the stillness. "We the only two here?"

"Yes, sir."

Where was Annalise? He wasn't asking.

"Dr. Annalise went to check on Miz Josie. She'll be back directly."

Matt nodded. If he'd been able, he would've taken advantage of her absence and gotten the hell out of there, but he couldn't even pull off his own hat, much less make it to the door. All he could do was stay in this bed, in this clinic, with this woman.

Knowing he was in no shape to leave didn't stop the resentment simmering inside him. He wasn't sure if it was directed more at Annalise or the fact that he couldn't help search for his attackers.

His back still burned with a razor-edged pain as if he'd been skinned. He sure would like to know what those injuries looked like. Staring at the glass gave him an idea.

"Hey, Andrew, does the doc have a mirror anywhere?"

The boy searched the examination room where Matt lay, then the front room. "I don't see one. I could go upstairs and look in her rooms," he said eagerly.

A little too eagerly, Matt thought. "No need for that. How about you run over to the Fontaine and ask Miz Lydia for a couple of mirrors? I want to get a look at my back and I think I can do it using those."

"Well…" Andrew hesitated.

"If you're worried the doctor will chew on you for leaving me alone, I'll take responsibility. Besides, you won't be gone even five minutes. I promise to stay just like this until you get back."

"Get back from where?" A whoosh of air accompanied Annalise's words as she opened the door and stepped inside.

The boy's blue eyes lit up at the sight of her. "I was

going to the Fontaine to ask Miz Lydia for a couple of mirrors."

"For what?" She straightened her bodice, which was the same deep green as her eyes.

"Mr. Matt wants to look at his back." Andrew's smile grew brighter, if that were possible. "Need me to do anything for you while I'm out, ma'am?"

"No, thank you. You don't need to run after those mirrors either."

At her authoritative tone, Matt's voice sharpened. "I want to look at my injuries."

"I can help you with that." She glanced at Andrew. "You'd best get on home for supper."

"Are you sure? I can stay if you need me to."

"I'm sure." She smiled. "You did a good job today, just as you do every day."

The boy flushed with pleasure and Matt huffed out a breath. She had that kid wrapped around her little finger.

"Well, good night then, ma'am," the boy said. "Mr. Matt."

"Good night, Andrew."

Fuming, Matt pushed up on one elbow, biting back a moan at the agony slicing through him. "Why didn't you let the kid get those mirrors? I want to see what those bastards did to my back."

"I might have an idea," she said coolly.

"You're going to draw me a picture?"

"No."

When she didn't explain further, he ground out, "Well, what is it?"

"You know I've been putting honey on your wounds?"

"So, that's what I smelled," he murmured. "Why did

you do that?" He knew why he would've put honey on her, and he knew what he would've done with it.

"It protects the wounds from dirt and helps with inflammation," she said briskly. "Back to your wounds, I think I can make an impression of them."

"An impression?"

"Yes, a likeness."

"I know what an impression is," he snapped.

"The idea is similar to tracing a pattern."

"I'll allow my head's fuzzy, so how would that work?"

"In effect, I'll make a paste to form to the injuries— it won't penetrate beneath the honey—then cover the wounds with a cloth soaked in a cornstarch solution. Once the mixture sets up, I can peel off the cloth and we'll see the pattern."

"What the hell kind of idea is that?" Resentment threaded his words. "That something you learned back east?"

"Yes," she said stiffly. "I learned it from one of my professors."

"What kind of medicine is that?"

"It's not medicine. It's an experiment he tried, a way to discover things like what kind of weapon might have been used on a victim."

"It would be easier to just get me a couple of mirrors."

"Yes, but this impression will be permanent. You'll be able to keep it. If you do find the weapon, you can compare it to the pattern on the cloth."

How damn smart was that? Matt was impressed in spite of himself. "And you're sure it'll be accurate?"

"If we do it now. If we wait for the wounds to start healing over, the pattern will change."

"I've never heard of anything like this. It sounds crazy."

"That's what people said to Professor Quackenbush, but it worked. He was always trying things like this."

Professor who? "Hmph."

"It won't hurt you or hinder your recovery."

He noticed *she* didn't say she wouldn't hurt him.

She shrugged. "You can think about it. Just remember what I said about the wounds healing over and changing the pattern."

"Do it," he decided.

"You're sure?"

"Yes."

"All right, then."

For a few minutes, she bustled around gathering supplies. He watched her through half-slitted eyes, noticing how the golden lamplight made her skin glow like polished pearl. Something hard clutched at his chest.

She glanced at him. "Is your pain any better?"

"If it is, I can't tell it."

"I'll be careful," she murmured.

She gathered a large piece of cloth, the pint-sized crock he'd seen earlier, some bowls, a pitcher of water and a tin of cornstarch. Walking to him, she placed all the items on the small bedside table.

"First," she said, "I'll mix up the paste."

As she poured a small amount of cornstarch and water into one of the bowls, he found himself staring at her slender, strong hands, remembering when they had been on him for reasons that had nothing to do with medicine or newfangled ideas. A time when he had looked at her with the same ignorant adoration as he'd seen in the Donnelly kid's eyes.

"Does Andrew work for you every day?"

"Most days after school and sometimes on Saturday if I need him."

"The boy's smitten with you and you're encouraging him."

"I am not," she dismissed, mixing a different amount of water and cornstarch in another bowl.

"If you don't make it real clear that you're only his friend, he won't stop."

Rather than reply, she dipped the cloth into one of the bowls then wrung it out.

"You say jump and he says how high."

She sighed. "He wants to learn about medicine."

"Maybe about anatomy." Matt's gaze slid over her. "*Your* anatomy."

"He's fourteen, Matt."

"So was I, at one time. I know what I'm talking about. I remember…things."

She flushed and he recalled how she had turned that pretty shade of pinky-peach all over the first time he'd gotten her naked. Despite his injury, his body tightened and he pushed the image away.

Being here with her in the shadows, teased by the scent of primroses, made it hard to remember how cold-blooded she had been.

When she moved to stand over him, he eased down to his stomach. She spread more honey on his wounds then picked up one of the bowls. "This is the paste. It may be cold."

Her touch was gentle, but he still flinched.

As she worked, she said quietly, "Russ said you'd been beaten up a couple of months ago, maybe by these same men."

He grunted.

"You've been chasing them for a while?"

He didn't know why she cared, but her interest—and her enticing scent—distracted him from the pain.

"Been after them about eight months. With everything fenced now, it's harder for them to steal the cattle, but they still manage to do it and rebrand them."

"Is the Triple B the only ranch to suffer?"

"No," he said in a grainy voice. "The Ross place, Riley's, too. Also a new ranch started by a Mr. Julius from Chicago. And several places from here up through the Panhandle."

"Now, I'll place the cloth over your wounds. It will need a few minutes to set up."

He nodded. Her questions hadn't been personal, but that didn't stop Matt wanting to ask her some that were. Starting with why had she returned? Was she planning to stay? Had she left a man in Philadelphia the way she'd left Matt?

But he kept his mouth shut.

As she cleaned up the supplies, he told himself to close his eyes, but he couldn't stop looking at her. The dark sweep of her lashes, the velvet of her skin, the lush curve of her breasts. He remembered the sweet taste of her against his tongue.

Hell, he wished he could pass out. He was more aware of everything than he wanted to be—the pain in his back, Annalise, the emptiness he felt just being in the same room with her.

"I think it's ready." It took a few minutes for her to slowly peel off the cloth. When she finished, she laid it carefully on top of the glass-fronted cabinet, saying excitedly, "I think it's going to work."

"Really?" He had thought the idea was half-baked. "Let me see."

"Hold your horses. I want it to set up a bit. While it's doing that, I'll clean off any remaining paste."

She gingerly wiped his back. As she spread a little more honey on his wounds, he turned his head away from her.

His thoughts about her were entirely too soft. He didn't want to feel anything soft for her. He wanted to ignore her, but as she began to bandage him, he knew it would be impossible.

Once his back was covered, she helped him sit up so she could secure the dressing by wrapping strips of cloth around him, under his arms and just above his hips.

The warm puff of her breath against his chest, his belly, had sweat breaking out across his face. His muscles tightened, sending a shaft of pain through him.

"There." With her gaze averted, she appeared unaffected, but Matt knew better.

Her pulse tripped wildly in the hollow of her throat and though her breathing was controlled, he'd heard it hitch more than once. Right now, though, he was more concerned with not passing out and tumbling off this cot.

She finally looked at him, then frowned when she saw his face. "We overdid it."

She helped him lie back down. Once she'd made sure he was comfortable, she left the room, returning a few minutes later to pick up the cloth gingerly and hold it up for his inspection. "The cornstarch mixture has set up enough now that you might be able to recognize the pattern."

Matt concentrated, but couldn't identify the jagged streaks. "Could you hold it farther away?"

She stepped back a few feet, keeping her hands beneath the cloth to support it. Distance didn't help.

"I don't recognize the likeness. Maybe Russ or one of the other men will."

Disappointment chased across her features.

"It was a good idea." Matt didn't know why he was reassuring her.

Pleasure flashed in her eyes then was gone. "I can't take credit for it."

"Don't know why not." She had possibly given him a bonafide lead, using a technique he had never heard of. "The idea to take the impression of my wounds was your idea, not your teacher's."

She shrugged, turning away to return the cloth to its place atop the cabinet.

It didn't escape him that Annalise had been able to help both with the weapon and with his injuries because she had left Whirlwind. Left him. And he didn't like it one damn bit.

For the last three days, the walls had been slowly closing in on her. Annalise was painfully conscious of Matt and had been since she had bandaged his wounds after making the impression.

As she walked out of Haskell's General Store after lunch, she admitted her pulse hadn't settled down since. Faced with his wide, hair-dusted chest, she wasn't sure how she had managed to keep a steady hand. His body was more tautly muscled than it had been when they had been betrothed, the plane of his stomach even more well-hewn. Looking at him, touching him, made her mouth go dry.

It was beyond vexing. It scared the daylights out of her. Why couldn't she view him as just another patient? After what he'd done, how could she feel anything for him?

Sometimes, when she was too close to him, her skin

stung with sensation. Andrew's presence helped dull the awareness as did J.T.'s and Cora's. But at night, it was just Annalise and Matt in quarters too close for her liking. She was upstairs and he was down, yet it didn't seem to matter. Nothing could stop the memory of those work-roughened hands moving slowly over her bare skin or the hot press of his mouth on her breasts.

His presence, their history, the low-thrumming tension wore on her. As she had done the last three days, she forced her thoughts to something else. Neither she nor Matt had yet been able to identify the weapon used on him.

After comparing the marks on the impression with those left by pitchforks, rakes and even a circular saw blade, she still had nothing to tell Matt, his family or the sheriff. The weapon in question also didn't match any blade pattern she'd checked on knives at Haskell's or in his Montgomery Ward catalogue.

Davis Lee, Russ, Jericho and Bram Ross had returned to Whirlwind frustrated and empty-handed. The men had found nothing to identify Matt's attackers or to indicate where they had gone. Matt had shown Russ and the others the impression she had made, but none of them could identify the pattern or the weapon either.

She walked past Cal Doyle's law office then stepped inside her clinic.

And found four women gathered around her patient, who was sitting up. Catherine Blue and two of her sisters-in-law, Deborah and Jordan. And a lone blonde named Willow. Annalise remembered her from the night she and Matt had run into each other outside the Fontaine. The woman worked for Russ and Lydia at the hotel.

Surrounded by females, Matt was saying something

that made them laugh. The smile on his face faded when he saw Annalise.

Even so, her heart thudded hard. She eyed him dispassionately. The last thing she wanted was for Matt Baldwin to know how much he still got under her skin. At first glance, he looked fit enough, but she saw strain around his eyes.

"Hi, Annalise." Catherine, a trained nurse who had quickly become a friend, walked toward her.

"Hi, Doc." The other three women chorused.

She greeted everyone, smiling at Catherine as the others took turns reading the latest edition of *The Prairie Caller* to Matt. Whirlwind's newspaper had the news about Josie being ordered to bed for the duration of her pregnancy. There was also the announcement of the arrival of a man known only as Cosgrove, the manager for the Eight of Hearts Ranch, owned by new resident, Theodore Julius.

Squashing a sudden burst of irritation, Annalise caught sight of a pie on the bedside table next to Matt's bed. She glanced at Catherine. "Cora's been here?"

The raven-haired woman nodded. "Also May Haskell as well as Chesterene Eckert and Zoe Keeler."

No wonder Matt looked tired, she thought crossly. "How's Evie?"

At the mention of her one-month-old daughter, Catherine glowed. "She's doing well, for as little sleep as she's getting."

"Is she colicky?" Annalise asked with a frown.

"No." The other woman laughed. "Her father seems to think he has to hold her every minute he's with her. When Jericho finally puts her to bed, she doesn't stay asleep long."

Despite the sharp pang of loss in her chest, Annalise

smiled at the image of the former Texas Ranger being so enamored of the infant. She used to wonder what kind of father Matt would've been to their son, but it hurt too much to consider.

Hearing his deep chuckle, she shifted her attention back to him just as Catherine asked, "Have you seen good results with the honey you've been using on his wounds?"

"Yes, and there's been no inflammation. Everything's healing nicely."

As she and the other woman talked, Annalise's irritation with Matt grew. She had told him not to tire himself out, yet here he was, sitting up, laughing and flirting. Of course he hadn't followed her orders. What had she expected?

Though he looked as if his energy was flagging, she knew he would never admit it. He would tire easily until he was fully recovered, but if his wounds still looked as good as they had yesterday, she planned to tell him he was free to leave. He was ready and so was she.

When her conversation with Catherine lulled, Annalise turned to the other women. "Ladies, I need to examine Mr. Baldwin, so maybe you could continue your visit later?"

"Yes, of course," Deborah Blue said.

Willow shared a look with Matt that spoke clearly of sexual knowledge between them. "I'll see you after awhile."

Annalise knew from the blonde herself that she was a former prostitute. It appeared Matt knew the same from firsthand experience.

A few minutes later, Annalise was alone with him. "I guess you ignored my suggestion that you rest."

"You didn't suggest." No charming smile for her. "You ordered."

She didn't respond, instead gathering fresh bandages and the crock of honey from the glass-fronted cabinet then moving behind his cot.

As she examined his dressing, he said, "Is this really why you ran them off?"

"I didn't run them off. You look half-spent and I need to change your dressing. Why else would I ask them to leave?"

The smug knowing look he threw over his shoulder had her bristling. Before she thought better of it, she snapped, "Yes, I wanted you all to myself. Haven't had nearly enough of that."

"Ouch!" He flinched as she pulled at his dressing a little too hard.

"Do you want some help lying down?"

"If you're changing my bandages, I'd like to sit up."

"All right."

As she peeled off the old strips of cloth, she wrestled with her aggravation. She wasn't vexed because she was jealous, which was what Matt thought, the arrogant cuss. She just didn't like him disregarding her medical advice.

During the last few days, it had been obvious he had moved on from their past. She wasn't letting on that his actions from seven years ago still hurt her. She wanted to avoid any reference to their history. So her only conversations with him thus far had consisted of advice, treatment and asking what he might want for his meals.

After applying a fresh layer of honey, she bandaged him as quickly as possible, not wanting to feel any of those flutters she had felt the other day. A sigh eased out of her and she stepped back. "All done."

"Good. When can I get out of here?"

It was impossible not to take that personally. "Today."

"Did Russ or Pa bring me any clothes?"

"Yes." She went to the other bed, fetching a gray shirt and a pair of old boots his brother had brought from the Triple B.

Matt declined her offer to help him dress, for which Annalise was glad. Gathering up the soiled linens she would later boil, she stepped around his cot and into the front room to deposit them in a burlap bag.

"Why did you come back to Whirlwind, Annalise?"

She froze at the question as much as the bleakness in the words. Turning, she looked into his blue eyes, hard with scrutiny. She had to speak around the catch in her throat. "Because this is my home."

"You sure didn't mind leaving it seven years ago."

He now wore the shirt and she couldn't stop her gaze from going to the tuft of dark hair visible in the unbuttoned placket of the garment.

"My plan all along was to come back and you know it," she said.

"Did you leave a man back there, like you did here?"

She stiffened. The hurt slicing through her quickly turned to anger, but she didn't let him bait her. "You can have your bandages changed by whomever you prefer. No need to come back here unless there's a problem."

"All you ever cared about was medical school."

"That isn't true."

"Well, it damn sure wasn't me. Or what we had."

"That's what this is really about, isn't it?" Annalise wasn't reminding him that the other thing she'd cared about was their life together. She curled her hands into fists. "Because I didn't change my plans after you proposed."

"No." He didn't hesitate, but she didn't believe him.

"You knew I intended to come straight back to you—back here after medical school, but after you proposed, with my father already gone, you thought I would stay in Whirlwind and give up my dream of becoming a doctor."

"I never said anything like that."

"You didn't have to say it. You made it abundantly clear once I was out of sight. You acted as though I didn't exist."

A muscle flexed in his jaw as he slowly got to his feet. "I cared for you," he ground out. "And our baby."

"*Our* baby!" She shook with outrage, disbelief. "You didn't care enough even to acknowledge my letter about the miscarriage."

"You're a fine one to point the finger."

"What's that supposed to mean?" she asked hotly.

"If you'd cared about me or what we had, you wouldn't have lied about the baby."

"Lied? About what?" Incensed, she marched over to him. "You think I wasn't expecting?"

"No, I believe you were."

"Then what?" Her heart pounded hard in her chest.

"I think you knew before you left Whirlwind that you were carrying my baby and in your letter you tried to make me believe you didn't."

Her breath jammed painfully in her chest. "You think I knew and went to Philadelphia without telling you?"

"Yes."

How could he believe such a thing? "Well, I didn't know."

"You're the daughter of a doctor." He took an aggressive step toward her.

She moved back, not out of fear, but from sheer reflex.

"You helped your pa from the time you were ten, and you knew more than most about medical things. How could you not realize?"

"I was distracted by my grief over my father's death. If there were signs of a child at that time, I didn't catch them."

The skeptical, scornful look on his face set off her temper.

"You are a piece of work, Matt Baldwin! Why would I lie?"

"Because if you'd admitted back then that you knew, you would've had to stay." His voice rose, too. "You wouldn't have been able to traipse halfway across the country, putting our baby at risk."

Pain and guilt knifed through her.

"If you hadn't been so all-fired set to get to medical school, our baby would be alive. You as good as killed him."

Before she even realized it, her hand flew up and she slapped him. Hard.

He grabbed her wrist, his expression stunned.

Tears blurred her vision. "How dare you."

Her hand print glowed red on his jaw. The blame was already carved into her heart, but coming from Matt, who had never even acknowledged their child? How could he have said something so cruel? Was there nothing left of the man she'd loved? If so, she couldn't see it in those steel-cold eyes, the rigid jaw.

She was shaking so hard her teeth chattered. Very quietly, she said, "Get out."

"You bet." He released her with a curse.

She registered the heavy thud of his boots on the floor, the slam of the door as her entire body went numb.

He'd brought up the past and she hadn't been able to keep her mouth shut. She wished she had because now she was forced to admit what she had denied for seven years. She'd never gotten over him.

Chapter Four

If you hadn't been so all-fired set to get to medical school, our baby would be alive. You as good as killed him.

Five days later, Matt's words still razored through Annalise, a black poisonous cloud on an otherwise lovely Saturday. She wished she could push his words out of her head, push *him* out of her head, but she hadn't been able to. So she'd done the only thing she could—she'd avoided him like he was a coiled rattler.

Sunlight streamed through the front window of her clinic, warming the space of pine floor between her and the patient in his wheelchair. J.T. Baldwin had come in with Cora, wanting Annalise to examine his leg and determine why he was still unable to walk.

"How's the pain?" Annalise asked him.

"Most days, it's just an ache, but if I do too much—"

"Or ride in the wagon for very long," Cora put in.

J.T. smiled at the older woman before turning to Annalise. "Then it hurts like the devil."

"Is the pain sharp or dull after you've exerted yourself?"

"Sharp. It's a good sign that I can feel something, right?"

"It can be good, yes. In your case, I'm not sure. Because there are times when you can feel yet still aren't able to make your leg move, I think you have a mass pressing on a nerve in your lower spine."

"Mass? Like a tumor?" he asked gruffly, apprehension on his craggy features. "Is it gonna kill me?"

Cora reached over and took his hand.

Annalise understood his concern. Matt and Russ's mother had died from a tumor in her stomach when Russ was ten and Matt was nine. "I don't believe it's a cancerous tumor. You don't exhibit other symptoms."

"So what do I do? Can you get it out of there?"

"I can do surgery, but there are risks."

"Like what?"

"Your right leg might be paralyzed for good. Both sides of your body might be. There's also a chance it could kill you. Any operation is risky, especially one this tricky." She shook her head. "And you should know that I've only assisted in this surgery, never performed it on my own."

"I trust you."

"I appreciate that, but you really need to think hard about having this operation. If you want, I can wire a doctor in Abilene and ask that he come to the ranch to give you another opinion."

"You and Dr. Butler have already given your opinions. I think two doctors hovering around me is plenty." He winked to take the sting out of his words.

"Are you advising against the surgery, Annalise?" Cora asked.

"No. I just want J.T. to think about it. Both of you. And discuss it with Matt and Russ."

The older man frowned. "But you won't, will ya? If they find out, I think I should be the one to tell them."

"Of course. I don't discuss my patients with anyone. You decide who you tell and who you don't, but I do think it's a good idea."

"So what do you suggest for now?"

"Give your recovery a little more time." At the impatient look on his face, one that reminded her too much of his youngest son, she said, "I know you're ready to walk again, but you can't rush it. You might damage a nerve permanently. If your pain becomes worse and longer lasting, you need to tell me."

"Dr. Butler never found this lump," he said quietly.

"He's been back east for a few months now with his wife's family, hasn't he?"

"Yes."

"It may not have been there when he last examined you. Or it may have grown from a non-detectable size."

He nodded and Cora reached over to pat his arm. Annalise had been surprised to find that her friend and J.T. were courting, but they had a lot in common.

"Any more questions?" Annalise asked.

"Not right now," J.T. answered.

Cora rose and opened the clinic's front door as the man rolled his wheelchair closer to Annalise and squeezed her hand.

"I'm glad you're home, girl," he said gruffly.

"Me, too." And she was, except for having to see his son. She picked up her bag and walked out with them, closing the door behind her.

At the other woman's questioning look, Annalise

explained, "I have to check on another patient. Should I fetch Russ to help you into the wagon, J.T.?"

Russ had lifted his father from the wagon to his chair when he had arrived at Annalise's. There had been no sign of Matt, which was good because she didn't want to be within ten yards of him.

"Both boys are planning to come over. The rustlers' trail has gone cold so Matt's going to ride out to the ranch with us. He's healed up enough now to come home."

"Ah." She gave a polite smile, which promptly faded when she saw her former fiancé standing on the steps of Haskell's General Store, talking to Jake and Bram Ross.

She focused her attention on the dark-haired Ross brothers, both broad in the shoulders and tall. Jake held a little blond girl in one arm. Annalise knew the toddler, Molly, was the half-sister of the rancher's wife, Emma. Held against Jake's wide chest, the child looked tiny.

Annalise was glad to see her friend with a family. It had been horrible for him, for everyone after Delia's death. The woman had been one of Annalise's closest friends, the first one she had told of her feelings for Matt. *Matt.*

Try as she might, she couldn't stop herself from looking at him. Those long powerful legs, the muscled chest she had rested against too many times to count. But not when she had needed it most, she reminded herself.

Looking up, she was startled to find his intense gaze moving over her like a heavy hand, stripping her inside and out. Even from yards away, she could see the anger in his eyes. She could *feel* it like a blistering wind.

He was still riled up? Well, so was she.

As he stepped down into the street from Haskell's porch and started for her clinic, Annalise said her goodbyes to J.T. and Cora. Rather than walking toward Matt and taking the alley between the general store and Cal Doyle's law office, she went around the other side of her building and made her way to Davis Lee's house.

There had been a time when she would've been too stubborn to let Matt Baldwin think she was avoiding him or to let on that he affected her that much. But after the horrible accusation he had made, she wanted nothing to do with him and she didn't care if he knew it. His blaming her for their child's death had caused her guilt to flare up. Of course, it was never far below the surface anyway. In the days since their set-to, that guilt had seeped through the anger and hurt. Always the guilt. But Matt wasn't innocent in this either.

She didn't want to think about him any longer. Pausing on Davis Lee's porch, she waited until her thoughts were focused solely on her patient. Several minutes later, she stood in Josie Holt's bedroom.

The woman was in bed, as Annalise had instructed and Emma Ross sat in a nearby chair, visiting. Annalise had met the petite blonde at church.

"Hello, Emma."

"Hello." The young woman rose and squeezed Josie's hand, saying, "Let me know if you need anything."

"I will." Aside from her paleness, Josie looked to be otherwise all right.

As long as she stayed put, the hemorrhaging shouldn't start up again.

Emma let herself out and Annalise turned back to her patient, pleased to see Josie's bleeding had long since stopped. "This is a good sign, though you still need to stay in bed."

The petite seamstress nodded. "If it weren't for the visitors, I'd be crazy as a Bessie bug. Catherine and

Jericho have come more than once as have Russ and Lydia. And Matt's been here several times."

Ignoring the sharp pang in her chest at his name, Annalise moved up the side of the bed to take her patient's pulse. "And I imagine Emma has visited a few times?"

"Yes. I'm so glad she found her way to Whirlwind. She's been good for Jake."

"From what I've seen, I think so, too. They seem very happy."

"You've known Bram and Jake a long time."

"All my life."

"So, you knew Jake's first wife?"

"Delia, yes." After her death, Annalise had wondered if Jake would ever move on.

Then last year he had found Emma. Or rather, she had found him. Annalise recalled him telling her that his wife had fled her stepfather's house with her infant sister and left the child on Jake's doorstep then hired on as the baby nurse. He was happier than Annalise had ever seen him.

She still hoped Delia's brother, Quentin, would one day stop blaming Jake for Delia's death and find happiness, too.

Annalise eased down into the chair next to the bed. "Have you had any pain?"

"Not since that first night."

"Contractions? Lower backache?"

"Sometimes my back does ache, but I think it's because of being in bed all the time."

Annalise gave her a sympathetic smile. "I know it's difficult, but this is best for you and your baby."

"I'm happy to do whatever I need to. I didn't mean to sound as if I was complaining."

"It's fine if you do. You're used to doing a lot. It's quite a change to be confined to bed."

Josie's green eyes followed Annalise as she placed her stethoscope on the woman's belly, listening carefully for the baby's heartbeat.

She smiled at her patient. "The heartbeat is strong."

"Thank goodness." Relief spread across Josie's face. "Did you always want to be a doctor?"

"Yes. My father was a doctor here for years and his work always fascinated me."

"Where did you get your training?"

"Women's Medical College of Pennsylvania, in Philadelphia."

The other woman's eyes lit up. "I've never been out of Texas. My home was in Galveston before I came to Whirlwind. Did you like Philadelphia?"

"Yes." It had given her a place to heal, to try and get over Matt.

"Did you have a special someone up there?"

Annalise thought about Travis Hartford, her dear friend who had wanted to be more, though she hadn't. "A friend, but we weren't romantically involved."

He was also a doctor. She had met him at the hospital where they'd both attended general clinics. Travis was one of the few males there who hadn't harassed her and the other female medical students.

Annalise packed away her stethoscope. "May I get you anything to drink or eat?"

"No, thank you. Emma brought me some lemonade." Josie paused, then said tentatively, "Davis Lee told me you and Matt were supposed to get married."

Annalise stiffened. She wanted to snap at the other woman, but there was no reason to take her irritation out on her. "Yes."

"But you didn't. Because you left to go to medical school?"

"That's right."

"He didn't want to wait?"

"He didn't want me to go," she said tightly.

"Matt didn't want you to be a doctor?"

At the disbelief in Josie's voice, Annalise gave her a small smile. "He thought I would change my mind after we were engaged."

Josie's eyes grew big. "Oh."

Annalise hoped Josie was finished discussing Matt, but she was disappointed.

"Matt says they're no closer to catching those rustlers."

"His father said the same." She liked Josie and they had become friends, but Annalise didn't want to stir up any more memories of Matt and their past.

After finishing her visit, she promised to check in the next day. She stepped outside, her gaze immediately going to the other end of town and the cemetery at the top of a small rise.

Talking about Matt, remembering Delia, had brought up Annalise's own dark memories. She thought about her time in Philadelphia after everything with Matt had gone so wrong. She had felt utterly alone, terrified out of her mind. Now, the memories and Matt blaming her for the miscarriage put her on the edge of erupting.

There was no sense in regrets, not now and not about this. His words shouldn't affect her as much as they had, especially since she had been saying the same thing to herself all these years. But his opinion did matter. She hated that he still had the power to hurt her like this.

Still, it wasn't his words that had her moving toward Whirlwind's cemetery. It was her own guilt.

* * *

Some minutes later, Matt sat in the Pearl with his pa, Cora and Russ. Annalise had practically run away from him. Now he was even more certain that his former betrothed had lied about knowing she was expecting when she left Whirlwind all those years ago.

And he wanted her to admit it.

Their conversation about the baby had been five days ago. Five days of solid mad for Matt. While his back had been healing, his anger had been festering.

After what she had done, it was no wonder she was avoiding him, but he wouldn't allow it. She should have to face him.

Matt drained his lemonade. He would've preferred something stronger, but this was what Pa wanted before they started for the Triple B. Matt wasn't done with Annalise by a long shot, but right now he was more concerned with his father and why the man had spent nigh on half an hour in her office. So far, J.T. hadn't said one dad-blamed thing about it.

Matt exchanged a look with Russ, urging his brother to start the conversation.

Russ settled back in his chair, dwarfing both it and the dining table. "So, Pa, what did Annalise say about your leg?"

"Does she know why you're still unable to walk?" Matt asked.

J.T. shared a look with Cora before answering, "Her opinion is that I should give my recovery a little more time. She offered to contact another doctor in Abilene and request an examination, but I don't need another one."

Russ, who blamed himself for the accident that had

crippled their father, nodded in agreement. "I'm sure Annalise knows what she's talking about."

Well, Matt wasn't so accepting of his family's blind trust in her. "Maybe you *should* talk to another doctor. We don't know if she has any experience with injuries like yours or any other kind."

"She knows enough to patch up your sorry self," Russ noted dryly.

"You're just going to take her word for it?" Matt asked his father. J.T. was aware of her lies to Matt.

"She knows more than you or I, son. I think she's more than capable." The older man glanced at Cora. "Ready to go?"

The hazel-eyed widow nodded.

And that, Matt knew, was the end of the discussion. For now anyway. When his pa decided he was done, then he was.

J.T. addressed his eldest son. "Russ, I want to see Cora home. You and Matt wait for me outside the clinic."

The woman harumphed. "J.T., I'm not going home, and if I were, I'm perfectly capable of seeing myself there. I have things to do in town. You get on out to the ranch. I know your leg is paining you."

Arguing with her was as futile as arguing with Pa. A few minutes later, J.T. was settled in the wagon with his wheelchair in the back. Matt planned to ride his mare, and if his father needed him to drive the wagon at some point, Matt would tie the gray behind the buckboard. As the wagon lurched into motion, Matt mounted up and guided Dove alongside the buckboard.

They headed down the street past Haskell's then the newspaper office. At the west end of town, the wagon rolled between the Fontaine and the livery. Matt glanced back and noticed the clinic was still closed. He wondered where Dr. Fine was, then dismissed the thought.

Once out of town, he caught a movement from the corner of his eye and looked over.

Annalise was at the cemetery. It was at the base of a small rise, shaded in a few places by trees and fenced in front by a low stone wall. She stood under a sprawling oak which he knew was near her parents' graves.

It still rankled that she had hightailed it away from him earlier. He'd had to live with her lie for years. She could damn well deal with him.

Matt must have unknowingly tightened his legs commanding his horse to stop because Dove had already come to a halt.

Pa slowed the wagon and glanced back. "What are you doing?"

"I'll catch up."

J.T.'s gaze went to Annalise. The older man nodded, as if Matt were doing something that pleased him. He probably thought Matt wanted to make amends with her.

He was stopping, but it had nothing to do with that. Guiding his horse up to the low stone fence, he dismounted and left Dove in the shade.

Annalise looked tiny. Frail. That was a word he had never associated with the woman he had once loved. The sun was bright and buffalo grass fluttered in the wind. In the endless stretch of prairie, she seemed so alone. So solitary.

He waited a couple of seconds for her to turn around and glare him away, but she didn't. She didn't respond at all until he walked up beside her.

Her head jerked toward him and he frowned at the

pallor of her velvety skin. The tortured look in her eyes carved a hole right through him.

"What do you want?" Fatigue etched her delicate features. "I was pretty clear a while ago that I don't want to see you."

He bristled. "Right now, what you want doesn't matter a lot to me."

"What a surprise," she drawled, the words slicing like a new blade.

He hated the bright flare of pain in her eyes. It was the same pain he'd seen at the clinic when he had accused her of being responsible for the death of their child.

"Go away."

She sounded…defeated and it pricked at his conscience. Still, he refused to lose sight of the reason he had stopped. "I'm not going anywhere until you admit that you knew about the baby before you left Whirlwind, that you lied."

She swayed. Startled, he automatically reached out for her. Jerking back, she steadied herself by grabbing hold of the grave marker in front of her.

Matt glanced down at her slender ungloved hand clutching the smoothly finished wood.

Wood? Her parents' markers were made of granite. Who was she visiting? He looked closer, read the name and date burned into the wood.

Hardy M. Fine. 1879.

It took a minute for Matt to register exactly what he was seeing, then an icy rage swept over him. "Does this belong to our baby?"

"Why are you here?"

"Answer me," he ground out.

"There's no reason for you to be nere."

"I have as much right as you do."

"No." Her voice shook, the word so low he had to lean in to hear her. "You don't."

"He was my child, too."

"Since when!" she burst out. "You wanted nothing to do with him, couldn't even acknowledge him after he was gone."

Matt's throat tightened. "I had a right to know you fixed him a spot here."

"Now you do. Leave."

Her imperious tone blistered him up even more. "You were wrong not to tell me."

"Why would I tell you anything? I was alone for the entire pregnancy, the miscarriage, all of it."

"If you hadn't lied—" The stricken look on her face killed his next words.

"Losing him *was* my fault."

Finally! "It's about damned time you owned up to it."

Every bit of color drained from her face. The utter stillness of her body revealed a searing depth of agony. Her eyes were haunted.

"Annalise?" His voice was a harsh scrape on the soft air. Instead of the smug satisfaction he expected at her admission, he felt a drum of apprehension.

She clenched her fists. "Like I said, I *didn't* know about the baby when I left, but if I'd waited, maybe even just another week, I might have realized. Then I wouldn't have pushed myself to reach Philadelphia before the new term began."

Tears rolled down her cheeks. The grief, the guilt ravaging her features brought home to him how his words had hurt her.

Five days ago, all he had cared about was ripping out her heart the way she'd ripped out his, but now it didn't feel right. Now, it felt like hell. *He* felt like hell.

He'd only ever seen such a desolate, lost look on her face after her father had passed and it rattled him to the core.

Her body trembled visibly. "I never heard from you again and I needed you."

For a moment, his brain seized up.

Her loss of composure, the deep sobs wracking her slender frame had his entire body throbbing with agony.

Her raw emotion stripped away everything, leaving a gaping hole inside him that hurt worse than anything he'd ever known. All he cared about was stopping her tears, plugging up the emptiness inside him.

He pulled her to him, murmuring, "I'm here, Angel."

She pushed at his chest. "I don't need you now!"

Something hot and sharp shoved up under his ribs and he wrapped his arms tight around her. She stiffened against him, her spine feeling fragile beneath his hands, but he didn't release her. He couldn't.

He hugged her closer and finally she sagged into him as though every bit of gumption had spilled out of her.

Her shoulders shook as she wept, her tears wetting his shirt. His eyes stung. He'd never seen her like this.

Her arms went around him and she clutched at him as though she needed his strength in order to stand. It scared the hell out of him. It also tore open a fierce protectiveness that had been buried deep for seven long years. "Annalise, please stop."

Her breasts rose and fell against his chest as she tried

to catch her breath. Seeing her like this made him bleed inside.

Assaulted by the soft feel of her against him, the teasing scent of primroses set off a strange sort of panic inside him. "Please, Angel," he begged gruffly.

She drew in a deep shuddering breath and looked at him. In that moment, all Matt cared about was erasing the devastation on her delicate features.

He framed her beautiful face in his hands, thumbing away her tears. She shook her head and curled her slender capable fingers around his wrist.

He knew she meant to throw him off; he expected her to. But she didn't. When he looked into her wet green eyes, there was no thought, only instinct as Matt lowered his head and brushed his lips across hers.

She drew in a sharp breath. For a heartbeat, he thought she might slap him again. Then her arms went around his neck. She kissed him back frantically. Her tongue touched his, searched his mouth.

The ground shifted beneath his feet and he deepened the kiss, needing to taste more of her.

She made a small sound in the back of her throat. Before Matt could do more than register her reaction, she suddenly pulled away.

"No," she panted, color streaking her cheeks. "I don't want this."

That damn sure wasn't how it felt. Feeling as though he'd had the wind knocked out of him, Matt tried to collect his wits.

"You aren't going to hurt me again." She gathered up her skirts, grabbed her medical bag and ran.

Watching her race down the hill and back the way they had both come, Matt stood rooted to the spot. What the hell had just happened? He should have wanted to punish her. Instead, he had cared only about comforting her, getting rid of the guilt and the shadows in her eyes. How had he ended up with her in his arms, his mouth on hers? Why had he done that?

He looked down at the marker, *his baby's marker,* and gripped the arched top.

What if Annalise really hadn't known she was expecting when she left him and Whirlwind? He didn't want to believe that, but seeing how she blamed herself played havoc with his anger. Could he have been wrong all these years?

Five days ago, Matt had accused her of causing their child's death. At the time, there had been a flash of doubt and he had crushed it, but he couldn't crush it now. His tiny whisper of doubt became a roar.

Chapter Five

Two days later Annalise's nerves were still humming from Matt's kiss. As mad as she was at him for kissing her, she was more mad at herself for kissing him back.

His mouth had touched hers and every thought in her head had scattered. For that brief moment, she had let herself give in, let herself be held and had been ambushed by the memory of the day she had left Whirlwind.

He hadn't liked her going to medical college, but he had driven her in the buggy to Abilene to catch the train. They had spent the night together for the last time and the feel of his hands and his mouth on her—all over her—was a memory she had never been able to bury. He had seen her off the next morning with the promise that they would always be together. Hah. That promise hadn't lasted three months.

She had been pregnant then. She hadn't known it, but Matt believed she had. He had cornered her in the cemetery for the sole purpose of getting her to admit it.

She still hurt over that so she understood the pain,

the betrayal in his blue eyes when he learned about the baby's marker. Even so, she refused to feel badly about not telling him. He had neither supported her nor acknowledged their baby, and his offer of comfort now didn't hold any water with her.

For the past two days she had tried to keep her thoughts from him. Besides purchasing a mare and riding to outlying ranches to check a couple of patients, she had read further about the tumor she suspected to be on his father's spine. She had also spent hours comparing the impression of Matt's wounds to different implements in Haskell's mercantile. So far, she had been unable to identify the weapon.

Now, just after noon, she went looking for and found Quentin Prescott outside *The Prairie Caller*'s office. In addition to laying type for the newspaper, he also kept bees and supplied honey to all of Whirlwind and Fort Greer.

After using so much on Matt's wounds, she needed to replenish her stock.

"I'll gather fresh honey in the morning and bring it over." The brother of her deceased best friend was crippled and in a wheelchair courtesy of a shoot-out with his former brother-in-law, Jake Ross.

"Thank you."

Though still whip-lean, Quentin had put on weight since Annalise's return. His sun-burnished features were sharp, but the cruelty she had noticed in his dark eyes when she had first returned was gone. "How are things going?"

"Very well." When she didn't have to be in the same vicinity as Matt Baldwin.

"Seeing a lot of patients?"

"I'm keeping busy. I guess you are, too, what with both your jobs."

Quentin nodded. Before his injury, the man had laid track for the railroad. While his job for the newspaper was quite a change from that, he still had a hard muscular torso and arms. His frame was more streamlined now, but just as strong.

He had shaved off his thin dark mustache, and his coal-black hair, while still neatly trimmed, was longer than Annalise could remember ever seeing it.

She wondered if he was still bitter about his injury. They hadn't talked about it since her return. "Have you thought any more about letting me take a look at your leg?"

Something indefinable flashed in his dark eyes. "I've thought about it, but I'm not sure I want to do it."

"If you change your mind, you know where I am." She smiled.

"I do." His eyes warmed. "I saw you coming from the cemetery the other day. Matt, too."

Annalise tensed. Had he seen them kissing? She steered the conversation away from the two of them. "Do you still ride out to Jake's to visit Delia's and the baby's graves every week?"

"No, not every week. I'm trying to move on. You're not the only one who's said I should."

The shadow that crossed his features at the mention of his sister had Annalise reaching out to touch his shoulder. She was glad to see he allowed it. There had been a time when he wouldn't have welcomed anyone's touch or advice. "Do you still blame Jake for Delia's death?"

He was quiet for a long moment. When he answered, his voice was hoarse. "I've learned some things about Delia, things Jake should've been told, but wasn't."

"Do you mean like her never telling him about the doctor's warning that it was too risky for her to have a child?"

Squinting against the sun, the man nodded. "Did she tell you that?"

"No. I asked her straight out and she ignored the question. That was my answer right there."

He nodded in agreement. "As much as I hate to admit it, I know if Jake had been aware of Delia's secret, he would've done anything in his power to keep her from conceiving."

"Do you still blame him for putting you in this wheelchair?"

"I admit I provoked him. He only returned fire because I almost put a bullet in his head. It's hard to let it go, but I'm trying."

"That's good."

His gaze went past her then returned. "Can I ask you something?"

"Of course."

"Is there anything going on between you and Matt?"

A sudden burst of skittishness had her wanting to say goodbye. "Anything like what?"

"You seem to be avoiding him."

"He's not in town enough for me to avoid him," she said drolly.

Her friend just looked at her, obviously aware she was trying to dodge the subject. He took her hand. "I saw you at his brother's wedding. I thought the two of you might—"

"No." She shoved away the memory of their kiss. "That'll happen when Sunday is the day after Wednesday."

His dark gaze scrutinized her. "That was over a long time ago, huh?"

"Yes." Annalise had to push the word past her suddenly tight throat. Thankfully, Quentin didn't appear to have seen what had happened between her and Matt at the cemetery.

Her friend brushed his lips across her knuckles. "I'll see you tomorrow."

"All right." She squeezed his hand then started back toward her clinic. Just as she passed Haskell's, Andrew Donnelly jumped down from the porch and ran to her.

"Doc!"

"Hi, Andrew." She smiled at the boy, who was flushed with excitement.

His sister-by-marriage, Deborah Blue, walked out of the mercantile with Bram Ross. The dark-haired rancher said something to make Deborah laugh as they stepped into the street.

"What are you all doing in town today?" Annalise shaded her eyes from the sun. She hadn't expected to be out this long so she hadn't worn a bonnet.

Bram thumbed back his cowboy hat, turning serious. "More cattle were stolen from our place and the Baldwins' last night. I came to report it to Davis Lee."

"But," Andrew said with an impish look at the couple, "He saw Deborah in the store and got sidetracked."

The young woman laughed, sharing a warm smile with Bram.

"Guilty." The big man grinned. "In fact, I rode to town with Matt, but I don't see him anywhere. I don't suppose you've seen him?"

"No." And she planned to keep it that way. "Why aren't you in school, Andrew?"

"The teacher let me take my lunch with Bram, so

he could go with me to Ef's. I just got my first pair of spurs!" The boy lifted a foot and turned it to the side so she could see the way the spur fitted his boot. "Bram said I need 'em if I'm gonna help him run cattle. He helped me tell Ef what I wanted. I paid for them with money I made doing chores for you."

"Hmm, those are pretty fancy." She gave a mock frown. "Maybe I'm paying you too much."

"Oh, no, ma'am!" The look of alarm on the boy's face had the adults laughing.

Flashing a good-natured grin, he knelt and removed one spur. He rose, stepping over to Annalise. "See these buttons on the heel band here? They have my initials on them."

She looked closer at the piece. "You say Ef made them?"

"Yeah." The boy flicked his finger down the toothed rowel, making it spin.

"He does excellent work." She knew he had done all the iron work for the Fontaine's balcony. Annalise smiled at Deborah. "Are you still thinking about getting your teaching certificate?"

"Oh, yes."

"I wish you'd consider becoming a nurse or a doctor. You have a way with people. You'd make a good one."

"I've told her the same thing." Bram smiled warmly at the woman next to him.

Deborah gave him a look of affectionate exasperation. "You say that about anything I want to do."

"Yeah, I guess so." Bram's blue eyes twinkled.

Annalise could tell the rancher was stupid in love with the young woman. She'd once been that stupid in love with Matt.

"We were heading over to the Fontaine for some lunch," Bram said. "Would you like to join us?"

Andrew set his rowel to spinning again, giving her a toothy grin. "Miz Naomi's supposed to have her special chocolate cake."

"That sounds delicious." Ef's wife oversaw the cooking at the hotel. "But I'd better get on to my clinic."

"I guess that means I have to go back to school now," the boy grumbled.

She smiled down at him, her attention again caught by the sun glinting off the still-turning wheel. "Are you allowed to wear your spurs in the classroom?"

"No, ma'am. Mr. Tucker says we aren't to scratch the floor or put gouges in it. I'll take them off before I go inside."

Gouges? Caught up short by a sudden thought, she stared at the rowel. The tips were blunted, but if enough pressure was applied, could they break the skin? Dig out someone's flesh? What kind of mark would they leave on someone? Could spurs be the weapon used on Matt?

Annalise pictured the impression she'd made of his wounds on the cheesecloth. She couldn't be sure unless she compared rowel markings side by side, but the sudden jump of her pulse said she was on to something.

"Something wrong, Annalise?" Bram asked.

She became aware then that the others were staring at her expectantly. "No, nothing's wrong. I just need to check on something. It was nice to see you all."

"You, too." Bram tucked Deborah's hand in his arm and clamped one hand on Andrew's shoulder, steering him toward the school at the east end of town. "Back to class for you, boy."

Annalise bade them goodbye. Once inside the clinic,

she carefully picked up the starched cheesecloth with the impressions on it, then made her way to Ef's smithy.

Under a side awning, the blacksmith had a fire blazing in his forge. A raised brick hearth was outfitted with bellows and a hood to let the smoke escape. As she neared, a wall of heat hit her smack in the face. A hammer lay atop the anvil and Ef's leather apron hung from a nail just outside the lean-to.

Seeing no sign of him, she walked to the front door and knocked. Ef answered, his massive shoulders filling the doorway as he wiped his mouth with a napkin.

"Oh, I've caught you at lunch," she said. "I'm sorry. I'll come back later."

"It's all right. I've finished. Naomi has already gone back to the Fontaine. What can I do for you?"

"Andrew told me you made him a pair of spurs."

"And you want a pair, too?" he teased. The smile he seemed to wear constantly since marrying Naomi grew broader.

She laughed. "I do want a pair, but it's so that I can compare the rowels to the impression I made of Matt's wounds."

"Are you thinking that spurs could be what made those marks on his back?"

She nodded.

Ef's eyes lit up. "I know a way we might be able to find out."

She waited as he went inside then returned a minute later with a clean white scrap of linen and a tin of blacking made from beeswax and lampblack. Taking down the lone pair of spurs hanging in the back of his lean-to, Ef coated them with the substance.

Annalise held the fabric taut against the side of the wall and Ef drew the blackened spur rowel down the cloth, careful not to tear it. He held it up as she brought the cheesecloth impression up next to it. Her breath caught as she looked over at Ef.

"You're onto something, Doc." He smiled. "It's not the same pattern, but it's similar enough to suggest you're right about the weapon being spurs."

"Oh, my." Excitement tightened her chest.

"How did you come up with the idea?"

"Andrew was showing me one of his new pair, spinning the rowel and I just wondered… Oh, my."

Ef studied the marks on his sample then those on the stiff cheesecloth. "One of the rowels in your impression is sharpened."

She stilled. "Which would explain why some of these gouges and cuts are more defined than the ones made by the blunted rowels."

"Yes." Ef turned solemn. "That sharpening is deliberate, probably done by the owner of the spurs. I don't know any spur makers who typically sharpen rowels like that. It ain't necessary for riding a horse. It hurts 'em. Getting spurred had to hurt Matt like the devil."

Annalise had just realized that, too, and she inwardly winced. While it didn't dim her excitement over possibly finding the weapon used by Matt's attackers, it was sobering. "May I take this sample you marked?"

"Yes. Are you going to tell Matt?"

"I…guess so." She didn't want to.

"I heard he was in town today, but I'm not sure where. Want me to help you look for him?"

"Oh, no," she said quickly. When he raised a brow at the vehemence of her answer, she hurried to add, "You're busy. I'm sure I can find him."

"All right," he agreed thoughtfully. "It's real smart how you figured that out."

"It wasn't due to any special effort. I hope we're right about the spurs being the weapon."

"Let me know if I can help any more." Ef took his apron from its peg and put it on over his head, tying the leather strings behind him.

She nodded as he got back to work. She hesitated in front of his house, debating about whether to hunt Matt down. She flat-out didn't want to. If she saw him, she would get mad and want to slap him again.

It was better for her to just keep her distance and find someone who could relay the information to him. Russ?

Her gaze went to the jail. Davis Lee. The sheriff would also need to know what she'd found and he could pass the information to Matt or whoever he saw fit.

Perfect. Now she wouldn't have to see Matt.

Matt sauntered over to the door of the jailhouse and looked out the adjacent window, glad to see Annalise and Quentin were no longer in the street. They were nowhere in sight, and despite the relief he felt, the tightness in his chest didn't ease.

He knew Prescott and Annalise were friends, but what did she have to talk to him about for so long? Why had she smiled at him like he was something special? And why the hell had they been holding hands?

Was their friendship turning into more? Had she done anything else with Prescott? Like kiss him? The thought had Matt's gut knotting up like rusty barbed wire.

He didn't try to tell himself he didn't care because he did. A heap.

Clenching his jaw hard enough to snap bone, he moved back to the corner of the room where he couldn't see out the window.

He wished it was that easy to get her image out of his mind. Despite sitting up two nights in a row to keep a watch over his cattle, he hadn't been able to forget the kiss they'd shared. And her sweet taste wasn't the only thing that had haunted him. His doubts about her lying wouldn't leave him be.

Was that kiss making him soft in the head? Had he been wrong about her all these years? The idea didn't sit well.

He braced one shoulder against the weathered pine wall, taking in the four shotguns lined up in the glass-fronted cabinet behind Davis Lee. The wanted posters for Reuben and Pat Landis helped Matt focus his attention on the rustling and not on his former love.

"A cow and her calf disappeared from our herd. I know those cattle were rustled, but I found no footprints, only cow hoof prints."

"What about horse tracks?"

"No. They hit the Circle R last night, too. In fact, Bram and I started trackin' those rustlers together at dawn and we found nothing."

Davis Lee opened his top drawer and pulled out a leather-bound book. Snagging a pencil, he eased down on the corner of his wide oak desk then flipped through a couple of pages. "How many head were taken from the Ross place?"

"Five. Two of those are unbranded calves." As the sheriff made notes, Matt continued, "Bram and I rode into Whirlwind together to report the thefts."

"Where is he? I would make a joke about him getting rustled, too, but I'm sick to death of these thievin' bastards."

Matt nodded grimly. "Bram saw Deborah Blue going into Haskell's."

"Ah, enough said." The lawman continued to scribble in his book. "It sure would be helpful if we could get a lead on these rustlers or even the two SOBs who attacked you."

"It was those damn Landis brothers who jumped me."

"We can't prove it, though."

"Provin' it is your speciality. I know where to set my sights." Frustrated and on edge, Matt dragged a hand down his face. "I'm going to the saloon. I need a drink."

Just as he straightened, the door opened. Annalise stepped inside in a swirl of yellow skirts, carrying two pieces of white fabric.

Matt froze, squelching the pleasure that flared inside him. Had she seen him come in here? Was she looking for him?

"Annalise." Davis Lee rose from his desk, his eyes dark with concern. "Has something happened with Josie?"

"No, she's just fine. I didn't mean to alarm you." She gave a reassuring smile. She didn't appear to have noticed Matt yet.

Well, he was noticing plenty about her. Even from here, he could smell her light floral scent and in that sunny dress she looked like a spring flower. Her wavy mahogany hair was down, sliding around her shoulders in a fall of deep brown silk. It was pulled back on the sides by a pair of combs, showing the soft curve of her jaw. The sunlight picked up dark and light shades of gold, even a touch of red. He wanted to bury his hands, his face in it.

She closed the door behind her. "I may have figured out what caused Matt's injuries."

Then she could dang well tell *him*. "What do you reckon it was?" he asked.

Annalise whirled toward him, the surprise in her green eyes quickly shifting to irritation. Ah, she hadn't known he was here and she was vexed that he was. Well, too bad.

When she didn't answer him, he let his gaze drift from the top of her gorgeous head over the square neckline of her bodice that bared a small patch of peachy skin to the tip of her black shoes. A slow burn started in his belly. On the way back up, he paused at her soft pink mouth. "Hello, Angel."

At the endearment, her eyes flashed. Lips flattening, she turned away.

He'd thought that might get more of a rise out of her, and only then realized that was exactly what he had tried to do.

Keeping her back to him, she moved in front of the sheriff's desk, laying the two pieces of cloth side by side. One had black marks and the other was the cheesecloth imprinted with the impression of his wounds.

He gave himself a mental kick. He should have been pondering on the weapon himself instead of on Annalise and that kiss. Just the sight of her put an ache inside him, so he stayed where he was.

Davis Lee stood beside her, slanting her a look. "I saw you talking to Quentin. Everything okay?"

"Oh, yes. I was just ordering some honey."

Since when did it take so long? Matt thought darkly. And why did it involve all that touching? And dammit, Quentin kissing her hand?

Gesturing to the stiffened cheesecloth, she explained to Davis Lee how she had mixed a paste of cornstarch and water to take an impression of Matt's wounds.

"So, now we have a likeness and we won't have to recall from memory," Davis Lee said.

"Yes."

"Hmm." He looked impressed.

It was impressive, Matt admitted. Even so, he pressed her. "It still doesn't tell us what made the wounds."

Her shoulders went rigid, but she didn't turn to look at him, just glanced at Davis Lee. "I think it was spurs."

"Well, I'll be! I can see it now."

Matt moved to stand beside the other man. He, too, could identify the pattern, but his relief at finding a possible answer was interrupted by the thought that Quentin might have helped her with the idea.

"Ef helped me test my theory." Smiling at Davis Lee, she indicated the other piece of fabric. "He put some blacking on a pair of spur rowels and we rolled them across the cloth. Look how similar the pattern is to the one I made from Matt's wounds."

There was a moment of silence as the two men studied the ragged short lines. The pattern was so similar that there was no doubt about the weapon in question.

"I'll be danged," Matt said, unable to keep the awe out of his voice. "You're right."

She didn't respond. Didn't nod her head, blink, anything.

Davis Lee grinned at her. "Where did you come up with this idea?"

"Andrew was showing me his new pair of spurs and it hit me."

Matt couldn't take his eyes off her. "So you decided to compare spur marks to the wound impressions."

Looking at Davis Lee, she said, "I'd already compared every weapon and implement I could, with no luck."

She was ignoring him, Matt realized with a flare of

irritation. Like hell. He moved behind her, standing near enough that his shoulder brushed hers. Near enough to feel her body heat.

He knew being this close would rattle her, make it impossible for her to pretend he wasn't in the room. But even when he leaned over to look more closely at the samples and brushed her hand with his, she didn't react.

The sheriff looked from one piece of fabric to the other. "Good thinking to make an impression of Matt's wounds. Is that something you learned in Philadelphia?"

"Yes." She smiled.

Matt's attention locked on her lush pink mouth, remembering the velvet slide of her lips beneath his. And the way she had pulled back.

Her gaze flicked dispassionately to him then away. As if she didn't know him. As if they had never kissed.

"A professor of mine taught me how to do it," she said.

"Quackenbush," Matt put in, well aware that her eyes narrowed at his intrusion. He explained to the sheriff how Annalise's professor had worked with the police on some criminal cases.

She took a step back, putting enough distance between them that they were no longer touching. She acted unaffected by him, completely unaware, but he knew she wasn't unaware.

The hectic flutter of her pulse in her neck and the slight flush on her creamy skin were more than enough proof. She saw him, all right. She *felt* him, just like he felt her.

She remembered that kiss every bit as much as he did.

He wanted to drag her into the back room and do it

again, until she melted against him the way she had in the cemetery.

His temper spiked.

"I'd like to keep both these samples," Davis Lee said.

"Of course. Just handle them carefully and keep them out of direct sunlight. I'm not sure if they'll fade, but it's better not to chance it."

"This is great, Annalise." Excitement underscored the man's words. "This is the first lead we've had since Matt's ambush."

"I hope it helps." Her full attention was on the sheriff.

Matt wanted her eyes on him. "It won't help us find the men who ambushed me."

"Maybe not." Annalise looked directly at Davis Lee. "But when you do, you'll be able to check their spurs, see if any of them match the impression I made. If so, that will prove who jumped him."

Him? He was standing right here! A red mist hazed his vision.

She walked to the door, smiling at Davis Lee. "I'd appreciate it if you would keep me apprised. I'd like to let my professor know if the method helped."

"Sure thing. And thanks again for leaving the samples. I'll be careful with them."

With a quick smile, she let herself out.

Fuming, Matt stalked to the window, watching the gentle sway of her hips, catching a glimpse of a white stocking when she lifted her skirts to go down the steps.

"It seemed like y'all were getting along just then." The lawman's voice came from behind him. "I guess you resolved whatever the problem was between you."

"She ignored me the entire time she was in here," Matt pointed out dryly, rubbing at the ache in his chest. She had never done that to him. Ever.

"True." Grinning, Davis Lee slapped him on the back. "Which means she wasn't really ignoring you."

Matt shook his head at his friend. It had sure felt real to him. He and Annalise hadn't resolved anything. In fact, seeing her had stirred up everything he thought he had gotten past.

Chapter Six

It was downright aggravating that Annalise had ignored him at the jail.

Working sixteen- to eighteen-hour days at the ranch should have crowded out all thoughts of her, but it didn't. And it only got worse when Pa proposed to Cora and they decided to get married right away.

Their announcement brought up the memory of Matt's proposal to Annalise. On a perfect spring evening, they had stopped at a special place on the ranch to watch the sunset and he had asked her. She had accepted, and once they arrived back in Whirlwind and found her father out, they had made love for the first time. Two months later, her pa had died and she'd left. Expecting their child.

The memory stirred up his anger all over again.

Four days after seeing her at the jail, Matt and Russ were dressing for J.T.'s wedding at the Triple B. Russ and Lydia had offered to have the ceremony at the Fontaine, but the bride and groom wanted to do it at the ranch.

Vows were set to be exchanged at sunset and the

guests would be arriving any minute. Russ and Matt had cleared out the barn that was closest to the house then constructed a wooden floor for the ceremony and for dancing. Now they stood in front of the wall mirror in Matt's bedroom, checking their string ties.

Cora was in a bedroom across the hall, getting ready with Susannah Holt's help. Susannah was standing up with Cora and her husband, Riley, was walking the older woman down the aisle. Davis Lee and Josie were the only people from town who wouldn't be present, due to the doctor's orders that the expectant mother stay in bed.

Russ bent to look in the mirror, fiddling with the buttoned-up collar of his white shirt. "Davis Lee told me Annalise figured out what weapon was used on you."

"Yeah." Matt shouldered his brother out of the way to inspect his tie.

"That gives us a great lead."

"Yeah."

Russ slid him a look. "You aren't pleased about it?"

"I am." Matt hesitated. He had sawed back and forth between gratitude towards her and regret over what he had said to her that day at the cemetery. "In fact, I can't believe she did it."

"Why not?" His brother eased back against the wall, waiting.

Matt yanked at the tie that already felt like a noose and began to retie it. "The day I came home with Pa, we passed Annalise in the cemetery and I stopped. I wanted her to admit she had lied to me about knowing she was expecting when she left Whirlwind."

Russ's gaze sharpened, but he remained silent.

"She still swears she didn't lie about that, but she did say it was her fault the baby died, that if she had waited even a week to leave, she might've realized she was expecting and postponed her trip to Philadelphia."

"If she's telling the truth, you can't blame her for the miscarriage."

"She blames herself plenty and I made things worse." Matt dragged a hand down his face. "She was standing in front of a grave marker and it belonged to our baby. She named him Hardy, after her pa."

His brother's brows snapped together.

Matt didn't know if the child's middle initial, *M,* stood for Matthew. He explained about getting angry over Annalise not telling him about the memorial and how she had let loose her temper on him.

Until he'd seen the wooden remembrance, the baby and the loss hadn't seemed quite real. It was more than real now. Matt felt the same emptiness he had felt when she had left years ago.

"After miscarrying, she got an infection and nearly died," he said hoarsely, still recalling too clearly the staggering anguish in her eyes. She had looked ravaged. "You should've seen her face."

He couldn't get the image out of his head.

"And she was alone through all of that," his brother said quietly.

Throat tight, Matt nodded. He thought he understood now a little bit about how alone she must have felt, how difficult it must have been to tell him, in the space of a single letter, that they had been expecting a child then lost him.

Russ shook his head. "It's amazing she didn't turn her back on you the night we brought you to her clinic— refuse to patch you up or help figure out what tore up your back."

"I know." And Matt had wrestled with it for days. He

owed her a thank-you for that. And an apology for what had happened at the cemetery. Not the kiss. No way in hell was he apologizing for that. "I understand why she didn't tell me about the baby's marker. Doesn't mean I think she was right."

Through his open window, he heard the rattle of wagons and people calling greetings to each other. He finished his tie and preceded Russ down the stairs.

"So what are you going to do?" his brother asked as they stepped onto the porch and halted in front of the door.

"I'm not sure." Matt faced the other man, running a finger under his collar. It was already tight and the wedding hadn't even started yet.

Still smarting from the way Annalise had ignored him at the jail, Matt wanted to confront her, force her to acknowledge that kiss. It would take some work to soften her up, but he could do it. Remembering the hurt and blame on her face made him question if he *should* do it.

Could anything between them be set right? There were so many years of blame and resentment, anger and betrayal. At the cemetery, Matt had seen her guard down, seen the pain and guilt she carried.

"I think...too much has happened between us. There are too many wounds. I don't want to hurt her any more."

"Meaning what?"

Staring blankly at the door, Matt took a deep breath. "I'm going to leave her be."

His brother arched a brow. "Really?"

"I'm going to apologize for lambasting her at the cemetery the other day and thank her for figuring out the weapon that was used on me during the ambush. Then I won't bother her anymore."

Russ's gaze flicked over Matt's shoulder. "She's here."

"I figured she'd come." He braced himself to turn and see her.

"With Quentin."

Quentin! Matt jerked around. She walked beside the newspaperman as he wheeled his chair toward the porch. The two of them weren't even touching, but a fierce heat clutched at Matt's gut.

A moss-green dress hugged her petite curves like a shadow, sleeking over a full bosom and down her taut waist. The lacy shawl draped loosely around her shoulders drew his eye to the creamy swells of her breasts bared by her square neckline.

The bodice wasn't cut daringly low, but Matt knew what the rest of her looked like, tasted like. His mouth went dry.

Slightly flushed, her skin glowed like a sun-kissed peach. Her hair was caught up high in the back then cascaded loosely in a fall of mahogany waves, revealing the delicate shells of her ears, the graceful line of her neck. Her mouth curved as she sent a soft smile to Quentin.

The look on her face, the memory of her slick, naked flesh against his set off a smoky explosion of lust in Matt's belly.

As Russ directed her and her escort to the barn for the ceremony, she barely glanced his way. Matt managed to do the same until the wedding was over and people were crowding around to congratulate the bride and groom.

Dusk had settled. As Matt finished lighting the lanterns he had hung around the barn, a hazy amber glow spread over the guests, edged into the corners.

From a few feet away, he watched her talking to Mitchell Orr, Charlie's nephew, and squashed the impulse to join them. Her wrap had slipped and Matt couldn't take his eyes off her. The memory of how her breasts had felt in his hands, against his tongue, hammered at him.

"Ah, Matt and Russ." Theodore Julius, who owned the Eight of Hearts Ranch west of town, walked up. "I'd like you both to meet my new ranch manager."

Matt forced his attention to the barrel-shaped man in front of him, shaking Julius's hand after Russ did.

Theodore Julius was the newest ranch owner in the area and had first come to Whirlwind to buy Russ's share of the Fontaine. The man had some ignorant notions about women, one being he didn't do business with them. When he learned Lydia owned the other half of the hotel, the deal had fallen through. Despite Julius, Russ had managed to pay off the note on the ranch and save the Triple B from foreclosure.

Julius indicated the stranger beside him. "This is Cosgrove. He's just taken over management of the Eight of Hearts."

"Cosgrove?" Matt asked. "That your first or last name?"

"Just Cosgrove," the man said in a deep voice. He stood about six feet tall with a muscular build, dark hair and dark eyes.

His fancy three-piece suit looked to be of tailored quality. Matt recognized that because all three of the Baldwins had their suits tailored. They were too big to buy ready-made clothing.

"Where were you before joining up with Theo?" Russ asked genially.

"A small ranch in Colorado."

The man looked them both in the eye, answered all their questions without hesitation, but something about him sat wrong with Matt.

After a few minutes, Julius took his manager around the barn, stopping to talk to other townspeople. Matt noticed that Annalise introduced them to Quentin.

It seemed to Matt that Cosgrove and Julius both spent an inordinate amount of time visiting with Dr. Fine. He didn't like it, and he liked it even less when the ranch manager led her onto the dance floor.

A growing unfamiliar impatience snaked through his belly. No matter who he spoke to or where he stood, he was aware of her. Cosgrove finally relinquished Annalise to Mr. Julius, and Matt didn't care for that either.

Bram Ross eased up beside him, frowning. "Deborah has spent almost as much time with that Cosgrove cuss as she has with me, and she came with *me*. Not that anyone would know it."

Matt tore his gaze from Annalise to find the oldest of Jericho Blue's raven-haired sisters. Bram had been sweet on the girl since her arrival a couple of years ago.

His friend had a point. Matt couldn't remember even seeing Deborah with Bram since the ceremony. Just then, Jericho interrupted the pair, leading his sister away from Cosgrove. She was plainly reluctant to go. "Looks like her brother doesn't care much for Deborah spending so much time with the man either."

"Good," Bram said. "Have you talked to that Cosgrove fella much?"

"Just a little."

"What do you think?"

"Something about him puts me off."

"Me, too," Bram said, "and it's not because he's spending so much time with our women."

"I agree." Matt didn't point out that Annalise wasn't his woman. "He's too…shiny. Too smooth."

"As a baby's butt," Bram agreed darkly before saying goodbye and making his way through the crowd to Deborah on the other side of the barn.

Matt wanted to apologize to Annalise, but if he was waiting for a chance to catch her alone, it wasn't likely to happen. As the night went on, he never came close to getting near her, let alone talking to her. She seemed always to be surrounded by a group of people. He didn't know if they were seeking medical advice or just making nice, but she was highly sought out by old friends and new acquaintances, usually from her spot beside Quentin.

As Matt watched, little Lorelai Holt tugged on Annalise's skirts and held up a rag doll. She knelt, looking serious as the blond-haired child spoke to her. When she straightened and took Lorelai's hand, Matt saw his opportunity.

He followed the two females out of the barn and into the house, careful to move slowly and quietly across the wooden floor. Once inside the house, the sounds of music and dancing faded. He stopped at the corner of the dining room as Annalise lifted the little girl into a chair and sat down opposite her, her back to Matt. Her light floral scent drifted around him.

"What seems to be the problem?" Annalise asked.

Lorelai thrust her doll at the doctor. "Margaret cut her finger."

Annalise took the toy and pointed to its right hand. "This one?"

"Yes." Lorelai nodded, blond curls bouncing.

Pulling his gaze from Annalise's profile, Matt noticed

the little girl had a bandage on the index finger of her right hand, the same hand Annalise examined on the doll.

"What happened?" she asked.

"Me, I mean her, was playing with Mama's fancy tea cup and her dropped it. I helped clean it up."

"Is that how you cut your finger, too?"

"Yes." The child's blue eyes were wide and wary as if afraid the doctor would see through her story that the doll and not she had broken the cup.

Annalise took a handkerchief from a hidden pocket in her skirt. As she cleaned the doll's hand, the little girl watched closely.

"Her's not s'pposed to play with that cup. I've told her a hunnerd times."

Matt saw Annalise bite back a smile. A strange heat prickled in his chest as he watched her with the child. Their son would be six now. What would he have looked like? Would he have had Matt's black hair or Annalise's mahogany brown? His blue eyes or her green ones?

The doctor wrapped the handkerchief around the doll's hand. "Keep this on until you get home then have one of your parents help you bandage it."

The little girl nodded emphatically as she carefully took her toy.

"Maybe Margaret will know better next time," Annalise said to Lorelai.

"Her will."

"Be careful to keep her hand clean, especially for the next week."

"Does she need medicine?"

"One kiss in the morning and one at night."

"Even if I already kiss her a bunch?"

"Yes." There was a smile in the doctor's voice. "That should fix her right up."

Kisses would sure fix him up, Matt thought.

The front door opened and he looked over his shoulder to see who was coming inside.

So did Annalise and when she caught sight of Matt, her lips flattened.

Riley strode into the house, his boots making a light scuffing noise against the pine floor. "Is Button in here? Ah, I see she is."

Matt grinned at the man's nickname for his daughter. Holt had called her that from the day she was born. She had been adopted by him, but no one thought of her that way, especially Riley. He loved the child as if she was his own blood.

"Papa!" The little girl jumped from her chair and ran to him. "Dr. 'Lise fixed Margaret!"

Smiling, Riley swung the little girl up in his arms. "Did the doc tell Margaret not to play with mama's china anymore?"

"Yes." Lorelai soberly clutched her doll tightly to her chest.

The rancher smiled at Annalise. "Thanks."

"Thanks," the child parroted.

"You're welcome."

Riley left, Lorelai chattering about the doctor's instructions to tend the doll's cut finger.

Skirts brushing against his trousers, Annalise started past Matt.

"Wait."

She didn't.

She was almost to the front door when he said, "You were good with her. You would've made a good mother."

She froze, making a choked sound. "I don't want to talk to you about that."

"I kinda got that message," he muttered.

She reached for the doorknob and all the frustration he had tried to tamp down got the better of him. Two strides brought him in front of her and he tugged her hand from the knob.

Shaking him off, she stepped back.

He got right in her face. "You can't keep pretending I'm invisible. There's still something between us."

She gave him a cool look. "We're connected by the death of our child. That's all."

Her words dug under his skin. "It's more and you know it."

"No, it isn't."

What little patience he had snapped, and he planted himself against the door, blocking her exit. "You kissed me, Angel. You can't pretend it didn't happen."

Her green eyes narrowed. "Move."

"You still want me. Why can't you just admit it?"

In the room's golden lamplight, her eyes were bright with anger. And tears. "It doesn't matter what I admit. I'm not interested in picking up where we left off. Whatever was between us died with our son."

Wanna bet? "That's a lie."

She reached around him and he wanted to pull her into him, make her stay. Instead, he stepped away so she could open the door.

Drawing in her enticing scent, he let her walk out although it took considerable effort not to go after her, haul her into Pa's office and kiss her until she admitted what they both knew.

As he watched her march away, her spine rigid, he realized he hadn't said any of the things he'd come to say.

Three hours later, Matt stood at the east end of town beside the Whirlwind Hotel, watching Quentin say good-night to Annalise. The moon was half hidden behind a cloud, but Matt could see just fine. She and Prescott were in front of her clinic, at the foot of the two steps that led to her stoop.

Matt had followed them from the ranch and had been watching them for almost ten minutes. How damn long did it take to say good-night?

Thinking about the way she had walked away from him earlier had frustration churning inside him. A frustration that only burned hotter as he observed her with the other man. Matt tried to calm the recklessness pumping through him, the possessiveness that had been sparked by watching her dance with and talk to other men.

She laughed, the full-throated sound like a punch to his chest and when Prescott took her hand, tension stretched across Matt's shoulders. He relaxed when the newspaperman did nothing more than squeeze her hand then bid her good-night.

The man waited until she got inside before steering his wheelchair down the main street to the other end of town where his house sat behind the livery. With Quentin gone, Matt expected the raw searing need to possess her would ease. It didn't.

In the front window of the clinic, a light flickered then grew. A curvy silhouette appeared and he started across the moonlit street. The breeze kicked up a swirl of dust around his boots. Surrounded by the noise of chirping insects and the distant bawl of cattle, the town itself was quiet. Everyone had turned in for the night.

He had things to say to Annalise and he wasn't leaving until he said them.

He didn't believe for one second that whatever was between them had died with their child and he knew in his gut she didn't either, but he still intended to leave her be once he'd said his piece. He would apologize for taking a strip off of her hide about the baby's marker and thank her for identifying the weapon that had been used on him.

Seeing her with Quentin made Matt want to do more than that, made him want to bind her to him in some way, but he wouldn't.

He paused on the porch, taking a moment to calm the rough tension inside him before he knocked. But when she opened the door, a tightness clutched at his chest. He was rocked by a savage elemental need to claim her. She belonged to him.

Taking himself completely by surprise, he demanded, "What's between you and Quentin?"

Shock flashed across her delicate features. "None of your business. What do you want?"

You. You. And you. Reminding himself why he'd come, he gentled his voice. "I wanted to apologize for what happened at the cemetery."

Eyes widening, she went still, wariness in every line of her body. "You mean, kissing me?"

"No." Without an invitation, he moved to step inside. When she didn't stop him, he entered then shut the door, leveling his gaze into hers. "I'm not apologizing for kissing you. I'm sorry for…sorry I jumped on you for not telling me about the baby's marker."

She eyed him disbelievingly, her pulse fluttering wildly in the hollow of her throat.

"I mean it," he insisted.

She let out a slow breath and silence ticked between them, scraping Matt's nerves raw before she finally said, "Well…all right. Now if you don't mind—"

"I also wanted to thank you for identifying the weapon that tore up my back." He'd thought getting this off his conscience would ease him, but his muscles were still tight. "You could've just let it drop and I appreciate that you didn't."

"What's really going on?" She folded her arms, the movement plumping her breasts up.

Damn, he wanted to touch her. He dragged his gaze from her chest to her face. "You beat all. I just told you what."

She shook her head. "There's something else."

"Those are the things I wanted to say to you at the ranch earlier, but you walked out before I could."

"So you came all the way into Whirlwind to tell me," she said skeptically.

Suddenly, Matt realized what he really wanted, what he *needed*. "There's one more thing."

"Ah, now you get to it." Turning away, she walked to the opposite side of the room, near the fireplace in the corner.

His gaze slid down the slender line of her spine. He itched to wrap his hands around her and pull her into him, but that didn't seem prudent at the moment. He closed the distance between them and stopped at her back, close enough for silky tendrils of her hair to brush his shirt. "I want you to look me in the eye and tell me it's over, that *we're* over."

She stiffened. "I already told you."

Her scent settled in his lungs as he bent to murmur in her ear, "Square in the eye, Angel."

The shiver of reaction that went through her had him going hard. Clenching his fists so he wouldn't reach for her, Matt didn't move. Tension knotted his gut. He had to go slowly here. His heart beat so hard he could hear it.

Straightening her shoulders, she faced him, her voice calm and steady. "We're over. Finished."

"No." He nudged her chin up with one knuckle. "My eyes, Angel. Look in my eyes. Not at my chin or my chest or anywhere else."

She pulled away from him, fists clenched at her sides. "Don't be ridiculous. I've already told you. Why do you want to make things more difficult?"

"You can't do it. You can't tell me."

"You need to leave."

Her refusal to admit what they both knew grated on him. "Is that really what you want?" he asked roughly.

"I...yes," she choked out.

It might have taken Matt's mind a moment to register that she hadn't flat-out told him to go, but his body got it right off.

Before he realized he had moved, he scooped her up and covered her mouth with his. Her resistance lasted two heartbeats then she sank into the kiss. Into him. Matt's mind blanked.

She was warm and soft and willing. All he cared about was getting more of her. Her arms went around his neck, her mouth opening beneath his. Curling her tight into him, he somehow managed to make it several feet over to the stairs. He sat and settled her in his lap.

Short nails grazed his nape as her fingers slipped into his hair. The years fell away. He had missed this, missed her. The quick flare of heat between them, the connection he'd only ever felt to her, what they had shared before things went south.

She shifted against his arousal and hard, hot want burned away his last bit of common sense. A savage hunger tore through him and he wanted to peel her out of her dress, touch her all over.

Locking her body to his, he speared one hand into the satin cloud of her hair, cradling her head. She turned full into him, her breasts pressing against his chest, her primrose scent swirling between them. Satisfaction spread through him. She could deny it all day long, but she wanted him. And he wanted her. All of her, not just in his bed.

He deepened the kiss, drinking in her sweetness before moving his lips to the silky curve where her neck met her shoulder. Nuzzling her throat, he touched his tongue to her collarbone, worked his way down. Her skin was like cream beneath his mouth, just the way he remembered. He brushed his lips across the swell of one breast then the other and a curious ache lodged in his heart.

She made a ragged sound that put a throb in his blood. He buried his face between her breasts, breathing her in as he fought the desperate driving need to strip her naked, take her upstairs and lie with her on her bed.

She was the only woman who had ever been able to make him go stupid inside of five seconds. She's always been able to spin him like a top.

His heart was pounding hard; so was his head. It kept pounding. Surfacing from the fog of desire, he realized the hammering wasn't in his head. Someone was knocking on the door.

She suddenly stiffened in his arms, the action striking

him like a whip. Matt struggled to remember why he had come to see her in the first place.

Before she could push him away and tell him— *again*—that there was nothing between them, he pulled back.

She blinked up at him, her green eyes smoky and dazed.

After a few seconds, when he could think past the fog of desire, he set her gently on her feet.

She wobbled a little and he steadied her with a hand on her taut waist. Breathing hard, he rose.

The banging came again and Annalise hurried across the room. The flickering golden-amber light showed a deep-rose flush on her face.

Matt followed, startled and irritated at being interrupted. "Why the hell is someone here this late?"

"Because I'm a doctor," she said breathlessly before opening the door.

Cosgrove stood there, sweeping off his hat. When he saw Matt, a look of surprise crossed his face before he turned his full attention to Annalise. "Dr. Fine, there's been an accident at the ranch. Could you come please?"

"Yes, I'll get my bag." Looking slightly dazed, she reached behind the door and picked it up from the floor.

The other man smiled, his dark eyes hot on her in a way that had Matt wanting to pull her behind him. "Do you have a buggy?"

"Yes."

"Good. I can escort you there and send a man back with you."

"Thank you—"

"I'll be taking her." Matt adjusted his gunbelt and settled a hand on the butt of his Peacemaker.

The other man's slit-eyed gaze went from Matt to the doctor. She drew in a sharp breath, her voice brittle with irritation. "I'll be right behind you, Cosgrove."

"Yes, ma'am."

She practically pushed Matt out the door then locked her clinic and started for the livery. The ranch manager mounted his bay and followed.

Matt had no trouble keeping up with her agitated strides. "You're not going out there alone," he said in a low voice.

She wouldn't look at him. Inside the livery, she led her mare from its stall to her buggy at the back of the building. "I am perfectly capable of driving myself."

"And now you don't have to." He took a harness from the weathered wall and went to her.

"I don't want you to come." she said hoarsely.

"There's no chance in hell you're going to Julius's ranch without me." His pulse finally steady, Matt hitched her horse to the buggy. "Not while Cosgrove is in sight and those rustlers are on the loose."

She shoved her bag under the buggy seat, looking as if she might explode. "It has nothing to do with you."

"Yes, it has."

"I said no."

"We're wastin' time arguin' about it," Matt pointed out, offering his hand. "You want that man to keep hurting, maybe bleed to death while we stand here?"

Biting her lip, looking torn, she finally grasped his fingers and let him help her into the buggy. Her hand trembled slightly in his. He climbed in and snapped the reins against the horse's rump. The buggy rolled out of the livery stable to join Cosgrove on his horse where he waited just outside of town.

The other man galloped ahead of them. They drove in silence, Annalise's shoulders rigid as she stared out at the moonlight-gilded prairie. Spoke-high grass swished against the wheels. Thanks to the size of the buggy, she was snug against Matt. She shifted a couple of times, her breast grazing his arm and he fought the urge to pull her tight into him and just hold her.

In the silver shadows, her face was pale marble. She was quiet. Too quiet.

Instinct kept him silent, too. He slid her a sideways glance. He had told Russ he would leave her be after saying his piece, but with her sweet body pressed to his and her taste still on his tongue, all Matt's good intentions went to dust. He wasn't done with her by a long shot. Leave her be?

Oh, yeah, he would. When there were rustlers in heaven.

Chapter Seven

She was no better at denying Matt now than she had been seven years ago. Who knew where they would have ended up if Cosgrove hadn't knocked on the door?

Annalise was afraid she knew where.

The buggy bumped across the prairie, the moon bright enough to guide their way. Cool night air swirled around them, but Annalise was hot. From the inside out.

She hadn't looked at Matt since he had kissed her. Seeing as how they sat close enough to share a button, it was a little difficult, but she managed.

Neither of them spoke as the horse kept a brisk pace. After the ranch manager explained that a visiting friend had fallen from the barn loft, they made the rest of the trip in silence. She was grateful Cosgrove was riding alongside the buggy because it meant she and Matt couldn't talk about what had happened.

Her irritation over his adamance about taking her to the Eight of Hearts Ranch was nothing compared to how shaken she was. Not only because of the way she had kissed him back, but also because of his apology.

The strength of her reaction caught her unaware.

How could she still want him? True, he had apologized for his harsh words about the baby's marker. But that didn't change the fact he believed she had lied when she'd left Whirlwind years ago. Even so, when she'd been in his arms, she'd felt the way she had that day at the cemetery, as if she could share with him, lean on *him*.

Who knew better than she how deceptive such feelings were? Matt hadn't been there for her when she needed him seven years ago. He wouldn't be there at any other time either and she would do well to remember it.

His kisses had made her ache, not just physically but with memories. With regret.

She didn't want to feel regret. She didn't want to feel *anything*.

Relief swamped her as they drove past the sprawling ranch house that had previously belonged to a cattleman who had moved north to Montana. Matt drew the buggy to a stop in front of the barn. Theodore Julius held a lantern, kneeling next to someone who lay unmoving in the dirt. In the circle of amber light, Annalise could tell it was a lanky, fair-haired boy who looked about the same age as Andrew Donnelly.

As she accepted Cosgrove's hand and stepped out of the buggy, she noted at least a dozen cowboys gathered around the young man just out of the circle of light.

"Thanks for coming, Doc." Julius's voice boomed as he straightened. "Stand back, men. Let her through."

The cluster of cowboys who smelled of sweat and cattle fell back to make a wide path for Annalise, their shadows weaving and separating. Matt was at her back, his massive body protecting her like a wall. She didn't need his protection. Or want it.

Glad to put her focus elsewhere, she knelt next to the boy. His ruddy face was twisted in pain.

Mr. Julius stood over her with the lantern. "Edward's family and mine have been friends for years. He's here to learn the ranch business from the ground up and was assigned chores in the barn."

"I fell out of the loft," the boy moaned.

"I didn't think we should move him," the ranch owner said.

"You thought right." Careful not to jostle her patient's neck, she slipped her hands beneath his head, finding a big bump. "Is this how you landed?" she asked.

"Yes."

"Have you moved since the fall?"

"No, ma'am." In the hazy amber light, he was pale, his skin sheened with sweat.

"Where is your pain exactly?"

"Low on my back," he said in a labored voice. "About as far down as you can go."

Annalise lightly patted his shoulder as she glanced up at Mr. Julius. "We need to get him into the house. Do you have a wide piece of lumber or a plank sturdy enough to hold him?"

"How about a door?"

"Yes, that would work."

With a wave of his hand, the man sent two men to remove the door to the bunkhouse. "What do you need the piece of wood for?"

"To keep him immobile while carrying him into the house." She had first learned that from her father then at medical college. "It should help prevent further injury to his back."

Annalise held Edward's head in a fixed position then asked two men to support the boy's back and ease him up enough to slide the door beneath him.

Cosgrove and another cowboy followed Annalise's instructions and Matt worked the plank into place. Mr. Julius watched, his brow furrowed in concern.

A few minutes later, Edward was in one of the spacious upstairs bedrooms. The mattress was firm, stuffed with Spanish moss like those at the Fontaine.

Once the patient was settled, she moved to the head of the bed, placing her satchel on a chair near the window.

Matt and the ranch hands who had brought the boy in moved into the hall. Cosgrove went downstairs. Mr. Julius remained in the room and thankfully out of the way.

Annalise could feel Matt's gaze following her every move. Dismissing a ripple of awareness, she turned her attention to Edward. "Do you have any tingling or numbness low in your back?"

"No, just pain."

"Any tingling or numbness in your arms, legs or feet?"

"No." Fear darkened his eyes.

"That's a good sign," she reassured.

After gently skimming her fingers around the painful area and feeling a slight bump on his spine, she stepped back a couple of feet so he wouldn't have to strain to see her. "You could have fractured a vertebrae or sustained a worse break."

"Does that mean his back is broken?" Mr. Julius asked tersely.

"It's too soon for me to tell how serious the injury is. Since he's feeling pain and has no numbness or tingling,

I'm hopeful it's a fracture. Those kinds of breaks usually heal on their own." Her gaze went to the patient. "You'll need to stay in bed for a while, flat on your back. I want to check you again in a few days."

"Yes, ma'am." His voice was thin, labored.

"So, he's just supposed to lay here, hurting?" Julius asked in a frustrated voice.

"I can give him some laudanum for the pain." She opened her bag and pulled out a small brown bottle.

The ranch owner sent someone down to the kitchen for a spoon and Annalise poured out a small amount of the medicine. The boy swallowed, grimacing at the bitter taste.

She handed the bottle to Mr. Julius, who frowned at the label. "Is it all right for the boy to have this? I've heard some people start taking it then can't stop."

"It does affect some people that way. Just be careful. You administer it. That way, you'll be able to control the amount and know exactly how much he's had."

Mr. Julius nodded. As she retrieved another bottle of the liquid from her satchel, she glanced out the window.

In the distance, a fire burned, causing a jump in her heart rate until she realized it was a camp fire, not a wildfire.

She closed her bag, glancing at Mr. Julius. "Does anyone else need a doctor?"

"Everyone's checked in and they're fine at the moment. All the hands are here at the house because they wanted to see if Eddie was going to be all right."

She nodded, smiling at the young man. After repeating her instructions to the patient, she followed Mr. Julius out of the room.

Matt was waiting quietly in the hallway, one shoulder

braced against the wall. He straightened and fell into line behind her as they went downstairs.

After the ranch owner paid her, Matt helped her into the buggy and they headed for Whirlwind. Sitting so close to him again had Annalise's nerves twitching. A wave of fatigue rolled over her as she pulled her shawl tighter around her.

He glanced over. "You cold?"

"No, I'm fine."

His big hands controlled the reins easily. Hands that could be gentle, as they had been on her earlier. A quick flash of heat under her skin had her looking away. She didn't have the energy to deal with him.

Wrapped in her shawl, she wished she had been able to change out of her evening gown, but there had been no time. At least Edward's accident hadn't involved blood.

The thought of blood reminded her of the attack on Matt. "How is your back healing?"

"It's comin' along."

"Good," she murmured, her stomach fluttering at the hard, hot feel of him all the way down her left side.

Every breath brought his soap-and-leather scent into her lungs. He adjusted his hat, drawing her gaze to the strong planes of his face. He'd been clean-shaven when the wedding began, but now whiskers shadowed his jaw. It softened his features, had her remembering the rough velvet feel of him from long ago.

As though he knew what she was thinking, he looked at her again. She shifted her gaze. In the shadows of night, his eyes were dark, heated, putting her in mind of those moments in her clinic earlier.

It seemed like days ago rather than hours, yet she still felt off balance. The night surrounded them, cool air rippling through the wheel-high grass. All was quiet except for the chirp of crickets and grasshoppers, the occasional squeak of the buggy. She felt his attention on her again, his gaze stripping through the layers to the heart of her, putting a quiver in her stomach and making her feel uncomfortably exposed. What was he doing? Determined to ignore him, she stared across the rolling hills of the prairie.

"You just beat all. What you did back there was amazing."

At the admiration in his deep voice, her gaze jerked to him.

"You kept everyone calm, explained everything clearly. You were born to do that. Your pa would've been proud. I was."

Since when? Irritation shot through her. "What happened to the man who was furious when I left for medical college?"

"I was wrong about that." His voice softened as his gaze met hers. "I'd like to think I've learned something in the time you've been gone, and that I'm man enough to admit a mistake."

Annalise barely kept her jaw from dropping. Had he ever apologized to her for anything? And now twice in one night.

Anticipation coiled through her then a sudden jarring instinct to protect herself. From what, she didn't know. "Thank you."

After a long moment, he slid her a look. "When you said I thought you chose medicine over me, over us, you were right."

The words put a pang in her chest. "I didn't choose medicine over you. I thought I could have everything I wanted, but such a thing wasn't possible. It was silly to think so."

"No, it wasn't. Your father was a doctor and you wanted to carry on his work. You had big ideas. There's nothing wrong with that."

His gentle smile had her stomach tightening. Why was he being so nice?

"The miscarriage," he said hoarsely. "I should've supported you in that, too."

Remembering all the years she'd been alone, that he had believed the worst of her, she set her jaw. She wanted to keep her guard up against him, but the memory of that day at the cemetery flashed through her mind. The hurt in his eyes had been genuine, just as his words were now.

Before she realized what she intended to say, she spoke. "I should've told you about the baby's marker. Now I understand that it hurt you. At the time, I really didn't think you would care or even take notice."

"I cared." There was no denying the ragged edge of pain in his voice.

"I know that now and I'm sorry," she said softly.

"You had cause to think it," he admitted gruffly. "Back then, I only cared about what I wanted. And I wanted *you*."

The fierce hunger in his eyes put a flutter in her stomach. And a quick flare of panic. She wanted him to stop talking about the past. "Maybe we were both selfish."

In the distance, she saw a few lights burning in Whirlwind. "Oh, look, we're nearly there."

"Do you ever wonder what things would've been like if we had stayed together? We had something."

Something *physical*. She blinked back tears. Infuriating man.

What had happened earlier tonight proved they still had the physical. That was how things had started years ago and it hadn't been enough to hold them together. Their problem had been—was—trust.

"I used to wonder how things would be for us." She tried to sound firm, but her voice cracked. "I don't anymore. And you shouldn't either."

"I can't seem to help it. I still want you," he said quietly.

She wanted him, too, and she didn't like it. "You still believe I'm a liar."

He pulled the buggy to a sudden stop, which had her heart kicking hard in her chest.

"No." His gaze burned into hers. "I should've made that clear earlier, but you turn me inside out. There were things that didn't get said. I believe you told the truth about not knowing you were expecting."

Feeling off balance again, she curled one hand around the seat. "No, you don't."

"I do, Angel." He put his big, callused hand over hers, holding on when she tried to pull away.

He was sincere, as earnest as he had been at her clinic earlier tonight and his words, the stark emotion in his eyes reached a place deep inside her that she had thought closed off forever, the part of her she had believed she would be able to keep locked against him.

She tried to look away, but she couldn't. The regret in his face was too raw. Too real.

"I'm more sorry about that than I can say. It tears my guts out that I brought more hurt on you at a time when you needed me."

All those years when she had hated him, *needed* him, circled viciously in her mind. The anger and hurt that had hardened inside her broke apart. Slightly panicked, she tugged her hand from his. "I don't know what you want me to say."

His gaze softened on her face. "I just wanted you to know. It needed to be said."

He snapped the reins against the horse's rump and the buggy lurched into motion.

They covered the short distance to town in silence. Annalise's mind whirled, her emotions swinging wildly from one to another—first sadness, then bitterness then a bone-deep longing for him and what they used to share. Which unsettled her to no end. Ruthlessly, she reminded herself that she hadn't been able to count on him before. Why would now be any different?

She had never expected his remorse or apologies. Or this sweet, sharp longing for what they used to be. She had no idea how to handle it. How to handle *him*. All she knew was she needed to get away from him because she wanted to be around him. And that terrified her.

Neither of them spoke for the remainder of the journey. Or when they unhitched her buggy at the livery. Or as they walked down the street toward her clinic. Matt offered to carry her bag, but she declined. She didn't tell him to leave her be, which he took as a good sign. Of course, she didn't talk to him either.

His gut said stay quiet so he did. Tension vibrated in every line of her body.

When she'd apologized for not telling him about the baby's marker, he'd thought they'd made some headway in getting beyond their past, especially when he expressed his remorse over believing she lied about knowing she was expecting. But she had withdrawn into herself.

Matt was glad he'd apologized, but it didn't appear to have made much difference.

He'd felt her surprise, her shock. Maybe she didn't believe him. She sure as hell didn't trust him and Matt didn't know if she ever would again.

"Who is that?" Her quiet voice broke through his thoughts and his gaze followed hers down the moonlit street to the clinic. Two tall men draped in shadow stood at the front door. They turned as Matt and Annalise drew near, and in a patch of pale light, he could see it was Davis Lee and Jericho.

Annalise recognized them at the same moment and hurried toward them. "Has something happened? Josie?"

Davis Lee shook his head. "Josie's fine and no one's been hurt that I know of."

Beside him, Matt felt her exhale in relief.

"But Jericho and I do need to talk to you."

"You, too, Matt," the former Ranger added.

Concern etched Annalise's features as she hurried up the steps and unlocked the door. All three men followed her inside and Matt closed the door as Annalise set her bag on the floor and lit the lantern on the table near the window.

Jericho began in his calm voice. "A man I used to ranger with stopped at my house a while ago. He's been on the trail of the Landis brothers."

Matt removed his hat, his muscles going tight.

"Dale tracked them through Indian Territory and lost their trail about five miles west of Whirlwind."

Dread knotting his gut, Matt shared a look with Davis Lee. "So the bastards are in this area?"

"That's what Dale thinks," Jericho answered. "Just after they crossed the Red River, he shot and injured one of them. He followed their blood trail for a couple of miles. Some time later, he came upon a bundle of bloody rags. He recognized the nearby hoof prints as belonging to their horses."

"So one of them needs medical attention." Biting off a curse, Matt shoved a hand through his hair.

Annalise looked from him to Jericho. "What's going on? Do you think they might come here to the clinic?"

"Or to Catherine," Jericho answered tersely.

"Like the McDougals did," Matt said. A pulsing abrupt silence came over all three men at the mention of the murderous gang.

Two years ago, Jericho had arrived at Catherine's house, shot and near dead. He'd been chasing Andrew Donnelly, who he believed had killed his partner after getting involved with those same outlaws.

Annalise frowned. "I don't understand."

Davis Lee shifted his gaze to her. "About two years ago, there was an outlaw gang wreaking havoc all through the state."

"They killed Ollie Wilkes, Cora's husband, among others," Matt added. "The leader took Catherine hostage because they knew she's a nurse and his brother needed to be treated for consumption."

"He roughed her up." A muscle flexed in Jericho's jaw, his words cold and controlled. "And almost got her killed."

Annalise frowned, concern in her green eyes.

Davis Lee pinched the bridge of his nose. "Riley, Jake, Jericho and I cornered them and killed three of them. The fourth escaped, but was later captured."

Matt's chest burned as though it was being crushed. What if one or both of the Landis brothers came to Annalise for aid? What if they took her forcibly the way the

McDougals had done with Catherine? The possibility raised the hair on the back of his neck.

He sent a look to the other two men. "Do y'all plan to join Dale in tracking the Landis brothers?"

"Yes," Davis Lee said. "As soon as we leave here. Lydia and Catherine have agreed to look after Josie."

Matt took a step toward Annalise. "You need to move to the Fontaine. Tonight."

"What? Why?"

"Did you hear what we just said?" he snapped.

"Yes, but there's no need for me to stay somewhere else. Do you really think these men would show themselves in town?"

"Don't be stubborn, Annalise. Just because I'm the one who suggested you go to Russ's hotel doesn't mean it's a bad idea."

She raised a questioning brow, her gaze encompassing Davis Lee and Jericho, not Matt.

"It might be smart," Davis Lee agreed.

Jericho's eyes flashed. "At least until we get back from scouting the area."

Matt opened his mouth to argue again for the hotel, but Annalise leveled a look at him. "Moving to the hotel would only put other people at risk as well."

"Staying in the clinic isn't the best idea." Why did she have to be so hard-headed about everything?

She ignored him, looking at Jericho. "If those outlaws needed medical attention and were nearby, wouldn't they have already stopped in if they were so inclined?"

"Possibly," the former Ranger answered. "It's hard to know."

Matt braced his hands on his hips. "You would only need to stay at the hotel until they're caught, Annalise. The three of us will head out shortly to see if we can find them or figure out where they're going. You shouldn't stay here alone."

Her green eyes flashed. "The sheriff lives right behind me."

Matt spoke through clenched teeth. "The sheriff won't be here tonight. He'll be scouting for these SOBs. Please move to Russ's hotel."

"I'd still be at my clinic during the day. What's to prevent them from coming then?"

Not one damn thing, he thought.

Davis Lee frowned at her. "Do you have a gun?"

"Yes, I had to carry one in Philadelphia when I went to unsavory areas."

"If you aren't already carrying it, you should start," Jericho said.

She nodded. Matt was ready to chew nails. The woman frustrated the fire out of him. He'd tried wheedling and cajoling. Neither worked. He sure as hell knew she wouldn't do it as a favor to him.

He fought to keep his voice level. "Annalise, please go to the hotel. If for no other reason than to…"

The stubborn slant to her jaw had his words trailing off. He knew that look and he was wasting his breath.

Davis Lee opened the door to leave. "We wanted you to be aware, Annalise. Keep your eyes open."

"I will, and thank you. You too, Jericho."

The former Ranger nodded. "Remember, Ef is nearby, too, if you should need anything."

"All right."

Matt followed the two men outside then stopped on the stoop and turned.

Before he could even open his mouth, she said, "I'm not going anywhere."

"I know that, you dad-blamed stubborn woman." He

wanted to grab her and shake some sense into her. "I was going to say watch your back."

"I will."

With one last look at her defiant expression, he muttered a curse and slammed his hat back on.

Short of slinging her over his shoulder and marching her to the hotel himself, there was nothing he could do. And yes, Ef was nearby, but how would that help if one of the outlaws managed to get inside Annalise's clinic without being seen? At least at the hotel, the risk of being spotted was likely too great for the outlaws to sneak in there.

Agreeing to meet Davis Lee and Jericho in front of the Fontaine in fifteen minutes, Matt started across Main Street for the Whirlwind Hotel where he'd left his horse.

For once, he fumed, why couldn't she do as he asked? Just the possibility of the rustlers being nearby had been enough for Matt to insist on escorting her to the Eight of Hearts Ranch earlier. Now that he knew the Landis brothers had been spotted outside Whirlwind, there was no way he was leaving her without some kind of protection.

Well, if she wouldn't take more precautions, then he would do it for her.

His mind quickly went through a possible list of candidates who could keep an eye on her while he was gone. He planned to ask Ef to watch over her during the day, but there should be someone for after dark as well. The other choices he considered were either too young to stay up all night watching the clinic or weren't good with a gun. Except one.

Matt stopped and turned, his gaze going to the newspaper office. It was dark. He hoped that meant Quentin was at home.

Just the thought of asking Prescott for anything had Matt's back bowing, but there was no doubt in his mind that the other man would do whatever he could to protect Annalise.

Before pride won out, Matt angled across the street and strode past the newspaper office, the saloon, then cut behind the livery to Quentin's modest white frame house. A light burned in the front window. Good.

Stepping onto the wide porch that stretched the width of the house, he knocked on the door. On the other side, the floor creaked, then the door opened. Quentin was still dressed in the white shirt and dark trousers he had worn to the wedding.

From his wheelchair, the sharp-featured man eyed him warily. "Baldwin."

"Could I talk to you for a minute?"

The man hesitated.

"It's about Annalise."

"Because she went to the wedding with *me?*" Quentin asked flatly.

Matt didn't like the thought that there might be more between Annalise and the newspaperman than friendship, but that wasn't what mattered right now. "No."

"All right." His sun-burnished features softening somewhat, Quentin rolled his wheelchair back so Matt could walk inside and close the door.

The other man gestured toward the small parlor off to the side. "Do you want to sit?"

"No, thanks."

"What's this about then?" Prescott rested his elbows on the chair arms, his dark eyes shrewd and speculative.

Matt explained about the Landis brothers being

spotted nearby. All he had to do was mention the McDougals for Quentin to understand Matt's concern.

When Prescott heard that Annalise refused to go to the hotel, he nodded. "What do you need me to do?"

"Watch her place tonight. Maybe more than to-night."

"What if they show up and give her trouble?" Quentin glanced at his crippled legs and a flush spread over the man's neck. "Will I be more of a hindrance than a help?"

The fact that the man was putting aside his pride to ask showed how fond he was of Annalise. Just how deep did those feelings go? Matt wondered.

He nodded toward the Spencer rifle standing in the corner. "You used to be a real good shot. Are you still?"

"Yes. I have to protect myself so I stay in practice," the man said stiffly.

"That's good enough for me. If there's trouble, you fire two shots in rapid succession, just like any of us do when we need help. Whoever is here will come."

"All right."

"There are several of us going out to scout. Depending on what we find, I might be back tomorrow. It could be longer."

Quentin stroked his thin mustache. "Does Annalise know about this?"

Matt shook his head.

"She wouldn't like it."

"Why do you think I didn't tell her?" he asked with a rueful grin that got a smile out of the other man. "I'm riding out now."

"Don't worry. I'll take care of her."

The possessiveness in the other man's voice didn't sit

Send For
2 FREE BOOKS
Today!

I accept your offer!

Please send me two free Harlequin® Historical novels and two mystery gifts (gifts worth about $10). I understand that these books are completely free—even the shipping and handling will be paid—and I am under no obligation to purchase anything, ever, as explained on the back of this card.

About how many NEW paperback fiction books have you purchased in the past 3 months?

❏ 0-2   ❏ 3-6   ❏ 7 or more
E9LY   **E9MC**   **E9MN**

246/349 HDL

Please Print

FIRST NAME

LAST NAME

ADDRESS

APT.#   CITY

STATE/PROV.   ZIP/POSTAL CODE

Visit us online at www.ReaderService.com

NO POSTAGE
NECESSARY
IF MAILED
IN THE
UNITED STATES

BUSINESS REPLY MAIL
FIRST-CLASS MAIL   PERMIT NO. 717   BUFFALO, NY

POSTAGE WILL BE PAID BY ADDRESSEE

THE READER SERVICE
PO BOX 1867
BUFFALO NY 14240-9952

well with Matt, but he forced himself to look past that. He might not trust Quentin to have *his* back, but he had no doubt the man would watch out for Annalise.

After shaking Prescott's hand, Matt returned to the Whirlwind Hotel and retrieved Dove. He swung into the saddle, staring for a moment at the clinic.

The downstairs was dark, but a light shone upstairs. She wouldn't be glad to see him again. He should ride on, but even as he thought it, he guided his mare to the building and dismounted.

He knocked on the front door, knowing she would answer in case the visitor was someone who needed help.

After a few seconds, he heard the tap of shoes on the wooden floor and the door opened.

She was still wearing her moss-green evening dress, drawing Matt's gaze to the velvety swells of her breasts where he'd had his mouth earlier tonight.

Upon seeing him, she exhaled loudly. "I'm not moving into the hotel."

"I just stopped to say be careful. Please."

She blinked. "Oh. All right."

Lantern light glided over her mahogany hair, skimmed the graceful curve of her neck. He curled his hands against the urge to brush his fingers down the same path. To press his thumb to the wildly beating pulse in the hollow of her throat, feel the powder-fine texture of her skin. "All right then."

He remounted and raised a hand in goodbye. She did the same. Just as he urged Dove into motion, Annalise spoke.

"Matt?"

He reined up, looking over to see her put one small slippered foot over the threshold, standing half in and half out of her house. Her arms were wrapped around her middle, moonlight polishing her skin to a pearly sheen. In the shadows, her eyes glittered like dark gems. "You be careful, too."

Something big and hot unfolded in his chest. There was real concern in her eyes, something more than a doctor's concern.

He gave her a slow grin and winked. "You bet."

As he kicked Dove into a canter, he heard her door shut. For the first time since her return, she had looked at Matt without censure or disdain. Just as she had earlier that evening after he had kissed her.

When he had followed her and Quentin back to Whirlwind, Matt hadn't thought further ahead than finding her and having his say. But now he knew what he wanted. Her. *Them.* He just had to figure out how to get her to want it, too.

Chapter Eight

Ever since their return from the Eight of Hearts Ranch, Annalise's emotions had been swept this way and that. Matt admired her for her doctoring skills? He now believed she had told the truth about being unaware of her pregnancy when she'd left Whirlwind?

She had been turning his words over in her mind. They weren't the only thing that had her topsy-turvy.

The past two nights, she had noticed Quentin across the way, watching. At first, she hadn't realized he was observing the clinic specifically so she hadn't given it a second thought, but when she became aware that his attention was trained only on her, Annalise sought him out.

She had asked Quentin what he was up to and he explained that he was watching out for her at Matt's request.

Her former betrothed obviously felt more strongly about the threat of the Landis brothers than she had understood. Than she had wanted to understand, she admitted. The sense of responsibility he felt toward her chafed. She had gone years without his attention, but how could she take exception to Matt's arrangement with Quentin? He was only concerned for her safety.

The Matt she used to know would never have spoken to, much less asked for help from, a man whom he and most of the town disliked.

Just when she thought she knew up from down, he went and did this.

About an hour after lunch, she took a lamp and went to the back of the house and down into the cellar. Her medical textbooks were stored in the dry, dusty space along with a box of her father's things, including the silver pocket watch he had intended her to give Matt after they were married.

She'd forgotten about that and thinking about it now she was swept with a fresh sense of loss over her father and what could've been with Matt. Pushing the thought aside, she reflected on her father's friendship with J.T. Baldwin, who was the reason she had come down here to start with.

After her arrival in Whirlwind, Davis Lee and Riley had helped her unload her belongings, storing the crates containing the majority of her medical textbooks down here. None of the crates on the floor along the wall held her surgical or anatomy textbooks. With a grimace, she eyed the two wooden boxes sitting atop a high shelf that ran the length of the wall.

Of course the books she needed would be in one of those two crates.

Pulling the wooden ladder from the corner, she leaned it against the wall and climbed up. She reached for the first box and tentatively tested its weight. Heavy, but not too heavy for her to move. If she balanced just right, she could manage.

After carefully lifting the crate, she slowly made her way down the ladder. Once on the floor, she pried the lid off, but didn't find the books she sought.

She positioned the ladder closer to the remaining crate and climbed up again. She wanted as much information on J.T.'s condition as possible; she also needed to make sure she had done everything she could for Mr. Julius's young guest.

The lamplight flickered as she moved, stretching her shadow across the wall. She wiped her grimy hands on her skirt then dragged an arm across her sweat-dampened forehead. She cautiously pulled the second crate toward her then lifted it into her arms, making sure she had her balance before starting down the ladder.

Three rungs from the bottom, the base of the crate gave. She caught at it and the abrupt motion jarred the ladder. Unable to grab for support, she fell.

She cried out, wood splintering and cracking as she landed on her back. Her head hit the dirt floor and her vision went black for several seconds.

"Annalise! Talk to me!"

Fuzzy-headed, she came to. Had she heard Matt? She opened her eyes and found him leaning over her.

In the dusky light, she could see the alarm on his face.

"Can you hear me? Talk to me."

She lay there winded and trying to breathe. "Just…a… minute."

As he lightly brushed pieces of wood from her skirts, she mentally catalogued her injuries. Her right shoulder and the back of her head throbbed. She would have bruises and a knot on her head, but no bones were broken.

Finally able to get a full breath, she started to sit up.

"Wait," Matt ordered impatiently. He slipped one strong arm beneath her shoulders and she gripped his other one, bringing it across her torso to help lever herself up.

A sharp ache pierced her skull. Drawing in a shaky breath, her fingers tightened on his rock-hard forearm. "I think I can stand now."

"I don't know." He looked her over critically.

"Nothing's broken." Her nausea was already passing. "There's a bump on my head and I'll probably have a bruised shoulder."

Still looking uncertain, he slowly got to his feet, helping her as well. Her head felt as if it were being split open.

"Ah, there," she said, satisfied at her progress. "See."

She promptly swayed and would've fallen if Matt hadn't still been holding on to her.

"Whoa." He carefully lifted her into his arms.

"Oh!" She clutched his shirt, inhaling his warm masculine scent. "What are you doing?"

"Getting you out of here. You need to lie down for a minute."

"You don't need to carry me. The dizziness is passing." Even as she spoke, a wave of skull-crushing pain had her squeezing her eyes shut.

He just held her closer and walked up the cellar stairs.

"Matt, really. You don't need to carry me. I'm sure I can make it on my own."

He snorted. "You can't even stand up."

"I can now. I think," she said faintly. "I certainly don't expect you to carry me."

"Well, this is your lucky day. I'm totin' all crazy women without being asked."

He cradled her against his chest. To avoid her arms bending at an awkward angle, she slid them loosely around his shoulders.

Nausea rushed through her and she turned her face into him, trying to stop the world from spinning.

Cushioned against his broad hard chest, she felt his arms warm and solid around her. The scent of man and leather slid into her lungs. Her nose brushed the strip of skin on his neck where whiskers gave way to smooth skin and his breathing hitched slightly.

She let her head rest on his shoulder. His steps were steady and sure as he carried her into the front room then back into her exam room.

He carefully laid her on the narrow cot, nuzzling her cheek before letting go of her and easing down onto the side of the bed.

"Are you hurt anywhere else?" Blue eyes dark with concern, he gently brushed her hair from her face.

She found herself wanting to do the same to his coffee-dark hair. "No. I'm really fine. I was just dizzy for a moment."

She raised up on one elbow and he laid a hand on her shoulder, barely using any pressure but firmly keeping her in place. "You need to stay still until the inside of your head stops pounding. You're pale as milk, too."

At the moment, she didn't have the energy to prove him wrong so she eased back onto the pillow. "What are you doing here?"

He looked slightly reassured. "Rescuing crazy women from ladders."

She smiled then winced at the throb in her head.

His gaze ran over every inch of her green-and-blue

calico dress to the tips of her boots then returned to her face. "I just got back from scouting for the Landis brothers and I came to tell you we lost them again. We picked up their trail between Julius's ranch and Fort Greer."

"So they headed west?"

"For a bit, then they turned back this way. It's the damnedest thing." Bracing his hands on either side of her, he leaned over, gaze narrowed thoughtfully on her face. "We tracked their mounts another couple of miles, then lost them. They were there, then gone. Just disappeared. We couldn't even pick up their horses' tracks, only the hoofprints of cattle."

Repressing a little shiver at his news, she said quietly, "I can sit up now."

Matt slid one steadying hand under her elbow, his work-roughened palm gentle on her softer skin as he helped her.

"Those outlaws never showed up here."

"Good," he said.

Just as she started to tell him she knew about his arrangement with Quentin, she spotted something behind him in a wedge of sunlight on the wooden floor. It looked like…flowers? "Where did those come from?"

He glanced over his shoulder, then rose to go over and pick them up.

Bluebonnets, Annalise realized as he walked toward her.

"I picked them for you." He curled her hand around the bunch of stems as she admired the purplish-blue blooms. "At the time, I didn't know they would turn out to be a get-better bouquet."

He had brought her flowers. She searched his face, intense and sober. "Thank you. They're beautiful."

"Glad you like them," he said gruffly.

Her chest tightened. Gestures like this chipped away at the wall she'd built against him. "You shouldn't have."

"I wanted to." He stared straight into her eyes and she knew he was remembering that he had brought bluebonnets the first time he had called on her.

The flowers set off a longing inside her. It was getting more difficult to stay on her guard around him. To remember to keep her distance.

Her gaze drifted to his mouth and she recalled the kisses they had shared the other night in her front room. How she had wanted more.

She'd told herself she had responded because he had taken her off guard, but it wasn't true. She had responded because she had been just as swept away by him as she always had. There was no dodging that fact.

Fingering the blooms, she slanted him a look. "Quentin told me what you worked out with him."

"He did, huh?" Matt's gaze went soft on her face.

"There was no need." Instead of sounding firm, she sounded breathless. "There wasn't even a hint of trouble."

"Maybe that's why," he said pointedly. "What were you doing in the cellar?"

"Looking for some of my medical books."

He eased back down onto the edge of the mattress, close enough that she could feel the hard hot line of his thigh through her skirts. One of his large hands rested next to her hip, setting off a low vibration inside her.

"How's your head?"

"Better."

"Your shoulder getting sore?"

She nodded.

"Why didn't you ask someone to help you?"

"If that crate hadn't broken, I would've handled everything fine."

"It was full of heavy books, Annalise."

"Well, you can't take your eyes off me for one second," she quipped. "There's no telling what I might get up to."

"Evidently," he murmured, heat flaring in his eyes.

She swallowed hard and redirected the conversation. "I'm not sure I like you getting someone to watch me while you were gone."

"Not to watch *you*. To watch your back. There's a difference, and if you think I'm going to apologize, you can think again."

She couldn't seem to stop looking at his mouth.

His gaze moved slowly over her, striking sparks under her skin. "Those outlaws were too close for comfort. Damn sure too close for *my* comfort and it didn't inconvenience you one bit."

"No, it didn't." She wasn't vexed about it. Like other things that had happened in the past couple of days, it confused her.

"It made me feel a lot better knowing you had someone here," he said gruffly.

Before she could tell him she understood, he said, "The only time I've ever seen Jericho Blue rattled was when his wife was taken by outlaws, and that isn't going to happen to you if I can help it."

Annalise melted inside. Oh, how could he slip under her guard so easily? He plainly felt a responsibility toward her because he hadn't been there when she needed him all those years ago.

"It's all right," she said.

"I don't care if you think I'm paranoid. I'm not apologizing for having your best interests at heart."

It wasn't the fierceness in his voice that had her pulse jumping. It was the frankly possessive look in his eyes.

"I don't expect you to apologize, Matt."

"You're wastin' your breath if you think—what?" He broke off, looking nonplused.

"I know you had my safety in mind."

A frown gathered on his brow. "So, you're not mad?"

"Mad? No." But she was quickly being overcome by the desire to lean into him, rest against his chest the way she had a few minutes ago.

Their new tentative truce tempted her to believe things could be different for them, but they couldn't. Could they?

She told herself she could stay away from him if she wanted. It wasn't true. His apologies and thoughtful gestures didn't make the past hurt any less, but because of them, she was afraid keeping her distance was going to be downright impossible.

Matt had thought a lot about Annalise last night. About her fall, about the way she kept looking at him, how she'd accepted the arrangement he had made with Quentin.

As aggravated as she'd been before he rode out to search for the Landis brothers, Matt hadn't been sure what kind of welcome he would get when he returned. It was a good thing he'd gone to her clinic anyway. He didn't want to think about what might have happened if he hadn't been there after her fall.

He had stayed in town last night, in Russ's old room at the Fontaine so that Pa and Cora could be alone a little longer. And because, after Annalise's accident, he wanted to be close.

She kept insisting she was fine and she probably was. All Matt knew was that when he'd seen her on the floor like a broken doll, his gut had snarled into a big knot, and it had eased only after a few hours.

Once he was convinced she would be all right, he made sure she didn't move while he carried the books from the cellar. Thick heavy volumes with headache-inducing titles like *Ashhurst's International Encyclopedia of Surgery* and *Leidy's Anatomy.* After he finished shelving the textbooks, he had asked her to dinner, but she had declined, saying she had accepted an invitation from Quentin.

As prickly as that made him, Matt thought there was only friendship between her and the newspaper man, and hoped he wasn't wrong.

When she'd informed him that she knew about his arrangement with the other man, Matt had expected anger. Indignation at the very least. Instead, she'd been understanding, which not only surprised him, but also encouraged him. Enough that he was going to push his luck today and invite her to lunch.

He spent the morning putting new shoes on Dove and helping his brother fix a problem with the gas lighting at the Fontaine. He caught sight of Annalise a couple of times. Once while she was visiting with Andrew Donnelly as he swept her stoop before school and the second time when she came out of Haskell's.

Just before noon, he left the Fontaine and walked toward her clinic on the opposite end of town. He happened upon Quentin Prescott along the way and stopped to speak. During their brief conversation, Matt saw his pa and Cora come out of the clinic.

He had thought they might want to stay at the ranch alone for another couple of days before making their first appearance in town. Seeing them now reminded Matt that he had also seen Pa coming from Annalise's clinic the day before the wedding.

His father and stepmother made their way across the street and into the Pearl restaurant. Matt decided to talk to them later. After lunch.

The day was sunny and clear with puffy white clouds floating in the blue sky. Matt knocked on the door of the clinic. When Annalise answered, he braced one arm above his head, his gaze sliding over the gray-and-white checked bodice that molded to her breasts and waist. Her skirt was of the same serviceable gray. There was nothing provocative about her practical daydress yet Matt's pulse thudded hard.

Her hair hung over one shoulder in a loose braid, the sun bringing out the dark rich color.

"Matt?"

The sharpness of her voice pulled his attention to her face. And the deep green of her eyes.

Eyes that stared warily into his. "What are you doing?"

He grinned. "I came by to check on my patient."

A half smile tugged at her lips.

"How's your head?" he asked.

"Much better."

"And your shoulder?"

"Bruised."

"I'm glad you're not worse."

"So am I." Curiosity streaked across her features.

"I saw Pa and Cora leaving your clinic." He thumbed back his hat. "Is anything wrong? Is Cora okay?"

Something flickered in Annalise's eyes then disappeared. "She's fine. The two of them stopped by for a visit. Why are you in town again so soon?"

"Never left. I stayed at the Fontaine last night. Thought the newlyweds might like a little more time alone, seeing as they're…newlyweds."

"Oh." Her cheeks flushed a becoming pink. "Is that the only reason?"

Her raised brow indicated she suspected he had stayed because of her. She wouldn't be wrong. Instead of answering, he shrugged.

Matt shifted, catching a glimpse from the corner of his eye of the flowers he had brought yesterday. The bluebonnets were in a small tin pitcher sitting in the front window.

She hadn't thrown them away. He took that as a good sign. His gaze hiked over her again, lingering on her mouth. He wanted to kiss her, thought maybe he should have last night. "Have lunch with me."

This close he couldn't miss the slight stiffening of her shoulders. Even so, he didn't expect her next words.

"I don't know if that's a good idea."

He deliberately misunderstood her. "It's always a good idea to eat."

"You know what I mean."

Yes, dammit, he did. And he didn't fancy it. His chest tightened. He had caught the hungry way she had looked at him last night, but he knew better than to remind her of that.

"I thought we were starting to put the past behind us."

"It's not that easy."

"Doesn't mean we can't try, does it? That *I* can't try?"

"No."

"What's the problem?" He grinned. "Afraid you'll like it too much?"

"I don't want to like it."

That hurt, but he managed to keep his voice light. "I can see where that would be bothersome. I hate enjoying things."

She rolled her eyes. "It can't be like it was before."

"I'm not asking for that." Yet. That would be like dancing two steps back for every one forward.

Before he could coax her into sharing a meal with him, he caught sight of Davis Lee coming from the alley between the mercantile and the law office next door to the clinic. The lawman headed toward them.

Matt tilted his head in the man's direction. "Davis Lee looks like he has something on his mind."

"Josie," Annalise breathed. She stepped outside, her skirts swirling around his trousers.

Matt shifted just enough to give her some room, but he didn't move away. His gaze caught on a wisp of her hair blowing against the graceful curve of her neck.

"Annalise!" The sheriff cleared the steps in one stride.

"Is Josie all right?" she asked.

"Yes. I mean no." He blew out a frustrated breath. "I think so. There's no emergency."

"Oh, good."

Matt felt the tension ease out of her, but before Davis Lee could tell her the problem, a masculine voice boomed, "Sheriff!"

Matt's gaze went past his friend to Theodore Julius and his ranch manager. The men dodged a wagon as they crossed the street from the jail.

Annalise looked up at Davis Lee. "Does Josie need me?"

"No. At least I don't think so."

Huh? Matt glanced at Annalise, who looked confused, too.

Julius and Cosgrove stopped at the foot of the steps, both men tipping their hats to Annalise.

The older man turned to Davis Lee. "Sorry to interrupt, Sheriff, but some of my cattle were stolen last night. I thought you'd want to know as soon as possible."

"You thought right."

Matt listened as the men from the Eight of Hearts Ranch reported the theft of five cows and two calves.

Davis Lee nodded. "Were they branded?"

"Yes," the owner confirmed.

"Did y'all find tracks?" Matt asked.

"Only those belonging to cattle."

Matt could feel someone staring at them and looked over Davis Lee's shoulder to see May Haskell. Standing in front of the mercantile, the store owner's wife was glaring in their direction so hard, Matt could practically feel his skin burn. Who was she riled at?

Davis Lee half turned to follow Matt's gaze then shifted so that his back was to the woman. "No boot prints, no horse tracks?"

"No," Cosgrove answered.

Matt growled in frustration. "How in the hell are they rustling without leaving any sign except that of the missing cattle?"

The sheriff shook his head. "I have no idea."

Matt noticed Pearl Anderson stepping out of the telegraph office. Her eyes went straight to Davis Lee; she turned up her nose and went back inside. What the devil was going on? Matt wondered.

Davis Lee had seen it, too. His jaw tightened as he focused on Julius. "I want to take a look around your spread."

"All right," said the barrel-shaped man. "Although I don't think you'll find anything. Cosgrove and I didn't."

After a few more questions, Davis Lee pinched the bridge of his nose. "I'll come out a little later."

"Very good," the rancher said.

As he and Cosgrove turned to leave, Annalise stopped the ranch owner. "Mr. Julius, how is Edward?"

"He's staying in bed, like you told him."

"That's good. I'll be out to check on him in a couple of days."

"I'll let him know." Julius tipped his hat then walked away with Cosgrove.

She turned to Davis Lee. "Is there anything I can do for you?"

Zoe Keeler appeared at the side of the clinic, seemingly coming from the sheriff's house. "Hello, Matt. Hello, Annalise."

Her gaze lit on Davis Lee and she frowned, continuing across the street toward the telegraph office without speaking to him.

Matt looked from the usually cheery redhead to the lawman. "What did you do to Zoe?"

"Nothing," Davis Lee muttered.

"What about May and Pearl? They're all put out with you for some reason."

"That's why I came to see you, Annalise." Davis Lee snatched off his hat, looking helplessly at her. "Josie cries all the time, no matter what I do."

Squinting against the sun, Matt noted his friend's eyes were red-rimmed and his face haggard, as though he hadn't slept. His usually neat hair stuck up in places from his hands raking through it, which he did now.

"She's crying *all* the time?" Annalise asked. "Tell me what's happened."

Davis Lee paced to the edge of the stoop then back, hitting his thigh with his hat. "She said she wanted lemonade and when I brought it to her, she started crying. She asked me to rub her back, so I did. Then she started crying. I couldn't find a pair of socks this morning and when I asked her if they were all dirty, she started crying.

"Hell, she asks for food she doesn't even like. Yesterday, she asked for grits. She hates grits!"

Davis Lee looked as though he was at the end of his rope. Matt could see why.

Annalise put a hand on the man's arm. "Josie isn't crying because of something you are or aren't doing."

"Well, that isn't how it feels and every woman in this town disagrees with you. You saw 'em. I'd rather face a rattler. They want to string me up by my ball—er, hang me."

"Pregnant women are very emotional sometimes."

"She didn't do this the other two times. What should I do?"

"Would you like me to talk to her?"

Looking defeated, the big man's shoulders sagged. "I don't know."

Matt frowned. "I can ride out and have a look around Julius's ranch, if you need to stay here."

"No. It might be good for me to get away from my wife for a while, since all I do is make her cry."

Annalise gave him a sympathetic smile. "I'm happy to check on her."

"Thanks, I'd appreciate it." The tight lines in his face eased somewhat.

Annalise looked relieved, too, Matt noted as she

pulled the clinic door shut. Why? Because she was anxious to get away from him?

He shifted his attention to Davis Lee. "Want me to ride out with you to the Eight of Hearts?"

"Yes, in a bit. Right now, there's something I need to do at my office."

Probably hide out from his pretty little wife, Matt thought.

As the man walked away, Matt saw Annalise fighting a smile before she turned to him. "I'd better get going."

He thought about offering to walk with her to see Josie, but she was already as skittish as a colt. "Maybe I'll see you later."

She hesitated. "Maybe."

He watched her disappear around the side of her clinic. Recalling the frustration on Davis Lee's face, Matt shook his head. He felt sorry for his friend even though what he had shared was kind of funny. Not that Josie was crying all the time, but that she was asking for food she didn't like and refusing things which she did.

He wondered if Annalise had been that way when she had been expecting. He had missed out on everything. His smile faded. He knew nothing about those months except that she had lost the baby. Their baby.

He wanted to know, but now wasn't the time to ask. Hell, he couldn't even get her to agree to a meal. It didn't figure she would talk to him about that time in their lives.

Still, they had made some progress. She had accepted his flowers. And his arrangement with Quentin. She'd said no to lunch, but he wasn't giving up.

A half hour later, after seeing her return to the clinic,

he took the basket of food he'd bought from the Pearl and went over.

He walked inside and she came out of the back room, her steps slowing when she saw him.

"What are you doing?"

He held up the basket. "Since you won't join me for lunch, I brought it to you."

Pleasure flared in her eyes before it was replaced by uncertainty.

Matt refused to give in to her hesitation. "It's just lunch, Angel. You have to eat. There's no reason you can't do it with me."

After a long minute, she nodded. "All right. Thank you."

He followed her down the short hall to the kitchen which shared the fireplace with the front room. His gaze went to her trim back and small waist, followed the gentle sway of her skirts. The fluid way the fabric swirled around her legs made him wonder if she was wearing more than one petticoat.

He'd had to pry his way in here, practically force her to eat with him. It was clear she didn't trust him not to hurt her again, but he aimed to change that. Somehow.

Chapter Nine

In the following days, Annalise learned keeping her distance from Matt wasn't the problem. It was getting him out of her thoughts.

The day after their impromptu picnic she received a note from him. He said he hoped her injuries were healing and told her how much he enjoyed having an inside picnic with her. He ended by asking if she would have dinner with him. She sent a note back saying no.

She might have been charmed by the picnic, but she wasn't sure about doing more than that with him.

The next day he sent a note with a cluster of purple prairie verbena telling her he would be at her clinic the following day to drive her out to the Eight of Hearts Ranch so she could check on her patient. Again, he asked if she would have dinner with him. She said no.

True to his word, he drove her out to Julius's ranch and on the return trip, he asked her to have dinner with him. She said no.

The day after that, a piece of butter cake was delivered

with a note. He knew the dessert was her favorite and the note said if she would have dinner with him, he would get her an entire cake. She said no. With difficulty.

The notes got to her. Matt hated writing anything, especially of a personal nature. His penmanship was terrible, but she could tell he had taken his time over the messages. The only thing he didn't hate writing was information about his livestock. He kept meticulous records regarding the number of animals and births, sickness, deaths.

The following day, Ef showed up at her clinic with newly banded wheels on her buggy, courtesy of Matt. Though moved by his thoughtfulness, she had protested. With a grin, the blacksmith said he had been warned Annalise would argue about the gift. He handed her a note in which Matt explained that he had noticed the worn bands on their trip to the Eight of Hearts Ranch. It wouldn't take more than hitting a hole to lose a wheel and possibly cause an accident.

He closed by asking if she would have dinner with him. This time, she said yes.

The next evening, he arrived at six and they walked down to the Fontaine for dinner. As she waited for him, she remembered how giddy she used to be when he would call for her. How she would dither about choosing what to wear. Just as she had tonight.

She had finally settled on a dinner dress in rose silk. The neckline was square and trimmed in the same white duchess lace as the elbow-length sleeves.

After they were seated at a quiet table in the corner and had given their order to Naomi Gerard, Ef's wife, Annalise and Matt admired the dark-paneled room. The dining tables were polished to a high sheen, set with sparkling crystal and silver flatware. Both agreed that Russ and Lydia had outdone themselves.

In the soft white gaslight, Annalise glanced at him. "I appreciate everything you've done over the last several days."

He grimaced. "You don't wanna talk about it, do you?"

She laughed. "Only to say thank you, especially for seeing to my buggy wheels. I never would've thought about checking them."

"Because your pa always did it for you."

She nodded, her throat tightening. "It was very sweet."

He covered her hand with his, rubbing his thumb across her knuckles. She went very still, but before she could pull away, he did.

"So I owe this dinner to a set of buggy wheels?"

"Yes."

"I'll have to keep that in mind." His blue eyes were warm. "Did you talk to Josie about her crying spells?"

"Yes."

"Did she cry during that?" Matt chuckled.

"Yes."

His eyes widened. "I was just joshin'."

"She felt as though she'd driven Davis Lee out of the house that day. I assured both of them, separately and together, that neither of them were to blame. This is just something they have to get through."

It had made her think about how she'd handled everything on her own when she'd carried her and Matt's baby.

He stared at her as if he expected her to remind him that he had let her down, but she didn't. She really did want to put the anger and blame of their past behind them. Still, she wasn't willing to look further ahead than tonight. Matt could have her throwing caution to the wind and she didn't want that.

As they ate, she chanced a few looks at him. She admired the square line of his clean-shaven jaw. A white shirt clung to his wide shoulders and made his skin a deep bronze. Dark trousers gloved his long, long legs. The passing years had made him more handsome. Maybe it was because there were now some hard-earned creases on his face, a new maturity in those blue eyes.

Lines of fatigue fanned out from his eyes, carved a groove around his mouth. She knew it was because he was working long hours, day and night, trying to catch the rustlers.

"I guess you're still alternating shifts with Riley and the Rosses."

"Yes. It's worked out well. We ride in twos and this way everyone gets a break."

As they waited for coffee and dessert, his gaze traced her features. "Is there anyone missing you back in Philadelphia? A man, I mean."

She swept away a loose tendril of hair that had escaped from her loose upsweep. There had never been anyone for her except him and she was afraid it might always be that way. She didn't have to admit it to him though.

She thought about asking if he'd had anyone special since she'd left, but she didn't. There had been plenty of talk about him and a lot of women.

It wasn't as though he had cheated on her, but she couldn't help feeling a little hurt.

"No, no one special." She took a bite of butter cake.

His gaze traveled slowly over her, paused on her breasts then rose to her lips. "You sure are a sight," he said for the second time since he'd called for her that evening. "I wanted to eat you up when I saw you."

There was nothing daring about her dress. Only her neck and the flat plane of her chest were bared, but he looked at her as if he could see her in the altogether. The heat in his eyes gave her a shiver and sent a tingle to her toes.

He asked about her injuries and she told him they were much better.

He cut off a corner of her dessert. "Pa has been really distracted. At first, I thought it was because he's a new-lywed, but he's been absent-minded and sometimes short with people."

Annalise was afraid it was due to his condition. As far as she knew, J.T. was no closer to walking than before, which made her think the man would probably be coming to see her again soon.

Naomi brought more coffee, saying in her soft South-ern voice, "Let me know if you need anything else."

Matt smiled at her. "We will. Everything was more than fine tonight."

"Yes, very good," Annalise added.

"Thank you."

As they finished their cake, Charlie and May Haskell stopped at their table to say hello. Both had pleased smiles on their faces as they walked away.

Matt watched her carefully. "By tomorrow, it's going to be all over town that you were out with me tonight."

Sipping her coffee, Annalise nodded. The thought had occurred to her before she had accepted his invitation. "Some things don't change, I guess."

Her gaze followed his as the Haskells made their way across the room. Just as the older couple stepped out of the dining room, Charlie reached back and pinched May on the bottom.

Annalise choked on her coffee, quickly putting down her cup before she dropped it. Matt's chuckle said he'd seen the same thing.

"Do you remember—" They both began at the same time.

She laughed. "The night of the pecan harvest dance when we decided to stop in the Eishens' grove."

"And not for picnickin'," he said in a low voice. "I was dyin' to kiss you proper."

She'd wanted that, too. But when they reached the well-known, well-used spot, it had been taken. By the Haskells!

She had never looked at the mercantile owner and his wife the same way again and neither had Matt.

She smiled into his eyes. "You were appalled."

"And you weren't."

"I thought it was sweet." She had also imagined her and Matt doing the same thing after spending many years together. Her smile faded a bit. "They still fancy each other."

Her gaze locked with Matt's and a long pulsing moment drew out between them. The flickering gaslight made it easy to read the desire in his blue eyes. Her entire body vibrated with awareness. He stared at her mouth and she felt his hand curl into a fist, as though he was trying not to touch her.

Part of her wanted him to reach for her. She sat there in a daze until he broke the tension by winking.

"I bet May and Charlie are going home to fancy each other all night long."

"Matt Baldwin!" She couldn't keep a straight face and dissolved into laugher.

He laughed, too, his eyes crinkling at the corners. "Annalise!"

She turned to see Davis Lee rushing toward their table. His dark hair was rumpled and his eyes wide. He held his hat tight, crumpling its brim. "It's time! Josie's having the baby!"

"Are you sure? How far apart are her contractions?"

"I know you told me what to do, but I can't remember a blamed thing. You said—" He broke off, his features pinched and anxious. "We've never gotten this far before. I don't know what to do!"

Placing her napkin on the table, she stood. "It's going to be all right. I need to get my bag."

Matt touched her arm. "Go on with Davis Lee. I'll stop by and get it."

"Are you sure? It's on the way."

"I think Davis Lee would feel better if you went now. I'll be right behind you."

She smiled. "Thank you."

He nodded. She gathered up her skirts and rushed out the door with Davis Lee. When the two of them angled behind the mercantile and toward his house, she saw Matt go past them and head for her clinic.

She realized she was still smiling. When was the last time she had done that while thinking of Matt Baldwin?

She couldn't remember.

After grabbing Annalise's bag and an apron, Matt rushed over to Davis Lee's house. His friend took the things in to Annalise, who was in the bedroom with Josie. Then the lawman stepped back out, frowning when the door closed behind him.

Matt rubbed the nape of his neck. Having never been in a situation like this, he wasn't sure what to do. Davis Lee walked to the center of the room and stopped.

He thumbed away a bead of sweat, his eyes dark with worry and confusion. "Josie kicked me out."

Matt's eyes widened. "Why?"

"She said I looked like I was about to pass out and she couldn't worry about me, too." His hat and knife sat on the corner of the dining table alongside a thick piece of pine. He picked up the knife and wood then propped himself against the wall beside the cupboard and began to whittle.

His friend looked disoriented, and Matt didn't feel right leaving him alone, but the man needed to keep his hands busy.

It made sense to him that Annalise and Josie would want to clean up at some point. They'd want to clean up the baby, too. He took a basin from the shelf above the sink and used the indoor pump to fill the bowl with water. After lighting the stove, he set the basin on it to heat.

The large front room was the center of the house. The stove behind Matt, and the sink and cupboard along the wall made the kitchen almost a separate room. The fireplace was beyond the stove and Josie and Davis Lee's bedroom was on the other side of that wall.

"I should be in there," Davis Lee said hoarsely, pausing with his knife held over the rapidly dwindling piece of wood. If he didn't stop whittling soon, all that would be left was a toothpick. "But seeing her in that much pain makes me hate myself. What kind of man can't help his wife when she needs it?"

"You're doing what you're supposed to be doing."

"What? Standing around like a lump?"

Matt hooked a foot under a chair leg and dragged it toward Davis Lee, sitting down. "I don't know any men who were with their wives for a birth. Do you?"

"No, but I know she wanted me to be there." His eyes were hollow, haunted. "This scares the hell out of me. Josie did everything Annalise told her to. We both did, but what if I lose her? And the baby?"

"Everything will be fine." He could hear Annalise's calm voice, the occasional pain-filled groan from Josie. "Annalise is with her and she knows what she's doing."

Davis Lee nodded, but he didn't look convinced.

"I sent Miguel to the Rocking H for Riley and Susannah. They should be here soon."

"Thanks. I've been so scatterbrained, I didn't even think about getting my family here."

"You've got other things on your mind."

The sheriff sliced another layer off the wood, then pushed away from the wall and paced to the door of his bedroom and back. Back and forth. Back and forth.

Matt shifted restlessly. "Have any chores I can help you with?"

"No." His friend stopped next to the stove, his blade flashing as he viciously slid it down the length of pine.

Matt had always been amazed at how well his friend handled the knife, but his strokes were so fast that he half expected the thing to fly out of Davis Lee's hand or for his friend to cut himself. "Wanna play cards?"

"I couldn't concentrate." Another forceful downstroke shaved off a curl of wood. The shavings littering the floor gave off the faint scent of pine.

"It might at least keep you from messing up Josie's clean floor."

"Oh, I'll sweep up before—"

A scream sounded from the next room and Davis Lee jerked so hard he nearly sliced off his thumb. Matt leapt up and grabbed his friend's arm, taking the knife.

The other man rushed to his bedroom door. "Josie!"

"Don't-come-in-here," she panted then moaned in pain.

Davis Lee turned away from the door and came back to his chair. He sank down, shoving a hand through his hair. "We've never gotten this far along with a baby and Annalise says that's a good sign."

Josie screamed again, making a chill shoot up Matt's spine.

"I had no idea it would be this harrowing." The sheriff's voice cracked. "I feel like I'm being skinned alive."

There was a very real chance his friends might lose another baby, and Matt had no idea what to say. What could be worse than going through the whole painful process of childbirth only to lose the baby?

He wondered how he would've been if his and Annalise's baby had lived, if he had been present for the birth. But he hadn't been there at all. Not for the beginning or the end. He wasn't sure he could ever forgive himself for that, and now he could see why Annalise might not either.

"Josie was right to kick me out. She would sense my doubt."

That was probably right, but how could the man feel anything else? He had absolutely no control over this, couldn't protect his wife or child from further pain. Matt would feel the same.

He *did* feel the same, he realized. He hadn't protected Annalise or their baby. Rationally, he knew he couldn't have stopped the miscarriage, but he understood his friend's sense of failure, of responsibility.

The patient groaned then cried out. The sounds began to run together in Matt's head.

Josie's obvious distress had him on edge. He could only imagine how much more trying this would be if Annalise was the one giving birth.

It seemed like hours passed before he heard a guttural moan then a lusty cry. A baby's cry.

The sound of that tiny voice had Matt's breath jamming in his lungs. Overwhelmed by a sudden urge to run, he gripped the table.

Davis Lee jumped up then froze.

The bedroom door opened and Annalise stepped out, looking weary, but smiling. "Josie's just fine and you have a girl."

The relief on the lawman's face was so stark, so raw that it twisted something in Matt's chest. He clapped Davis Lee on the shoulder. "Congratulations, Papa."

The other man moved then. He rushed into the bedroom as Annalise came into the kitchen. Matt studied her face, not understanding the panicked reaction he'd had upon hearing the baby.

Lines of fatigue fanned out from her green eyes; her apron was bloodied. She still wore a smile, but he sensed a heaviness in the air. He wasn't sure what it meant.

"It was good of you to stay with Davis Lee," she said.

"I don't know that I was any help, but at least he wasn't alone." Matt reached for the basin he'd moved to the table.

"Here, I pumped some water."

"Thanks. I cleaned up the baby some before I gave

her to Josie." Annalise washed her hands then dried them with a nearby square of toweling.

Uncertainty hammered at him. "Everything okay?"

"Josie did very well. No problems at all." She glanced back at the bedroom and lowered her voice. "I was concerned about that."

The door opened and a beaming Davis Lee came to the doorway holding a blanket-wrapped bundle. "Matt, come see her!"

He covered the short distance between them, staring down at a perfect upturned nose, a tiny rosebud mouth. Her face was scrunched up and she had a head full of dark hair.

"We're going to call her Tannis, after Josie's grandmother. Isn't she beautiful?"

Matt smiled past the crushing weight in his chest. "She sure is."

"Luckily, she takes after her mama." Chuckling, Davis Lee carried his daughter back into the bedroom.

Matt shoved an unsteady hand through his hair. He was shaky, unsettled. What was going on? His ears were ringing as if he'd been kicked in the head by a horse, and he couldn't breathe.

Hearing that baby, looking at her, made him feel all jostled up inside. His own child had never cried, never even taken a breath. He had to get out of here, grab some fresh air.

He backed away and walked out to the porch, noting absently that the front door was already open.

Darkness had settled while they waited for the baby. Now a crescent moon hung high in a clear sky dotted with stars. The air had turned comfortably cool yet Matt was hot inside. His chest felt prickly.

An urgency, a desperation rose inside him to find

Annalise, but a look back inside the house told him she was gone. He hadn't taken three steps from the porch when he heard a sound to his left. Coming from the direction of her clinic.

In the shifting moonlight, he could see the white lace on her dress sleeve. She stood at the corner of the building. Her shoulders shook.

He strode to her, his heart pounding. It took some effort to speak past the hard knot in his throat. "Annalise?"

He heard a muffled sob. He touched her shoulder, startled when she turned and buried her face in his chest.

"I don't understand why I'm crying." The tears thickening her voice put a burn in his throat.

He thought he knew why she was crying. The same sense of loss gripped him, too, for the child they'd lost.

"Let's go inside. Come on, Angel."

Retrieving the key from the pocket of her bloodstreaked apron, he unlocked the door and guided her inside.

Chapter Ten

Annalise felt as if she was falling apart. Grief and loss sat on her chest like an anvil. Matt guided her past the cellar and up the hall, bypassing the kitchen then the front room to turn toward the stairs.

Moonlight rippled across the pine floor just beyond the front door, casting pale shadows into the dark corners.

"Here," Matt murmured, easing her to a stop at the foot of the stairs. "Let's get rid of this."

He untied the strings of her blood-streaked apron and carefully pulled it over her loosely upswept hair then dropped the garment to the floor. Striding over to the table that sat beneath her front window, he picked up the unlit lamp and came back to her. He struck a match and light flared. He put a hand at the small of her back, urging her upstairs and into her bedroom.

He steered her toward the big bed in the center of the room and sat her on the edge of the mattress. The oilskin shade was up, the moon visible from this position.

She stared blankly at the full white globe, vaguely

aware that Matt had disappeared with the lamp, leaving her to sit in dim light.

He returned with a cool wet cloth and pressed it into her hands as he set the light on the bedside table. "You got any liquor?"

"There's a bottle of Old Tub bourbon in the parlor. Bottom drawer of the cupboard between the two chairs."

While he went across the hall to her small sitting room, she ran the rag over her sweat-dampened face and neck, then pressed the moist cloth to her swollen eyes.

In a few seconds, Matt was back with a small glass and the bottle of dark-amber liquid. He splashed some into the glass and handed it to her.

She wrinkled her nose at the strong smell. "I don't know."

"You're trembling," he said quietly, pushing the glass to her lips. "Drink."

When she did, she sucked in a breath at the burn in her throat. It wasn't long before warmth spread through her limbs.

She should be stronger, not lean on Matt for support, but at this moment, she couldn't find it inside herself. He poured more liquor and downed it himself, then refilled the glass and offered it to her again. She took a sip as he settled beside her.

Their shoulders touched and she found the power and heat of his body reassuring. Taking the glass from her, he swallowed half its contents in one gulp.

"I'm surprised you had liquor," he said.

"It was here when I bought the place. I don't know if Jed mistakenly left it when he and Lizzie moved out or if she left it in order to keep it away from him."

The rawness inside her began to ease. Trying to steady

herself, her gaze moved absently around the room, to the wall mirror over her dressing table. Her hairbrush and ribbons, the wardrobe in front of her with its door open enough to see the dresses she'd tried and discarded before deciding on the one she'd worn to dinner with Matt.

He reached up and gently edged a tendril of hair from her eyes. "How're you doing?"

"I don't know what came over me. That baby isn't the first one I've delivered since I lost ours." Annalise noticed Matt held the glass of whiskey so tightly that his knuckles were white.

And now that she looked, so was he. His face was cloud-pale beneath his bronzed features. "Are you okay?"

"When I heard Davis Lee's baby cry…" He shook his head then tossed back the remaining bourbon in his glass. "Our baby never cried," he said hoarsely. "Never even breathed."

The hurt ravaging his strong features dug deep into a place Annalise thought she would never let him into again. New tears burned her eyes. She could tell this was something he hadn't thought much about until now.

He searched her face. "Can you talk about it? Expecting our baby, I mean?"

"What do you want to know?"

"All of it. Were you sick every morning? Davis Lee said Josie was."

"Not every morning, but several times. I thought it was just nerves from leaving…Whirlwind." She bit her lip. She'd almost said 'leaving you.' "From moving so far away, where I didn't know anyone."

"Did you cry a lot, like Josie?"

"A fair amount."

"That's hard to imagine. You never were much for tears."

That seemed to have changed, she thought wryly as she wiped her eyes.

"And cravings? Was there any of that?" He set the empty glass on the bedside table. "Or hating things you normally liked?"

"I wanted nothing to do with coffee. Just the smell made me nauseous." She gave a small laugh. "What I couldn't get enough of was lemon. Lemonade, lemon drops, lemon cake, just plain lemons."

Slipping his big hot hand into hers, he threaded their fingers together. "I never knew you liked lemons."

"I didn't. I still don't."

He smiled faintly at that. "When did you realize you were expecting?"

"The lemon craving made me suspicious, but I wasn't sure until the miscarriage."

Matt winced, his blue eyes dark and troubled.

"I woke up bleeding and couldn't get it to stop." She paused when his hand tightened on hers. "There was a midwife in the boarding house where I stayed. She helped me through it then I got an infection."

He cursed.

"Are you sure you want me to talk about it?"

"Not if you don't want to, but I need to hear it. I need to know what you went through."

She told him how the infection had nearly killed her, how she had missed a few weeks of medical college in the middle of first term. "I made them up the following term."

The self-loathing, the torture on his face made her stop.

"What is it?" she asked softly. "It's more than hearing about the miscarriage and what happened afterwards."

He felt as if he'd been trampled by a herd of cattle—aware of a pulsing pain down deep but too numb on the surface to really feel it.

"You probably think I don't have the right even to feel the loss. And I'm not sure I do."

She squeezed his hand. "He was your son, too."

"But I wasn't there when either of you needed me."

She laid her head on his shoulder and the silent comfort she offered tore a hole in his heart.

"I was a real bastard to you." The words were thick and he had to clear his throat in order to continue. "I really let you down."

Taking him by surprise, she tugged her hand from his and put both arms around his neck. His eyes stung as he lifted a hand and curled it lightly over her forearm. "I understand why delivering Davis Lee's and Josie's baby upset you. I can't believe you felt like this and had to be alone after the miscarriage."

"But tonight, I'm not alone. Neither are you."

Her green eyes were soft with understanding and shared grief, somehow soothing the jagged edge inside him. He wanted to thank her, to apologize over and over, to promise he would never turn his back on her again.

He couldn't spit out one single word.

When a fresh tear rolled down her cheek, he pulled her onto his lap and buried his face in her neck. The faint scent of primrose along with a womanly musk swirled between them as he tried to steady himself. The warm, wet feel of her tears released something inside him and he pressed her closer.

They stayed like that for a long time, until she settled and lay soft against him.

He nudged her chin up with a knuckle, wiped at the dampness on her face. "Can I get you something? Water? More whiskey?"

"No," she whispered. Her eyes, deep green and wet, met his. "I don't need any of that."

She looked as lost as he felt. Lost and hurting. And he recognized something else. Need. Stunned, he slowly realized that she needed him. And *he* needed *her*.

He didn't know who moved first, but their lips touched. And when she leaned fully into him, it blew every thought out of his head. The kiss was slow and searching, filling him with something he couldn't define, but he knew Annalise was the only one who could give it to him. She wanted this as much as he did. To be held, to know she wasn't alone.

The press of her breasts against him, the feel of her fingers delving into his hair had reckless desire shooting through him. He wanted her until the hunger was a sharp throbbing ache. But she hadn't asked for that.

She drew away, her mouth wet and red from kissing his, and he realized he was squeezing her too hard. Loosening his hold on her, he flattened his hands on her back and lightly kept her in place.

Her fingers slid gently down the side of his face. "I don't want to be alone. I don't think you should be either."

Blood pounded in his ears, his groin. "I can stay for whatever you need."

"I...need to feel close to you."

"I'll be here as long as you want."

Searching his eyes, she pressed a soft kiss to his lips. "I need *you*."

He went still inside, trying to think past the haze of desire and need and comfort. Did she mean—

She kissed him, sweet and hot, a little desperately. There was no way he could turn away from her, especially when her hands slipped into his hair again and her mouth parted beneath his.

This was real. He was holding her. He had wanted to be with her, had imagined it, but in his mind, it hadn't been this bittersweet give and take.

The pull between them, the longing, was physical, yes, but there was also a sharp desperation clawing at him.

His lips glided down her slender neck. The soft sound of surrender, of encouragement, she made went straight to his heart then lower.

Neither of them spoke. The only sounds were of his rough breathing, her sighs, the occasional sweep of the wind outside of the clinic.

She clasped his face in her hands and kissed him again. Compelled to taste the rest of her, Matt's mouth moved to the sensitive spot behind her ear, the silky hollow of her collarbone.

He wanted to say something, but no words seemed enough for this sobering, extraordinary moment. The emotion rushing through him was like nothing he'd ever felt. It was freeing. And terrifying.

Pulling the pins from her hair and dropping them on the bedside table, he buried his hands in the thick mahogany cloud and held her still for a deep kiss. She melted into him, and a sense of possession surged through him.

All he wanted was to keep her close and, for a moment, it was enough.

Then she made a sound of need deep in her throat, her small hands tugging his shirt from his trousers and slipping beneath to touch his bare, hot skin. When she dragged the fabric up to his shoulders, he reached back and jerked the garment over his head, tossed it on the floor.

Laying her on the bed, he propped himself up on one elbow beside her so he could thumb open the buttons on her dress. He got it off, leaving it in a pool of rose silk on the floor, then her corset. There was a slight whisper and hiss as he pushed off both her petticoats, then her stockings as she toed off her slippers.

She pulled her chemise over her head and reached for him. Aching, he nearly groaned when he felt her lotion-smooth flesh against his. His lips glided down the satin length of her throat then to the sweet creamy swells of her breasts.

Her fingers fluttered over his back, a barely-there brush over his healing scars.

Mesmerized, he watched his weathered hand slide over her pale velvet skin washed in golden lamplight, a pretty pink flush rising in his wake. He wanted to touch every inch of her—the tight dusky nipples, her soft flat belly, the wet heat between her legs.

He stroked the curve of her breast then closed his mouth over her.

"Matt." Her smoky voice broke on his name.

Compelled by the rush in his blood as she opened her thighs to him, he levered himself over her—breast to chest, heart to heart. When her dreamy green eyes locked on his, he felt bored open, stripped raw. He wanted to give her all of himself. Fleetingly, he wondered if it would be enough.

Urging him to her, she stroked his hot, rigid flesh. She met his kiss, her arms and legs wrapping around him, and he sank into her, muscles quivering as he fought to

go slowly. Every nerve ending pulsed with nearly painful sensation.

He had never needed her like this, never needed
anyone like this. She took him in, her hands gliding
down the long line of his back then holding on tight so
there was no space between their bodies. He brushed a
kiss across her forehead, her eyelids.

Rocking her gently, his mouth covered hers and a tiny
sob shuddered out of her. His chest ached as though it
was too small for his heart. Their loving was slow and
deliberate and reached into the place only Annalise had
ever been able to touch.

The end was more than a physical release. It was a
sharing. A cleansing.

Matt rolled to the side, holding her tight with one arm
around her shoulders, the other resting on her bare hip.
He stroked her downy-soft skin.

Neither of them spoke for a long moment. She was
quiet as her breathing leveled out.

A sliver of doubt wormed in. "You did want that?"

"Yes." She nodded, her silky hair sliding over his
chest.

He inhaled her clean floral scent. After another long
moment when she still hadn't spoken, he pressed a kiss
to her head. "Do you want me to stay?"

"Yes."

Good. He wasn't sure he would've been able to make
himself leave, no matter how badly he wanted to do
whatever she needed.

She relaxed against him as he drifted off. Curling her
into his side, he whispered, "I'm sorry, Angel. For all of
it."

She didn't speak, just stretched her arm across his
chest and held on.

He wanted to take away her pain. Maybe he had, a little bit. She had certainly done that for him.

It had taken a while to work their way back to each other. Matt didn't kid himself that things would be sunny from here on out, but they were together. That was what mattered.

What had she done? The next morning, Annalise lay in bed watching pink-gold light push around the edges of the oilskin shade. She had thrown caution to the wind, exactly what she had said she wouldn't do.

Matt's side of the bed was empty, but she could hear someone moving around downstairs. The white dress shirt and his boots in the corner were a clear sign he was still here.

Last night, she had been taken aback by the emotional flood unleashed after delivering Davis Lee and Josie's little girl. When she saw that Matt was as affected as she was, she had reached out.

For the first time, they had grieved together over their child. She hadn't realized they needed that, needed each other. But if she hadn't gotten so upset over the Holt baby, Annalise probably wouldn't have slept with Matt. She had let herself be swept away and now she wasn't sure where she wanted things to go from here.

Just as she sat up, he padded barefoot into the room. *Ohhh*. He was bare-chested and her breath caught at the sight of his massive frame. When they had been together last night, the golden lamplight had softened the width of his brawny shoulders, the hard bands of muscle across his stomach, the sharp definition of his arms. But in daylight, she could clearly see all of that. She was amazed all over again by how big he was. And how gentle.

She had touched every inch of his bronzed supple flesh; he had done the same to her. At the memory, heat swept her body.

The ends of his hair were damp and a drop of water glistened in the dip of his collarbone. Her gaze traced over the dark hair on his chest, followed the narrow strip that disappeared into his unbuttoned trousers then went lower.

"Angel, you better stop looking at me like that or I'll climb back in there with you."

The wicked grin on his face sent a shiver through her.

He walked to the bed and sat on its edge, his hot thigh burning hers through the sheet. Leaning forward, he dropped a kiss on her naked shoulder. "How are you this morning?"

"Fine," she said in a raspy voice.

Matt moved his face into the thick tumble of her hair, his morning beard tickling as he nuzzled her neck. "There's some water heating downstairs. I washed up and thought you might want a bath."

His deep voice had her melting inside despite her uncertainty about them. "Thank you. I guess I should get up."

He scooted back so she could slide out of bed, his gaze flashing hotly as she rose, gathering the sheet around her.

As she walked to her wardrobe, he leaned back on his elbows, making an appreciative sound deep in his throat.

Well aware of his heated gaze doing a slow glide down her body, she struggled to stay covered as she slipped on her floral cotton wrapper. He'd already seen—and touched—every inch of her. Annalise supposed it was silly to hide her body from him, but she couldn't help it.

She glanced over her shoulder to find him staring in arrested silence. "What are you doing?"

"Just lookin'." The glitter in his eyes set off a hum in her blood. "I thought I'd fix us some breakfast."

"Oh." The sheet slithered to the floor and she turned, finishing the last of her buttons. "I don't know."

"You don't trust my cookin'." Chuckling, he stood and strolled to the dressing table where she had moved to brush her hair. He eased up behind her, curling a silky lock around his finger. "I can go get something from Pearl's or take you there to eat."

Her silent refusal was immediate. She was still disconcerted from last night, but her edginess came from her uncertainty about them.

In the mirror, her gaze flickered to his then away. "I really need to go over and check on Josie and little Tannis."

Concern darkened his blue eyes as his big palms closed over her shoulders. "Want me to come with you?"

"No," she said quickly. Too quickly, she realized when she saw his mouth tighten. "I'll be fine."

He frowned as he slowly lowered his hands. "If you don't have time for breakfast, what about coffee?"

When she hesitated, he cupped her elbow and turned her toward him. Matt realized with no small irritation that she looked half-spooked. "We obviously have a problem. Why don't you tell me what it is?"

She searched his face for a long moment before saying, "We needed each other last night."

Disquiet snaked through him. He already didn't like this. "Yes."

"I don't regret it."

What the hell? Stiffening, his voice turned gruff. "Glad to hear it."

The pained look on her face drew his body up tight. "You've balked at every suggestion I've made this morning. Do you not want to be around me?"

"It's not that."

"Then what?" Aggravated, he braced his hands on his hips as she stepped around him.

"I think we should…slow things down."

His jaw went slack with disbelief and he barked out a laugh. "We slept together last night, Angel. Kinda hard to unthrow that rock."

"Yes, because we needed each other."

"You already said that." He sliced an impatient hand through the air. "Was it only about comfort for you?"

She didn't answer immediately and he went still inside.

Her gaze wouldn't meet his. "I'm not sure."

"It was more than that for me." Did she think he had found her last night, taken care of her, so he could have her? "It was a fresh start."

"I'm not sure one night is enough to build a reconciliation."

"Build—" Reining in his frustration, he nudged her chin up, made her look at him. "We're already reconciled. What do you call our making love? We were both in that bed, Annalise. There's no way you would've slept with me if we weren't together again."

"Maybe."

Maybe? A searing tightness gripped his chest.

She backed away and returned to the mirror, picking up a pale pink ribbon to tie back her hair.

He moved up behind her, his gaze finding hers in the mirror. There was wariness and doubt in her pretty face, and her hand trembled. Things fell into place with a sickening thud. "You still don't trust me."

She winced slightly. "I want to, but no, I guess I don't."

"I know I made a mistake." His gut started to churn. He wasn't losing her. Not again. "I've already admitted that."

"Yes. You appear to have changed, but I'm not sure. I can't go through what I did before." She faced him then, clasping her hands together. "It like to have killed me, Matt."

"I know that," he said hotly. Frustration and resentment made his voice harsh. He didn't want that. He wanted her.

Curling his hands into fists so he wouldn't reach for her, he gentled his tone. "I apologized. What else do you want me to do?"

"Nothing."

"Yet you can't forgive me."

"I can. I have. I'm just not sure I…want what you want."

His heart slammed into his chest. "You mean *me*. You aren't sure you want me or a future together."

During her brief pause, he was ambushed by a crush of hurt and denial.

After a moment, she nodded, turning back to the mirror.

Matt's world skidded to a halt. How had they gotten from their loving last night to this? Determination filled him. He wasn't letting her go. Sliding his arms around her from behind, he said quietly, "I want you and only you. You want me, too."

"But I don't want to."

Hell. If her voice had wobbled, he would've known how to reassure her. But she was dead quiet. And she sounded dead certain. The realization sliced through him like a blade.

"Do you think you'll ever be able to trust me?" The words actually hurt his throat.

Her green eyes were stormy and she let out a shuddering breath. "I need time."

"Fine, I'll give it to you, but I'm not going anywhere." He squeezed her lightly. "What I did years ago was a mistake and I'm not making it again."

She shook her head.

He wanted to kiss her, take her back to bed and love the doubts out of her, but no one knew better than he did that it wouldn't work.

Resting one hand on her stomach, he pulled her into him, his fingers brushing the undersides of her breasts.

Leaning down, holding her uncertain gaze with his, he murmured in her ear, "You're mine, Angel. The only person standing in our way is you, and come hell or high water, I'll regain your trust."

He knew he had to let her go for now so he slid his hands to her hips. His hold tightened when he felt her shiver against him. "You go on and get your bath. I'm going to fetch us some breakfast. Just breakfast," he said when she opened her mouth to protest. "That's all."

For the moment anyway, he thought. As he watched her walk out of the room, he snagged his shirt and dragged it over his head. He was standing by her this time. He wouldn't turn his back on her again. No matter what it took or how long, he would convince her.

Tugging on one boot, he realized he would have to go one step at a time with her. He hoped he could move as slowly as she needed.

Chapter Eleven

You're mine, Angel. The only person in our way is you,
and come hell or high water, I'll regain your trust.

After Matt's vow, Annalise hadn't known what to
expect, but it certainly hadn't been the ache that lodged
deep inside her. The sensation was so unfamiliar that it
took a couple of days to realize it was desire.

They were both busy, her with patients and him with
the ranch so he couldn't come to town every day. On
the days he did, he spent most of it with her, going on
a drive or to church or for a meal. She expected him to
take advantage of the desire that she knew was probably
plain in her face but he didn't. He never did anything
more than give her a light kiss on the mouth.

When he wasn't in Whirlwind, he sent her silly poems
or wrote her letters recounting his day. One day, he had a
silver hand mirror delivered. Another time he surprised
her with a gorgeous silk fan.

She realized she actually missed him when he wasn't
around. One afternoon, while checking on Josie and her
baby, Annalise had been hit hard again with a sense of

sadness and loss. The memory of how sweet Matt had been to her the night of the baby's birth helped her get through the visit. While she enjoyed being with him, she didn't want to depend on him or trust anything more than the moment.

She needed to remember he was still the same man who had hurt her all those years ago. Not because she was holding the past against him, but because she wasn't ready to make the same commitment he was. They should get to know each other again and take things one day at a time.

Still, she was let down one afternoon when he sent a ranch hand with the message that he wouldn't be able to see her that day. More Triple B cattle had been stolen and he would come to town when he could.

The depth of her disappointment told Annalise she was moving too fast with him, but that didn't stop the flutter of her nerves the next afternoon when she heard his deep voice behind her.

"I need a doctor real bad."

"You've come to the right place." Smiling, she turned from folding bandages in her examination room and saw him in the doorway. Holding his hat, his blue gaze darkened as it traveled over her. His white work shirt was tucked into worn denims that emphasized the muscles in his powerful thighs. His black boots were filmed with red dust.

When she moved toward him, the afternoon sunlight showed the fatigue etched on his rugged features. "Why don't you come in and sit for a minute?"

He grazed a knuckle down her cheek. "I would, but I came to ask something of you."

Curious, she tilted her head. "All right."

"You got my note about the stolen cattle?"

"Yes." She resisted the urge to hug him or caress his face. "You look as though you were up all night."

"I was, and that's what got me to thinking about how you took an impression of the wounds on my back. Do you think you could do it with hoofprints?"

"I don't know why not. I could try."

A light flared in his eyes. "I'm at the end of my rope. These rustlers never leave any boot prints and there's something funny about the hoofprints I find. I can't figure it. I found a place where I think they were yesterday. Could you come right now?"

"Let me get my hat and the things I'll need."

"I'll bring your buggy 'round."

"All right."

Ten minutes later, they were on their way. She had expected Matt to ride alongside her, but he'd climbed into the seat, too. He snapped the reins against the horse's rump, urging the animal into motion. Leaning forward with his elbows resting on his knees, he kept the mare to a steady pace as they left Whirlwind behind.

Annalise's gaze was drawn to his strong bronzed neck, the dark damp hair peeking out from beneath his hat.

He gave her a crooked grin. "I really appreciate this."

"Maybe it will help in some way."

He linked their hands and brushed a kiss across her knuckles. "Tell me what you've been doing the last couple of days."

She told him about treating a guest at the Fontaine for a cold and that Davis Lee and Josie's baby was thriving. Made him laugh with a story about how their friends were both so nervous as parents that they had rushed little Tannis over when she sneezed.

His hold tightening slightly, Matt shared a look with her that said he was reminded of their own loss. "It's not hard to see why they'd be so spooked, is it?"

"No."

The trip passed quickly as they traveled a well-worn road from town. Occasionally, they saw large patches of bluebonnets, the purple-blue color vibrant against the green of grass and brush. They crested a rise that Annalise recognized as the western border of Triple B land.

The buggy bumped off the road into the pasture. Buffalo grass swished against the wheels as Matt guided them into a shallow valley. After a minute, he pulled the carriage to a stop and came around to help her down.

From under the seat, he pulled the satchel she'd filled with cornstarch, cheesecloth, a canteen of water and a medium-sized bowl.

With his hand at the small of her back, he steered her through the knee-high grass.

From under the wide brim of her hat, she looked up at him. "I'm no expert on cattle, Matt."

"You aren't on spurs either, but you figured out they were what tore up my back."

Pleased, she smiled as he led her to a blackened spot in the pasture. The grass was trampled flat or burned away around the remains of an old fire.

He moved to a place at the edge of the circle. "Here are the tracks I told you about."

She stepped up beside him, spying a clear set of hoof-prints in a large patch of gouged earth surrounded by a mish-mash of other animal marks.

"Do you think there's enough of an imprint for you to make an impression?"

"I think so."

While she mixed the paste, Matt took out his pocket

knife and cut some small branches from a nearby pine tree. More than once, her attention wandered to the flex of muscle along his arms and shoulders as he worked to fashion a crude box.

Using his blade, he dug out a shallow trench of red earth around the set of prints and fixed the flimsy box into the ground as a frame for the small area where Annalise would work.

She laid down a piece of cheesecloth then poured the mixture of cornstarch and water. "It will need to firm."

"You are so damn smart."

Glancing up in surprise, she paused at the look in his eyes. She hadn't seen it before. It was more than admiration. It was respect.

"Are there any other cattle prints I can compare these to?"

He nodded. "We'll take a look once your paste sets up."

He snagged a lap robe from under the buggy seat and spread it on the ground. As she sat down beside him, she pointed at the remains of the fire. "Is this where the rustlers would've changed the brands on the stolen cattle?"

"Yes." Matt drew up one knee, draped his arm over it. "And I can't figure out why there are no human prints. At first I thought it was because the rustlers stayed on horseback or even in a wagon to move the cattle, despite how that would've slowed them down, but there's no sign of horses or wheel tracks. It just doesn't make sense."

"Maybe we'll be able to determine something when we look at the impression." She glanced around the rolling terrain. "It seems risky to light a fire. Someone patrolling the area could easily see the flames."

"Not with the fire being in this spot." He hooked a thumb over his shoulder. "We're at the base of a rise and that big mesquite tree just behind you hides pretty near everything. A person would have to top the hill to see the fire."

"Do any of you burn a fire while you're patrolling?"

"No, it would give us away."

She thought about Julius's cattle being stolen and the fire she had seen the night she had doctored Edward at the Eight of Hearts Ranch. "You said you had more cattle stolen last night. What about the Ross and Holt ranches?"

"They did, too."

"Has Mr. Julius reported any more cattle being stolen?"

"Not since the day after you treated his visitor."

Her heartbeat quickened. "Hmm."

"What?"

"The night I was there, I saw a fire from the second-story window. Until you said the rustlers wouldn't risk building one, I thought it might've been them." She shrugged. "Maybe Julius had hands out patrolling, too, and the fire I saw belonged to them."

"If so and they were waiting for the rustlers, it wouldn't be very smart."

"Well, I definitely saw one. And Mr. Julius specifically told me all his cowboys were at the house and accounted for."

"Have you seen anything since then?"

"No. The boy is healing nicely so I haven't been out there this week."

Matt thumbed his hat back. "Maybe the rustlers were on his land. It's worth checking into."

"Are you and the other men still patrolling in shifts?"

"Yes, and starting tonight, we'll be rotating Whirlwind in there, too. Davis Lee thinks it won't hurt to take the precaution and I agree. Two men will be assigned to the range and one to town."

He grinned and tossed off his hat then did the same to hers. "Now, let's stop talking about livestock."

"What do you want to talk about?"

"This." He tumbled her back onto the blanket and kissed her.

"This isn't talking," she murmured against his lips.

He chuckled, nuzzling her neck and waking up all her nerve endings. "You're not sore at me for missing last night, are you?"

"Of course not." She would have preferred to see him, she admitted.

He kissed her again, slow and deep. When he raised his head a long moment later, she was breathing as hard as he was. With one finger, he traced her lower lip. "You know Founder's Day is coming up."

"Yes." No one was exactly certain of the day in April when Whirlwind had been founded. Some said it had been in the first few days of the month and others swore it was toward the end. As a result, the citizens celebrated both dates, alternating one year with the early one and the next year with the later one.

Matt buried his face in her hair, his breath tickling her ear. "I want you to spend the day with me."

The warmth moving through her had her wanting to agree to anything he said, but she shook her head.

He drew back, eyes flashing with surprise. "Why not?"

She smoothed her hands over his broad shoulders. "Pearl and May decided we're going to have a tie party."

He groaned and dropped his forehead against hers.

Laughing, she said, "So, you'll only get to spend the day with me if you happen to pick the tie that matches my dress."

He toyed with the top button of her white shirtwaist. "Tell me what you'll be wearing."

"That would be cheating."

"You really aren't going to tell me?"

"No." She gave him a look from under her lashes.

"Well," he said in a deep rumble, "I have you now. Guess I'd better make the most of it."

He brushed his lips over hers and kissed her, hungry but tender. It wasn't only his touch that had her head spinning. He had asked for her opinion, valued it. It was heady stuff.

He slid a hand under her skirts, moved it over her knee and up her thigh. She could feel the calluses on his palm through her muslin drawers.

"I shouldn't start anything I can't finish," he muttered. He sat up, dragging a hand down his face.

For a moment, her mind blanked. She lay there watching him until he stood and pulled her to her feet with a grin.

"Let's go check your work before I get myself in trouble."

"All right." Her heart was still pounding, her skin flushed from his touch. She didn't want to stop, but that was her body talking, not her head.

The fact that Matt had called a halt surprised her. She had always been the one to set boundaries.

All the way back to Whirlwind, she studied him. He had stopped before going too far physically. He had asked for her help and had actually respected her opinion.

Annalise had to admit he *wasn't* the same man who

had hurt her all those years ago. This new man reached places inside her that the old one never had, and she wanted to think he was changed enough not to make the same mistakes, but she just didn't know.

Matt sensed that asking Annalise for help with the hoofprints had changed something between them, in a good way. On the drive back to Whirlwind, she had studied him with open curiosity, as if she saw something she hadn't seen before. Until now, she hadn't seemed any closer to reconciling with him, but Matt thought she was ready to move things along.

That was only one reason he wanted to be the first to arrive for the Founder's Day festivities. Unfortunately, Pa had bent the wheel on his wheelchair and Matt had to hammer it out before they could leave the ranch.

As a result, he was late to the Pearl Restaurant where the day would kick off with the tie-picking party. Most of the ties had already been chosen from the basket being guarded by May Haskell. Later in the day, the tables here would be moved to clear the pine floor for dancing, but before that there were horse races, games, a picnic and buggy races on the schedule. Matt had every intention of doing all of that with Annalise.

He stopped in the doorway of the restaurant, searching the throng of people until he saw her. She stood across the room talking to Bram, Jake and Emma Ross. Her thick mahogany hair hung in a braid down the back of her blue-and-white calico dress. The garment molded to her high breasts and nipped in at her waist. Just looking at her put a kick in his blood.

He made his way to the corner of the room, but the fabric matching her dress wasn't in May's basket. Finally, he caught a flash of the pattern over by the open door.

Andrew Donnelly had it, and he was showing it to his friends, Creed Carter and Miguel Santos.

Grinning, Matt started across the floor, joined along the way by Russ.

"I was starting to think you weren't going to make it before everyone paired off."

He explained to his brother what had delayed him, noting Russ already wore the matching string tie to Lydia's red-white-and-black calico dress.

The other man glanced at him. "You don't have a tie."

"That's where I'm headed right now."

"May's over there." Russ pointed to the opposite corner.

"Yeah, and the tie matching Annalise's dress is over here. I need to get it before the pairing-off starts."

He strode to the three boys with Russ behind him. Miguel and Creed went outside to talk to Zeke Keeler, but Matt stopped Andrew before he could do the same.

"Hey, Andrew, why don't you switch ties with me?"

The husky boy shook his head, blue eyes sparkling. "I have the one I want. I'm spending the day with Dr. Annalise."

Over my dead body. "C'mon, what do you want for it? How about fifty cents?"

Andrew's gaze went to Annalise then sharpened on Matt. "You're real sweet on her."

"Yeah." Expecting the kid to ask for candy or maybe another fifty cents, he said, "So, name your price."

"Let's start at ten dollars."

"Ten dollars!"

His brother chuckled and Matt glared at him. "That's robbery!"

"You said name a starting place."

He threaded his hat brim through his fingers. As he considered handing over that much money, Jericho Blue walked up.

The tall quiet-spoken man looked from the boy to the man. "What's going on?"

Grinning like a possum, Russ gestured toward Matt and Andrew. "Your brother-in-law is bartering with my brother."

"More like robbing me," Matt muttered, then said to the boy, "Five dollars."

"I'm not going down from ten."

"This is supposed to be a negotiation, kid."

"It is. I'm negotiating up."

Russ and Jericho laughed.

Matt hated being pulled over a barrel like this, but he really wanted that ribbon. "Well, ten dollars then."

"Is that all it's worth to you?"

What the hell? "I just met your price."

"You met my *first* price."

Miguel and Creed came back inside, watching with wide smiles from several feet away.

Matt eyed the Donnelly boy, who was more shrewd than he would've guessed. "Jericho told me you're planning to buy a horse."

Andrew's blue eyes lit up, but his face gave away nothing. Matt couldn't help but admire that. "I can help you choose one."

"I've got Jericho for that."

The murmurs of appreciation behind Matt aggravated him. "How much more money do you need in order to buy it?"

"Just your ten dollars."

Other people were starting to take notice of the negotiation. Trying to be patient, Matt pinched the bridge of his nose. "Then why don't we make a deal?"

"Because I don't have any tack."

Russ barked out a laugh.

Matt threw Jericho a dark look. "What are you teaching this kid?"

The former Ranger just grinned.

"All right, everyone." May clapped her hands, speaking loud enough to be heard above the noise of the crowd. "We're ready to begin."

Matt shoved a hand through his hair. Confoundin' kid. "I'll pay for your horse's first pair of shoes."

The boy thought for a minute. "I'll also need a bridle and a saddle blanket."

It was on the tip of Matt's tongue to tell the lad to get lost, but he wasn't passing up this opportunity to spend the day with Annalise. "Okay," he said grudgingly.

"And a saddle."

Matt nearly cussed. "Are you kidding?"

"One made by Jake."

Hell, no, he wasn't kidding. The boy obviously knew quality because Jake Ross made the best tack in the state. Despite Andrew's age, he wasn't wet behind the ears.

Well aware of his brother and friend laughing, Matt's eyes narrowed. He pointed his hat at Andrew. "You know I could just take it?"

"But you won't, not in front of Dr. Annalise."

He scowled because the kid was right.

"Matt, you're holding us up," Pearl called out.

The men began to gather on one side of the room and the women on the other.

Andrew waggled the ribbon. "Mrs. Haskell's fixin' to start pairing everyone off. What do you say?"

Matt couldn't help but admire how the boy had turned

the situation to his advantage. He had no intention of letting Andrew know that though. "You've got a deal."

Stepping over to the kid, Matt counted out the money. "Talk to Jake about your saddle sometime today. I'll tell him to send the bill to me."

"All right. Thanks!" Andrew gave Matt the string tie, grinning down at the money in his hand. With a sly look, he said, "I would've let you have it for just the bridle."

Matt bit back a smile. "I would've bought the horse for you, too."

"Shoot!"

Matt laughed along with Russ and Jericho.

The boy extended his hand. "I still think I got a pretty good deal."

"Better than good," Matt agreed wryly. He shook Andrew's hand, chuckling as the boy ran over to May and grabbed another tie from the basket.

All eyes seemed to be on Matt as he took a place beside Russ and put on the tie.

His brother clapped him on the shoulder. "I hope what you just paid is worth it."

"It is." His gaze went to Annalise who was watching him with a little smile. A little smile that had him thinking about getting her alone.

Feeling suddenly targeted, he dragged his attention from her and saw the other women were whispering and looking at him. Their intense scrutiny made him feel as if he was standing there in the altogether.

He wasn't crazy about the women knowing he'd paid to spend the day with the doctor, but he didn't mind if the men did. It saved him staking a claim on Annalise to every man he saw today.

Once they'd paired up, he tucked her hand into the

crook of his arm and they walked outside. The sun shone from a clear blue sky.

Shading her eyes with a flat-brimmed straw hat, she looked up at him, green eyes dancing. "I can't believe you bullied a boy into giving up the tie."

"Bullied? If anyone was bullied, it was me. That boy bargained better than a lot of men I know."

"You're too good at negotiating for him to best you."

"Not today, but it was worth it to get what I wanted."

She flushed with pleasure. "You've always been good at getting that, too."

Yes, and he wasn't stopping now.

The morning passed quickly. Matt won a couple of the horse races. They rooted for Quentin in the horseshoe toss; he and Cora tied for the win. After watching the wheelbarrow race, Matt and Annalise participated in the sack race.

They came in dead last because they fell once and Matt was content to lie there with Annalise on top of him. He was enjoying the feel of her soft curves until she smacked him on the arm and whispered that everyone was looking.

Her cheeks stayed rosy with color until they joined their friends for the noon meal under a copse of trees on the northeast side of the church. Matt spread a blanket and they ate the potluck lunch provided by the ladies of town.

Davis Lee and Josie sat down with baby Tannis and it wasn't long before Riley and Susannah and Jake and Emma joined them. Davis Lee's child was too small to do anything except sleep. Matt thought she already looked completely different though she still had a lot of hair.

The Holt and Ross girls played together. The young girls, two and one respectively, were both blond, but Lorelai had blue eyes and Molly had green.

At one point, Matt caught Annalise watching the new baby with sadness. He reached for her hand and she gave him a small smile. When the children began to fuss, the other couples took their leave.

Annalise showed no sign of being ready to go so Matt leaned back against an oak tree, content to study her. The sun lent her skin a peachy glow and her eyes sparkled with vivid color. As his gaze lazily roamed over the curve of her lips, the stubborn slant of her jaw, heat prickled in his chest.

She watched the people who milled about town. "I noticed Mr. Julius and Cosgrove are here."

"Yeah. Cosgrove paired up with Zoe Keeler. He probably wanted to be with Deborah Blue, but Bram managed to get the tie matching her skirt."

"Probably by doing what you did." Annalise smiled. "I'm glad. He's crazy about her."

Dragging his gaze from her chest, he said, "I went out to the Eight of Hearts yesterday and I did find evidence of a fire where you said, but all I could tell was it wasn't fresh."

"So the remains could've been from the one I saw or a much older one."

He nodded.

"Did you use the impression we made to compare with other cattle prints?"

"Yes, and what I found was strange. The prints in the impression are uniform, all the same width and depth. There's no way the stolen cattle left tracks that perfect. Some were calves, some bulls."

"And the animals' weight varies too much for the prints to be the same. Some would be deeper or wider."

"Right." Matt huffed out an exasperated breath. "It beats anything I've ever seen."

"You'll figure it out," she said confidently.

"With your help." He took her hand.

She smiled, gently tugging from his hold to lean back on her elbows. She tipped her face to the sky, the leafy branches blocking the sun from her eyes. A slight breeze stirred the hem of her skirts. "It's a beautiful day."

"Mm-hmm." His gaze traveled over the elegant line of her throat, bared to him, making him want to press his lips there, then lower. Later, when they were alone.

"Pa's been talking about having surgery on his leg. Is that why he's been coming to see you?"

"What did he tell you?"

She didn't look at him, didn't move, but Matt felt a sudden tension in her. "He hasn't said much. Is it dangerous?"

"There are risks, yes."

He noticed how carefully she answered and he felt a pinch of some emotion he couldn't define. "We're talking about some doctor going inside him. It could mess up his innards and who knows what. I want you to convince him not to do it."

"I can't do that. I can only tell him the options and risks, Matt." She looked at him then. "It might enable him to walk again."

"And it might not. It might kill him."

"True."

He sat up, resting his arms on his bent knees. "He listens to you. If you tell him it's too dangerous, he won't do it."

"Is that all he told you?" She sat up, too. "That he was thinking about having the surgery?"

"Yes. He hasn't mentioned it in a while. Russ and I are hoping he's put it out of his mind."

She didn't respond and Matt realized she hadn't answered his questions or agreed to discourage J.T. from the operation. Maybe she didn't want to talk about this when they were supposed to be having fun.

He let it go for now. Later in the day, they competed in the buggy races and danced until well after dark, when Annalise told him she was ready to go. He was, too.

Since their night together, he'd been trying to show her that she could depend on him, that he could be patient, and he thought she'd recognized that.

He bypassed her front stoop in favor of the back door. He couldn't kiss her the way he wanted if they were in plain sight. He gathered her to him, widening his stance so he could bring her right against him. Moonlight skimmed over her velvety skin, made her eyes dark and liquid.

Brushing his lips across her forehead, he worked his way to her jaw, nuzzling her cheek with his. "Have a good time today?"

"Yes, thank you," she said softly.

He settled his mouth over hers. She melted against him like hot wax, sending a scalding rush of desire through him.

He wanted her. He had wanted her all damn day.

Bracing his back against the wall, he bent his knees until her breasts were pressed tight to his chest, her stomach cushioning his erection. Even now at the end of the day, he caught a whiff of her primrose scent.

He spread his hands on her back and held her to him as he set his teeth on her neck then grazed her ear.

She sighed, pulling him to her for a kiss. Her hands were in his hair. She was his, all his.

He dragged his hands to her waist, his thumbs feathering over her tight nipples. He wanted to take this inside, but what did she want?

I love you. The words were on the tip of his tongue, but something held him back.

She stared up at him, her fingers touching his mouth. "Stay with me tonight."

He hesitated. He wanted her until he ached, but he wanted all of her—mind, body and soul. Her heart. She had his.

If he stayed, he would at least have her for a time. He knew she wouldn't take him to her bed if she didn't still love him, but she wasn't ready to say the words.

"Matt?"

For now, this had to be enough. He closed the door behind them and followed her upstairs.

They made love slowly and when she fell asleep against him afterwards, he stayed awake staring at the ripple of moonlight on the ceiling.

An edge of frustration had gnawed at him all day and he'd thought it was because he wanted to get her alone, but now he knew the real reason. If she was any closer to trusting him, he couldn't tell. They might be in this bed together naked, but she was still holding him at arm's length.

She wouldn't let him in past a certain point and he wasn't sure she ever would.

Chapter Twelve

In the following ten days, Matt wondered more than once if Annalise would ever trust him again. Since the Founder's Day celebration, they had been together as often as he could get to town. They were getting along well. Sometimes he stayed the night; sometimes he didn't. But as far as he could tell, things weren't any different now than they had been then.

Each time he saw her, touched her, he looked for something in her face besides desire and fondness. He told himself to be patient every damn day, but his nerves were twitchy.

If he didn't get some space from her, he would start pressuring her and his gut said don't. She would get as jittery as a spooked horse.

A low, simmering frustration grew. She never came to him for anything except sex. While he had no complaints about that, he wanted her to discuss things with him or ask for his opinion or lean on him for support. The fact that she didn't told him louder than words they hadn't made any progress.

Until now he hadn't considered she might view this time together as a trial run, but perhaps she did.

The situation between them wasn't the only thing that had him setting his teeth. He was no closer to catching the rustlers and he still hadn't been able to figure out why the hoofprints in the impression Annalise had made were so uniform. All of it buffaloed him.

For the next several days, he was needed at the Triple B and while he had no intention of calling it quits with Annalise, he was glad he had to be elsewhere. Putting some distance between them would give him a second wind as well as clear his thoughts, and he needed both.

She hadn't said one thing about the future; it was only about now. If he didn't take a break, Matt was afraid something stupid would come out of his mouth.

Like the nonsensical thoughts that were running through his head. Last night, he'd considered proposing just to get a reaction out of her. That would've been a mistake.

That evening, on their way back to her clinic after having supper with Russ and Lydia, Annalise had asked if he would mind stopping at the cemetery.

As the sun sank into the horizon, they stood side by side, staring at the wooden marker she had placed next to her parents' graves. Regret filled him, the same tearing regret he always felt over the loss of their child as well as the way he had misjudged Annalise.

Hardy M. Fine. Matt touched the smoothly finished wood. "I wish my name was on here. If I hadn't been such a bastard, maybe it could've been."

Beside him, she went still. Did she hate the idea? His

heart sank as he frowned down at the marker. "You made yourself a target for scandal and left me out of it."

"I actually thought about giving him your last name."

Surprised, his gaze sliced to hers.

"But when I first returned to Whirlwind, I was angry. At the time, I didn't think you wanted anyone to know you were his father. You didn't respond to my letter about the miscarriage, so I assumed you didn't want to claim him."

"That's not how I felt." His voice was hoarse, his chest tight.

"I know that now," she said softly.

He stared for a moment at the baby's marker. "We could have a new one made, of stone. Not to put my name on it, just to have a more permanent one. I bet Ef could do it."

"That's sweet."

"So, you wouldn't mind?"

"No, and I don't mind putting your name on there either." She slipped her arm through his and hugged it to her. "Anyone who's seen the marker now knows I was expecting. They would also know you were his father."

They stood there in silence for a long moment squinting into the glare of the day's last light.

The sunset painted the prairie a red-gold; a brighter orange slanted across the wooden symbol.

The fact that Annalise was willing to let Matt add his name to their child's marker gave him hope that perhaps they had a chance at a future together, but he didn't want to ask. Not yet.

Partly because he didn't want to pressure her and

partly because he was afraid she might say she had decided they should go their separate ways.

"I'll talk to Ef about the stone," Matt said.

Annalise nodded, leaving her hand tucked into the crook of his arm as they walked out of the cemetery.

They moved down the rise and angled behind the livery toward her clinic, her skirts brushing against his trousers. On the soft night air, he caught the clean scent of primroses. Her mind seemed to be elsewhere and he wondered what she was thinking about.

"I won't be around for a few days," he said.

She glanced up. "Why not?"

"We're moving the cattle to the south pasture."

"All right."

Disappointment stabbed him. Her easy acceptance suggested she was nowhere near where he was in their relationship. Hell, would she even notice or care that he wasn't here?

They reached her clinic and after she unlocked the door, he opened it and followed her inside.

"Do you have any idea how long it might be before you're back in town?"

He shrugged, closing the door. Late-day sunlight spilled through the window. "Maybe as long as a week. Depends on the weather and if there's any trouble."

"I've gotten used to seeing you more often." She reached up to remove the dark-blue bowler hat that matched the stripe in her dainty pink dinner dress.

His gaze roamed over her full breasts, the gentle flare of her hips silhouetted by the fiery gold light of the setting sun. As usual, the sight of her set off a low throb in his blood.

Tendrils escaped from her upswept hair and teased the velvety flesh of her neck. He wanted to put his mouth there. Or anywhere, he amended as his attention moved down the buttons of her fitted bodice.

"Matt?"

"Hmm?" His focus shifted from her chest to her face.

She smiled at him, a soft smile that hinted at something besides desire. "Thanks for giving me the time I asked for to decide about us."

He stiffened. This sounded like a lead-in to something. Was she going to tell him that she wanted even more time? He hoped not, but he could do it. He'd *been* doing it for what felt like a damn long time.

"When you're ready, I'll be here. No matter how long it takes."

She was quiet for a moment. "It's meant a lot that you haven't pressured me even though I imagine it's sometimes been difficult."

This sounded a lot like goodbye. "Annalise—"

"Let me finish." She closed the distance between them and laid a hand on his chest, her green eyes searching his. "What you said earlier about wanting your name on the baby's marker meant a lot to me, as did the fact that you asked about replacing it."

Covering her small hand with his, he asked hoarsely, "But?"

"While we were in the cemetery, I realized something."

What? That they were finished? His heart hammered hard.

Before he could speak, she put a finger against his lips. "You've been supportive, strong. Dependable."

"You sound like you're describin' a horse." He couldn't keep the edge of frustration out of his voice.

Her mouth curved in a smile. "You've changed.

Enough to admit your mistakes and enough not to repeat them. I know it's been hard on you yet you haven't pressured me. You said you didn't blame me for losing the baby and I see now that's true."

"You've been coming to terms with a lot."

"Yes."

"So, what are you sayin'? Are you trying to get shed of me?"

"No!" She slid her arms around his waist.

Okay, this was a good sign. He put his arms around her, too. Beneath his hold, he felt her tight waist and the heat of her body warming his hands.

"I believe you intend to stick by me this time."

Well. At her unexpected words, he stared down at her.

She drew back, her green eyes dark with concern. "Have I waited too long? Have you changed your mind about us?"

"I haven't changed my mind."

"I want us to try again." She stroked the dark hair showing in the V of his shirt.

Something big and hot unfurled in his chest.

"I'm sorry for doubting you."

He grinned, sliding his hands up and down her arms. "Don't be sorry for finally coming to your senses."

She laughed, pressing herself right up against him. "I want you."

The feel of her sleek curves had tension coiling inside him. It took a moment for his common sense to work its way around the hard, hot want pounding inside him.

He held her shoulders, searching her delicate features. There was no mistaking the earnestness there. Or the heat in her eyes. "Is it because we just visited the cemetery?"

"What do you mean?"

"Things were pretty emotional back there. Losing the baby still hurts." Maybe he was an idiot for even asking, but if all she wanted was sex, he had to know. "Do you only want me for comfort, like the first time? Because that's not what I want."

"No." Taking his hand, she tugged him into the shadowed corner behind the stairs where they were hidden from anyone who might come in or see from the porch.

She didn't want him to have any doubts about why she wanted to be with him. Staring into his blue eyes, her fingers skimmed his bristly jaw. "It's not about the baby or the past or for comfort. It's because I want to be with you. This is about us, you and me."

"This is a real reconciliation?"

"Yes, if you still want one."

"I do." His eyes flashed and warmth curled low in her belly.

She smiled. "You've been such a gentleman. Very patient."

"Not anymore," he growled, backing her into the pine wall.

He crushed his mouth to hers, thumbing open the buttons on her bodice. He folded back the fabric, pushing it to her waist. Her breasts swelled over the top of her corset and he muttered something. He smoothed one hand over the satiny fullness while his other hand undid the hooks down the front.

He tossed it aside and untied her chemise, pushing the loose undergarment off her shoulders. He stared down at her with a muscle clenching in his jaw. The fierce possessiveness on his face had Annalise's breath jamming in her lungs. She slid her hands under his shirt, stroking his supple skin, the long line of his spine.

He reached back and pulled the garment over his head, dropping it on the floor.

Bending, he ran his tongue around one nipple then closed his mouth over the taut rosy flesh. She made a sound deep in her throat, sliding her hand down his muscled stomach to unfasten his trousers. She released the last button on his pants and reached inside, curling her hand around him.

His muscles clenched and he kissed her harder, deeper. "Now," he grated out. "Here."

He pushed her skirts up, his hand going between her legs to cup her through her drawers.

She pressed into his touch, whispering his name. That seemed to calm something inside him because he slowed. He dragged his mouth to her neck and gently nipped the sensitive spot where her shoulder met her neck. He worked his way slowly, too slowly down her throat to the valley of her breasts.

She shivered. "Don't stop."

"I'm not. Just want to enjoy it a little longer."

A finger delved into her silky heat, his thumb pressing the knot of nerves there. "Oh!"

He watched as she broke apart, the tenderness in his eyes making her knees weak.

Over the past weeks, he'd gotten past her guard. She'd enjoyed their time together and seeing him with baby Tannis had turned her to mush. She couldn't help but be moved by it, couldn't help seeing that he *had* changed.

The only time she'd wavered had been at the Founder's Day celebration when he'd started talking about his father and wanting her to discourage J.T. from the surgery. She wished the older man would talk to Matt and

Russ about it, but he was doing things in his own time, his own way.

If pushed, Annalise would have to tell Matt she couldn't discourage his father if the man decided he wanted the surgery, but he hadn't brought it up again.

And that had nothing to do with this.

When Matt had told her how much he regretted not having his name on their child's marker, something had settled inside her and she'd known she was ready. At some point, she had begun to trust him again.

She wanted to be closer to him in every way. Reaching between them, she urged him to her, melting at the feel of his hot rigid flesh against her slick softness.

In the dusky gold-tinted light, she could see his blue eyes glitter with emotion and her heart ached.

Holding her gaze, he lifted her and slid inside, deep and sure, then began to move. She met every stroke of his body. His hair-dusted chest heaved against her smooth one. For the first time since she had returned, she felt as though she were really home.

She gave all of herself to him, held nothing back. The raw vulnerability on his face made her realize he'd been holding back, too. She saw a burning need in his eyes, the same need that burned in her blood.

It had always been this man for her. It always would be.

He steadily drove her up a dizzying peak. When she felt the tiny urgent pulses deep inside, his muscles bunched and he went over the edge with her.

With his whole weight pressing into her, his head rested beside hers on the wall. His breathing was ragged, his flesh slick on hers.

She moved her hands over the tough sinew of his shoulders, his granite-hard arms, and held him close.

The coarse surface of the wall scratched her back; her hair had fallen down. She didn't care.

He shifted, murmuring in her ear, "I missed you, Angel."

Tears stung her eyes and she clasped him tighter. Finally, they had found their way back to each other.

Matt hadn't been able to make himself leave until after midnight. Two days later, he was still thinking about their reconciliation, smiling about it even though he was riding the back end of a cattle line, moving livestock.

He was hot, sweaty, eating red dust and surrounded by the fecund odor of cow flesh and manure and dirt. He had to pay attention. A calf could wander off or a cow could step in a hole or something could spook the herd.

But Annalise was right there in his mind.

If there were no problems, the cattle would be settled in the south pasture by tonight and tomorrow he'd be able to see her.

They were really together, for good this time. She'd left him in no doubt she was ready and not just physically.

He recalled the unguarded look in her green eyes when they had made love. There had been no hesitation, just openness and love. He'd seen it there. He'd felt it.

In her kiss, in the slide of her silky-soft flesh against his, her slender legs wrapped around his hips, the tight grip of her body.

If he didn't stop replaying how they'd spent the other night, it would become obvious to everyone that he was thinking about a woman. His woman.

She *was* his. He wanted to make it permanent, he realized.

He could take her to the Fontaine or bring her out

to the ranch, to that stretch of land she loved near the big oak tree with the patch of bluebonnets and Indian paintbrush.

They'd wasted enough time. They had resolved their differences about the baby so he couldn't think of any reason to wait.

The baby. Matt went still inside. *Baby*. Annalise could be pregnant right now. What if she was?

Had she even wondered? He couldn't believe *he* hadn't considered it until now. The possibility made him want to propose even more.

"Matt! Matt!"

He became aware of someone calling his name and the thunder of hoofbeats at the same time. He turned and saw Cora bent low over her black mare, Prissy, flying across the ground toward him.

Something was wrong. Matt hollered to one of his hands to take over his spot and spun Dove around to head toward Cora.

The older woman reined to a stop in front of him, her black mare jolting to a stop hard enough to dig dirt. "It's your pa!"

"What's wrong?"

"The pain is bad." Her hazel eyes were wide with concern. "He can't get out of the wheelchair, not onto the bed or the sofa."

Matt kneed his horse into a flat-out run, Cora's horse keeping pace with him. They reached the ranch and Matt rode right up to the front porch and jumped down, slapping Dove on the rump to send her toward the corral.

Cora was right behind him, dismounting before he could help her down. He rushed inside, saw his pa in the wheelchair looking as white as death. Deep grooves bracketed his mouth; pain etched his features.

The only other time Matt had seen him in this much pain was the day of the accident that had caused his injury.

"Pa!" He rushed over, not sure what to do.

"Help…me…get to the bed," J.T. panted, his blue eyes cloudy with agony.

Matt yanked off his leather gloves and jammed them in the pocket of his denims before pushing the chair around the dining table and to the large bedroom on the bottom floor where Pa and Cora had moved after they'd married.

She hurried ahead of them and turned down the bed. Her usually calm features were pinched with worry. Between the two of them, they got the big man into bed.

He groaned, sweat glistening on his craggy face. "That already feels better."

Cora sat on the edge of the bed, holding tight to his hand. "I'm sending Matt for Annalise."

J.T. didn't argue, didn't even shake his head which told Matt the older man must be hurting like blue blazes.

Cora looked up at Matt. "I'll stay with him."

"I'll be back as quick as I can." He glanced at J.T. and Cora laid a hand on his arm.

"He'll be all right," she mouthed.

He looked into her hazel eyes, so steady, and nodded. He turned on his heel and strode out the door, riding hell bent for Whirlwind.

An hour later, he and Annalise drove into the yard in her buggy. Because the rustlers were still on the loose, he had no intention of letting her travel alone. Later, he would take her back to town, where he'd left his horse. He helped her down and followed her inside.

He and Cora hovered in the bedroom doorway as

Annalise examined J.T. More than once he caught himself tapping his fingers against the frame. What did Annalise think?

As she quietly questioned her patient, she turned him so she could reach his back. Despite her careful touch, Matt saw his pa's fist clench in the white bedsheet. That and the fact that his lips were bloodless were a clear sign his father was in excruciating pain.

The older man continued answering Annalise's questions. She took a bottle from her satchel and asked Matt to fetch a glass of water. He did, handing it to Cora as Annalise measured an amount of medicine into a spoon then fed it to J.T. Cora held his head as he sipped at the water.

Annalise glanced at them. "It's morphine. It will ease the pain."

The tightness across his chest eased as he watched her tend to his father.

"I don't want to give you too much morphine or you'll go to sleep and we need to talk."

The older man nodded. The distress in his face began to ease and Matt drew his first full breath since helping his father into the bed.

Annalise motioned Matt inside. Cora stroked J.T.'s thick shock of silver hair. Annalise placed the medicine bottle on the bureau at the foot of the bed.

Matt crushed his hat in his hands. "Why is the pain so bad? It hasn't been like this before."

Her look encompassed him and his stepmother. "The tumor has moved and I think it's grown."

"So what do you recommend?" J.T. rasped in a strained voice.

"I think it's time for the surgery."

"He's not considerin' that anymore," Matt said. "Are you, Pa?"

The older man winced, asking Annalise, "What are the risks?"

"It could paralyze you."

"What else?" Cora's voice shook.

"There's a chance you might not make it, J.T."

"How much of a chance?" Matt asked harshly, his gut knotting.

"Your father's in good health—"

"What are the chances?" he insisted.

She met his gaze. "Fifty-fifty."

"And if he survived, would he walk again?"

"There's no guarantee."

The chances were as good that his pa might die as they were he wouldn't and if he did survive, he still might not be able to walk.

A buzz started in Matt's ears. Annalise continued to answer questions from the two older people, but all he could hear was that the surgery might kill his father. Matt felt as though he was being slowly suffocated.

"There are other options, right?" he interrupted.

"Yes. We can manage the pain with morphine or laudanum, but that's a short-term solution."

"No surgery," Matt said quickly.

When she frowned at him, he glanced at J.T. "Right, Pa?"

"You think I really need the surgery, Annalise?" The man's voice was thready with pain.

"Yes."

"But that could kill him!" Matt burst out.

Cora looked away, but he saw a tear roll down her cheek. Her first husband had been murdered three years ago by an outlaw gang and now she could lose J.T., too. He and Russ could lose J.T.

A knife-edged dread stabbed at him. They had lost their mother to a tumor. They couldn't lose their father, too. "Pa, you can't have surgery without talking to Russ."

J.T., his strong features drawn and pinched, looked from his son to his new wife.

When his gaze moved to Annalise, she said quietly, "You shouldn't wait much longer. The tumor will probably continue to grow."

Giving her a sharp look, Matt clenched his fists, trying to stay calm. "The chances aren't good enough, Pa."

His father's blue eyes were bleak as he looked at Cora. "What do you think, honey?"

"I want whatever you want, but—" She broke off, biting her lip.

The strongest woman he knew was afraid and that hit Matt like a kick to the gut. "Pa."

After another long look at Matt and Cora, J.T. nodded, saying to Annalise, "Do you have more of that medicine?"

"Yes. I'll leave some and I'll also give you a little more before I go. It will help you rest."

"I guess I'll try the medicine option for now."

"All right." She patted his hand.

The crushing band around Matt's chest eased, but a feeling of heaviness still hung over him.

She took the small bottle from the bureau at the foot of the bed and showed Cora the amount to administer. Matt tried to rein in the frustration churning inside him.

Annalise picked up her satchel and squeezed her patient's shoulder. "Send for me whenever you need more medicine or if something changes. If *anything* changes. I've left enough morphine with Cora for a week. That should give you time to talk to your family and decide what you want to do."

"Thanks, girl," he said in a raspy voice.

Cora echoed her thanks as Annalise followed Matt outside. He helped her into the buggy, taking his seat beside her. Urging the horse into motion, he clenched his jaw, struggling to get past the anger chewing on him.

He could feel Annalise looking at him, but he couldn't talk yet.

After a long moment of silence broken only by the occasional creak of buggy wheels and the swish of prairie grass, she reached over and curled a hand over his knee. "Are you all right? I imagine it was hard to see him like that."

He grunted, telling himself not to say anything, but he burst out, "I can't believe you told him to have the surgery!"

"Why not? He asked me what I thought."

"You said you were going to tell him the options and the risks. All I heard in there was you telling him what to do."

"He asked my opinion and I gave it to him." She frowned, slowly removing her hand from his leg. "You're mad because I did that?"

"He could die," Matt bit out.

"Do you want him to live in pain the rest of his life?"

"I want him to have a life," he said hotly. "If it was your father, would you be so quick to let somebody butcher him up?"

She winced. "It's not butchering, Matt. I'm not a butcher."

He knew that. He heard the hurt in her voice, but fear rode him hard. "Would you recommend it for your father?"

"I think so, yes."

"Well, I don't think you would. And I don't want you taking any chances with *my* father."

"It isn't your decision, Matt."

That had him seeing red, but before he could speak, she continued, "And it isn't mine. It's his."

"He wasn't in his right mind. He was out of his head with pain until you gave him the medicine and that helped him. He was restin' easy when we left."

"That's only a short-term solution."

"What if he has the surgery and doesn't survive? What about Cora? What about me and Russ? Can you guarantee Pa won't die?"

"No," she said quietly.

"Then you can't do it. You can lessen his pain with the morphine. That's what he wants."

She appeared to struggle with something for a long moment before looking at him, understanding in her green eyes. "I think he only said that for your benefit. He saw how upset you and Cora were."

"He's going to give a lot of weight to your words."

"I never promised I wouldn't give my opinion."

"You sure as hell did. During our picnic at the Founder's Day celebration. I don't want you to tell him that again."

"Matt." She tried to take his hand, but he gripped the reins even tighter.

She pulled back, edging away from him. "I know this is frightening. It is for him, too. He needs your support."

Afraid of what he might say, he clamped his mouth

shut and reined up in front of the livery. "Well, here we are."

In short order he had her horse unharnessed and rubbed down, the buggy stored.

Annalise's gaze followed him the whole time.

He couldn't look at her or he would get mad all over again. He led Dove out of the livery and tied her to the hitching post.

"Matt?" The hurt in her voice grabbed at his chest.

"I gotta find Russ."

"When will you finish with the cattle?"

"Probably tomorrow."

"Will I see you then?"

"I don't know."

She angled her chin at him. "I can't believe you're mad at me about this."

He didn't want to be, but he couldn't seem to get shed of it.

"If your father needs more morphine or decides he wants me to operate, you know where I am."

"Yeah," he growled. "I do."

Her eyes narrowed and she studied him for a moment. Then she went up on her tiptoes and took his face between her hands, kissing him hard. Surprised, he stiffened, but then her mouth softened, invited.

Before he could push her off or kiss her back, she pulled away, her green eyes sparking with challenge. "You think about that, Matt Baldwin, and you remember who we are to each other."

Picking up her satchel, she stepped around him and started across the street for her clinic.

He watched her go, feeling as if his chest was being crushed.

Maybe the surgery was the best option, but Matt didn't

see any point in cutting his father open when there was another way to help him. Pa obviously agreed because he'd told Annalise he wanted the morphine.

Matt wasn't crazy about his father taking the drug either. He knew the risks, had heard of men and women who had become addicted to it, but in this situation, the medicine was the best thing.

Wasn't it? He thought so, but he wasn't sure. What he did know was that Annalise had done something she had told him she wouldn't.

Their reconciliation had already hit a bump and so had his earlier plans to propose. Right now, that was just fine with him.

Chapter Thirteen

Annalise didn't like how she and Matt had left things. She didn't like how he had accused her of breaking her word either. It had been two days and she hadn't seen hide nor stubborn hair of him. She'd had about all of his silence she wanted.

She had racked her brain, thinking back over the conversations they'd had during the time they spent together at the Founder's Day celebration, particularly over lunch. He believed she had told him she wouldn't give her opinion about the surgery to J.T., but she hadn't said anything of the kind.

I want you to convince him not to do it.

I can't do that. I can only tell him the options and risks...

If you tell him it's too dangerous, he won't do it.

Not once had she said she wouldn't give her opinion if asked.

She knew he had spoken to his brother about the disagreement they'd had over J.T.'s surgery because Russ and Lydia had come over that same night asking questions. Annalise answered all of them, had even gotten out her *Ashhurst's International Encyclopedia of Surgery* and *Leidy's Anatomy* to show them what the operation would be like if she did it. Russ had been as opposed to the surgery as his brother and, even after quizzing Annalise, he hadn't come around.

Still, she would offer the same to Matt. If she ever saw him again, she thought in exasperation staring out the clinic window as dusky light settled over Whirlwind.

Tucking in the bottom of the sheet she had just put on one of the cots in the examination room, she heard a knock on the door.

She turned at the same time it opened.

"Hi, Annalise." Lydia Baldwin stepped inside and closed the door, carefully handling a stiff-looking piece of cloth.

Was that what Annalise thought it was? She hurried toward the tall raven-haired woman who carefully laid the piece on the table in front of the window. Smoothing her pale-blue skirts, she turned to Annalise.

"Is that the impression Matt and I made of those hoofprints?"

"Yes." The other woman fanned her face, color flushing her pearly skin. Her black eyes flashed with humor. "I was threatened to within an inch of my life if I let something happen to that."

"What are you doing with it?"

"Matt wanted J.T. and Russ to look at it and see if they had any ideas as to why the prints are so uniform, but neither of them did. Matt wondered if you would show it to Ef and Davis Lee. Maybe one of them will come up with something."

Annalise's heart sank. Was that Matt's only message?

Show the impression around? Why couldn't he have brought it himself? "I'll do that tomorrow."

"Thank you again for taking the time to answer all of Russ's and my questions last night."

"Of course. It didn't seem to settle your husband's mind. Matt's certainly isn't settled either."

"They are two stubborn men, but I've found them to be reasonable." A mischievous light flared in her dark eyes. "Most of the time."

"Russ seemed as opposed to the surgery as Matt."

"Russ doesn't want to take the chance because he feels it's his fault J.T. is in the wheelchair to start with."

Annalise nodded. Matt had told her the same thing.

"If he had this surgery and died, Russ would feel responsible for that, too."

Annalise didn't know what to say to that. She couldn't promise the man wouldn't die or be paralyzed.

"We went out yesterday evening and spoke to J.T. about it. Russ hasn't changed his mind completely, but because of what you told us, he was able to give some good information to J.T. and Matt."

"I'm glad." What bothered Annalise wasn't that Matt didn't agree with her, it was that he thought she had broken her word.

"You might want to send the impression out to the ranch with Miguel or someone. I don't know when Matt will be back here, if ever."

Lydia tucked a stray strand of black hair behind her ear, smiling. "He'll be back. In fact, he started into town yesterday with us to see you, but then he came upon a long section of downed fence in the pasture where the cattle were just moved to. That's like giving the rustlers an invitation. Russ stayed to help him and the other hands fix it."

Annalise was encouraged that Matt had started into town to see her yesterday. Maybe he didn't like this silence any better than she did.

Lydia reached into her reticule and pulled out a piece of paper. "J.T. also wanted me to give you this note."

"What does it say?"

"I don't know. He folded it in half twice so I don't think he meant for me to read it."

Annalise nodded as she took the paper and slipped it into her skirt pocket.

"I'd better get over to the hotel now."

Annalise smiled and walked the woman out. "Thanks, Lydia."

"You're welcome." She stepped into the street and angled the short distance to the Fontaine.

Once back inside, Annalise locked the door and finished putting clean sheets on the other cot in her examination room. Then she took the lamp and went upstairs, waiting until she reached her bedroom before reading J.T.'s note.

She frowned down at the masculine scrawl and eased onto the mattress. He wanted to do the surgery. He wanted her to do it at the ranch in two days when Matt and Russ would be finished repairing fence, and could be there with him.

It sounded as though J.T. had discussed it with the boys. Did that mean they had come to agree with his decision? Part of Annalise was relieved; she really did believe this was best. She hoped Matt would feel that way when all was said and done.

The next morning when she woke, she was still thinking about him. She moved the impression out of the sun, placing it on the kitchen table that sat away from the window and out of the light. She would take it to the sheriff and blacksmith this morning and get their thoughts.

After fastening her cotton wrapper, she set about making coffee and eggs, then sat down to eat. She wondered if Matt would make it to town today. It was past time to discuss the fact that he believed she had broken her word.

Her gaze landed on the cheesecloth and she rose to go look at it. Why couldn't anyone figure out what was so strange about it? Sipping her coffee, she stared absently at the pattern imprinted on the cornstarch-stiffened cloth.

She had looked at this thing a dozen times and she still hadn't found any new answers. Noticing what she thought was a mark, she leaned closer. Had Matt or someone gotten something on it? Was that dirt?

It took a moment for her brain to register what she saw on the fabric. It looked like the impression of…a nailhead.

Placing her coffee on the opposite end of the table, Annalise sat down and pulled the cloth toward her. It *was* a nailhead! She hadn't noticed it before and she knew Matt hadn't either or he would've said something.

Why would a cow have a nail in its hoof? And if a cow did have a nail there, wouldn't the animal be limping? That would make the pattern irregular, not uniform.

Did it mean anything? She couldn't quite put together exactly what, but she was sure it was important. She had to tell Matt, whether he wanted to see her yet or not.

Even if he wasn't willing to discuss his father's surgery, he would discuss this.

She opened the window and poured out the remainder of her coffee, then hurried upstairs to dress. After stepping into a lilac-and-white-checked daydress, she pulled her hair back and twisted it into a low chignon. A heavy knock rattled the front door.

"Coming!"

As she rushed downstairs, she hoped whoever was here wasn't anyone who had a serious problem. She was anxious to get out to the ranch. Before she could do that, she would have to find someone to drive out with her. Going by herself wouldn't be prudent, what with the rustlers still on the loose. And Matt would be even madder at her if she traveled alone.

Sunlight glittered through the front window and when the visitor peered inside, she saw it was Matt.

She hurried to the door and unlocked it. "Hi," she said breathlessly. "I was planning to come find you."

"You were? So you're still talking to me?"

"Yes."

"Can I come in?"

"Of course."

He stepped inside, hanging his hat beside the door and adjusting the Peacemaker he carried on the gunbelt slung low on his hips. He had never been one to go unarmed and since all the trouble had started with the rustlers, a lot of other men in town followed his example.

She relocked the door. "Is your father all right?"

"Yes. The medicine gives him relief." A muscle in his jaw flexed as he met her gaze. "I didn't like how we— I—left things the other evening. I want to apologize."

The words were so unexpected she blinked.

"For accusing you of saying something you didn't say. I've been trying to come to terms with the surgery."

"I wanted to talk to you about something, too."

"I know I should let you go first, but I need to say this. I need you to hear it."

She nodded, encouraged when he took her hand. "I thought back over our conversation at the picnic."

"So did I."

"I know now you didn't tell me you wouldn't give your opinion. I guess that's just what I wanted to hear."

The relief was so great her stomach dipped. "Thank goodness."

"You been worried about this?"

She smacked his arm. "Of course I have. I don't want anything to come between us again. It hurt that you believed I broke my word to you."

"I don't think that. I knew it yesterday, but I couldn't get to town to tell you."

"Yes, Lydia told me about the fence that needed repairing."

"The idea of that surgery lathered me up good. And I'm still not sure about it, Angel."

"I understand, but I'm so relieved to hear you say you know I didn't break my word."

"I knew better," he admitted, caressing the line of her jaw with his thumb. "The whole thing had me out of sorts."

"It's a very serious situation. Some things are hard to hear."

"Why won't Pa heal up the way Edward has?"

"It's not the same type of injury. The boy cracked a vertebra. Your father has a tumor that's pressing on his spine."

He nodded and she thought he might ask more questions about J.T.'s condition.

Instead, he pulled her into him. "So you forgive me?"

He must not want to discuss his change of heart about J.T.'s surgery. "Yes."

"It's a good thing. I feel like I'm askin' for forgiveness every time I turn around." He brushed a kiss across her lips. "So, why were you coming to find me?"

"I want to show you something."

He looked her up and down, causing that familiar warmth to spread through her. "I want to show you something, too."

She laughed. "Not *that* kind of something. Come on."

"Is this something upstairs? Please say yes."

"No." Anticipating his reaction at learning some new information about the impression, she took his hand and pulled him behind her into the hall, down to the kitchen.

"Well, you're not takin' me upstairs so I guess this isn't what I was hoping for."

"No, it isn't." She threw him a look over her shoulder.

He tugged on her hand, pressing her back into his front and dropped a kiss on her neck. It would've been so easy to relax against him. Or take him upstairs. But this was important. At least she thought it would turn out to be.

She drew him to the kitchen table and he stopped behind her, resting his hands on her hips. His clean soap scent mixed with a hint of the outdoors and a faint whiff of leather.

Nuzzling her cheek with his rougher one, he looked over her shoulder. He stood close enough for her to feel his warmth, the powerful width of his chest.

Sliding one hand around her waist, he flattened it on her stomach and held her to him while he gently sank his teeth into the spot where her shoulder met her neck.

She shivered. "Stop that. Look at what I'm showing you."

"I like where I'm looking just fine."

"You'll be glad."

"All right," he grumbled, leaning over so that his chin rested on her shoulder. His gaze followed hers to the impression. "I've seen this. I was with you when you did it, remember?"

"Look closely." She pointed to the spot she'd spied earlier. "Do you see it?"

"No—wait." Using one finger, he shifted the cloth slightly to the right. "There's an impression in the hoof. It looks like a nailhead."

"I think it is," she said excitedly.

"I'll be." He studied the likeness. "But a nail would make the hoof prints more irregular."

She frowned. "I think so, too. This means something—I'm just not sure what."

Together, they studied the cloth for a long moment.

She tilted her head. "It's almost as if someone nailed a hoof on the bottom of a shoe."

It sounded so preposterous that Annalise laughed, but Matt bent closer, scrutinizing the cheesecloth.

He straightened, his big hands closing over her shoulders. "That's exactly what they did! That's why there haven't been any human footprints or horse tracks. Angel, you're brilliant!"

She allowed the pleasure a brief moment before asking, "How will you find something like that?"

"Just have to start looking. And now I have something to look for. I'll tell Davis Lee and all the other ranchers who've lost cattle. They need to know about this, too."

Matt pressed against her back, obviously aroused and

murmured in her ear, "Now, take me upstairs so I can show *you* something."

"Well, I don't know," she said nonchalantly. "I'm pretty busy."

"I plan to keep you that way." He turned her in his arms and covered her mouth with his.

Annalise sank into the kiss and her heart began to pound so hard she could hear it in her head. It kept pounding. Finally, she realized the pounding was coming from the door.

She pulled away. "I have to answer that."

"We could hide back here. No one would know."

She kissed him lightly and started for the front door. "Someone might need help."

He followed, muttering that this better be important or else. They should've headed upstairs when they had the chance.

"It's Davis Lee." She unlocked and opened the door, surprised to see the lawman so early.

Matt grinned at his friend. "Thanks to the doctor here, we may have figured out why the hoof prints left behind after the rustlers hit are so strange."

"I'm afraid my news isn't as pleasant." His somber blue gaze went from Annalise to Matt. "Just got a wire that the Landis brothers broke out of the Abilene jail."

Beside her, Matt went as stiff as a wagon axle. "All of them?"

"Yes, the other five."

"So, in addition to Reuben and Pat being on the loose, now the others are, too."

"I'm heading up a posse. The SOBs were last seen going west, toward Whirlwind. Doesn't mean they're coming here, but I think we should be prepared. I told Marshal Clinton that we would start from halfway between here and Abilene and fan out in all directions."

"Which men are staying behind?"

"Quentin, Charlie, Pete Carter, Tony Santos and Penn Wavers. Jericho just left with Catherine for a trip back East."

"Andrew, Miguel and Creed can serve as extra eyes and ears." All three boys knew how to handle a gun. "They all shoot pretty well, too."

"We're heading out in ten minutes," Davis Lee said.

"I'll be there."

The sheriff looked at Annalise. "We don't know if the Landis brothers will come here, but Josie and the baby are going to stay at the Fontaine with Lydia and Naomi."

"All right."

After their friend said goodbye, Matt turned to Annalise. "Please stay at the hotel as well. I know you don't want to, but it would ease my mind."

She hesitated.

"Please."

The concern in his eyes and the softness of his voice had her nodding. "Okay."

"Thank you." The relief on his face was so strong that Annalise reached for his hand.

He brushed his lips across her knuckles then pulled her to him. For a long moment, he just held her. She laid her hand on his chest, feeling the steady thump of his heart.

"When will you go to the hotel?" he asked.

"Tonight, before dark."

"All right. One of us will send word when we can."

"Promise you'll be careful."

"You bet." Cupping her face in his hands, he gave

her a slow kiss, as though he were storing it away in his memory. And then he was gone.

She watched his long-legged strides eat up the distance across Main Street between here and the jail where Jake and Bram Ross and Riley were gathered in the bright morning sunlight.

The men mounted up. Half of them headed west, the other half went east past Annalise. With any luck, the posses would find the Landis brothers and no one would be hurt.

As Matt galloped by, he winked at her. She waved, thankful he had his friends to watch his back. She was glad he hadn't wanted to let anything come between them either. Thank goodness they had patched things up.

As she watched Matt ride off, Annalise knew things between them would be okay.

Late the next evening, Matt sat around a campfire with his brother, Riley, and Jake and Bram Ross. Annalise was on his mind. He was glad they had set things right between them and relieved she had agreed to stay at the hotel. Knowing she was with other people at night kept him from worrying too much.

He'd rather be there protecting her himself, but this was where he was needed.

After a supper of beans and biscuits, the men passed around a fresh pot of coffee. The night was clear, the sky an inky black dotted with diamond-bright stars. He and the others had met up with Marshal Clinton about five miles outside Abilene. He and the three men with him shared that the Landis brothers were definitely traveling west and one of them had been shot and wounded.

Matt's party had turned back toward Whirlwind,

tracked the outlaws past Triple B land as well as Riley's. The trail turned slightly north and he figured the outlaws were headed for the Panhandle.

They had ridden until dark again today then stopped for the night. It occurred to Matt that because of the jail break he hadn't told Davis Lee or Russ what he and Annalise had discovered about those hoof prints.

He explained to the others how Annalise had made the impression of the cattle tracks after the rustlers' last visit to the Triple B. All of the men who had lost cattle had been confused as to why the thieves weren't leaving any human tracks.

Matt described the uniformity of the hoof prints on the cheesecloth impression. "Yesterday, Annalise showed me the imprint of a nailhead in the dead center of the hoof."

"What're you sayin'?" Riley asked, tossing his straw cowboy hat onto the bedroll beneath him.

"The rustlers are nailing real cow hooves to the soles of their boots or shoes."

Exclamations sounded around the small fire.

Riley tossed a twig to the side. "Well, those tracks make sense now."

Davis Lee shook his head. "That's a trick I haven't heard before."

Bram stretched out on his bedroll, using his saddle as a pillow. "Sounds like you and Annalise came to terms."

"Yes." And Matt was damn glad. She hadn't won him over with her argument about the risky surgery she recommended for his pa, but he knew things would work out.

"What does the doc say about your pa's leg?" Davis Lee rested one arm on a bent knee.

Russ shared a look with Matt before answering, "She thinks he has a tumor low on his spine and it's grown. She thinks cutting him open is the way to go."

"As opposed to what?" Jake spoke for the first time, unfolding his bedroll next to his brother's.

Matt stared down into his coffee. "Giving him morphine to ease the pain."

Davis Lee looked across the fire. "For how long?"

"As long as he has the pain."

"Doesn't sound likely he'll ever get rid of it."

The quiet man was right, Matt admitted.

Riley looked up from checking his gun. "How does your pa do on the medicine?"

"Fine."

"He's not himself," Russ said at the same time.

Matt shot him a sharp look.

His brother shook his head. "When I saw him a couple of days ago, his axle was dragging and his reflexes were slower than a hobbled horse."

"I haven't witnessed that."

"Maybe you haven't noticed because you've been around him the whole time he's been taking that medicine. The other day was the first time I have."

Hell. Was his brother right?

"It's like he's sleepwalking, aware but not all that alert," Russ continued. "That's how Lydia described it."

And it was the truth, Matt realized with a jolt. He imagined his father living like that the rest of his life and the thought made his stomach knot up.

Annalise made a good point about the morphine not being a long-term solution, but Matt wasn't sure surgery was the answer either.

He looked at his brother. "You think Annalise is right about operating?"

"The thought of it scares the hell out of me."

"Me, too."

"But she might be right."

Matt wasn't quite ready to go that far.

"Lydia and I talked to her for a while about it." Eyes dark with worry, Russ set his tin coffee cup on the ground beside him. "Annalise showed us some pictures in a couple of her fancy surgery books."

"And?"

"It still scares me, but she sure seems to know what she's talking about."

"Is that enough? She said herself she can't guarantee something won't go wrong."

"I don't know, but I don't like seeing Pa the way he is on that medicine."

Matt felt that way, too. "Annalise thinks he only chose the morphine because the talk of surgery upset me and Cora."

"She might be right about that, too." His brother looked grim in the flickering orange firelight.

"When we get back, I'll talk to her again. Ask her to show me the pictures she showed to you and Lydia."

Russ nodded.

"It's a hard decision," Davis Lee said from the other side of the fire. "I'm glad I don't have to make it."

But he had, Matt realized as the other men murmured in agreement. Davis Lee had dealt with something equally as difficult.

"You and Josie had to make a decision like that, didn't you?" Matt asked. "I mean, a decision that hard. About trying to have another baby."

"Yes, and if we hadn't taken the risk one more time, we wouldn't have Tannis."

Matt looked through the curl of smoke at Jake. The man had lost his first wife and child.

"What about you, Jake? What do you think about having a baby with Emma?"

"We argued about it, especially after Dr. Butler said he thought it would be all right." Jake chewed the inside of his cheek. "No matter how quiet my wife is, if she gets something in her head then it's gonna happen. I guess I'm all right with it, but I'm glad she isn't in the family way yet."

Matt glanced at Davis Lee. "Would you take the chance again?"

"I really don't know. Josie had to do a lot of talking to convince me, but I'm not sorry we decided to try. I'll never be sorry," his friend said quietly. "Maybe you should figure out if you can live with your pa *not* having the surgery."

He exchanged a look with his brother. Russ's observation of their father's sluggish condition while under the influence of the morphine rattled Matt. At first, all he had focused on was getting rid of J.T.'s pain and keeping it to a minimum. Now he could see that the morphine wasn't best for the long term. He didn't know what was best and he wasn't sure Annalise knew either.

Chapter Fourteen

It had been two days since Annalise had seen Matt. There had been no word from any of the men who were hunting the Landis brothers, but she wasn't worried yet.

Today was the day J.T. had wanted to have surgery. With Russ and Matt away, Annalise assumed he would now rather wait until his sons returned. She learned differently when Henry Goforth, one of the Triple B's most seasoned ranch hands, showed up at her clinic about mid-morning.

He'd been sent by J.T. to find out why Dr. Fine hadn't arrived at the ranch for his surgery. Surprised at the unexpected summons, it took her an hour to gather her surgical set, medical bag and her volume of John Erichsen's *The Science and Art of Surgery.*

Driving her buggy, she followed Henry and his bay out to the ranch. He would escort her back to Whirlwind when the time came.

She wished J.T. would wait for his sons' return. For

one thing, it would give her a chance to talk to Matt again about the operation.

Once they reached the edge of Triple B land, Annalise steered the horse and buggy off the road and into the prairie grass. Unless there had been a drastic change in J.T.'s condition, she hoped to talk him out of doing the operation today. His sons should be there when it happened.

But within minutes of arriving at the ranch, she learned that J.T. was adamant about proceeding. Annalise stood in the Baldwins' large front room, exchanging a look over the patient's head with his wife.

"I'm not of a mind to wait," he said. "There's still pain in my back, but my leg is numb. That can't be a good sign."

It wasn't, Annalise admitted silently. "Are you sure you don't want to wait for Russ and Matt to return?"

"Who knows how long that'll be," the older man groused.

Cora walked around to stand in front of him. "You don't think you can wait?"

"I'm ready to get this done, honey." Lines of pain carved J.T.'s weathered features and his blue eyes were shadowed by discomfort.

Annalise observed that his speech wasn't slurred nor were his features lax. Which meant he hadn't taken any morphine today. Before she could ask why not, he locked his jaw and looked at her defiantly. "That medicine makes me feel like I'm not even in my own body."

Cora turned to Annalise. "I hate seeing him in this much pain, but the surgery makes me nervous."

"The only way to get past that is to just do the operation," J.T. insisted. "But, honey, if you want me to wait, I will."

Annalise could tell it had cost him to say that.

The older woman touched his hand. "No, let's go ahead."

Her voice sounded sure, but there was uncertainty in her hazel eyes.

"Are you sure?" J.T. searched his wife's face.

"Yes." She kissed him hard and fast, saying fiercely, "You do everything Annalise tells you before and after, do you understand?"

"Yes, ma'am." The quick grin he flashed reminded Annalise of his youngest son.

"All right, then," she agreed. "The best place to do this is in a bed where you'll be comfortable resting for a few days."

"We can use our bed." He wheeled past them to the lone bedroom on the first floor.

Annalise and Cora managed to get him into the bed and on his stomach. Though she would've preferred to wait for Matt and Russ, this would be fine. When the boys arrived home, their father would already be feeling better.

Annalise glanced at the small bedside table she would use for her instruments then at the inhaler she would use to give anaesthetic. Cora had agreed to assist and she would need room to move.

The woman watched as Annalise laid out the blades from the surgical set.

Then she took her Junker's inhaler and filled the reservoir with chloroform. Using a hand-bellows, Cora would pump air through a tube into the chloroform and a second tube would carry the mixture of air and anaesthetic to the patient as a gas. Annalise would administer the drug.

J.T. winked at Cora. "Everything will be fine, honey."

"It better be. I haven't forgotten that you promised to fix me a swing on the porch."

When the patient was settled comfortably, Annalise placed a rubber mask over his nose and mouth then Cora began a careful and slow pumping with the hand-bellows. In short order, he was unconscious and Annalise got to work.

Though there were butterflies in her stomach, her hands were steady. She had only assisted with this surgery, never performed it herself, but she had studied it extensively and the textbook was here if she needed it.

Hoping she didn't look as nervous as she felt, she cut into J.T.'s lower back and easily located the tumor. As she had cautioned both J.T. and Cora, the operation took a couple of hours and she worked meticulously, painstakingly, explaining the procedure as she went.

When she was certain she had gotten all of the growth, she stitched him up then bandaged him.

She looked at Cora. "I removed the whole tumor and didn't find anything else to cause concern."

"Oh, that's good news." The woman hugged her tightly and Annalise returned the embrace.

"You can sit with him until he wakes up, if you'd like. It will probably be an hour or so."

Cora eagerly agreed and pulled up a chair beside the bed, taking her husband's hand.

But, after an hour, J.T. hadn't stirred. Cora gave Annalise an anxious look.

"Maybe it's just taking him longer to come to," Annalise said quietly. "Because of his size, we had to use a lot of chloroform."

Cora nodded, but after another hour when J.T. still

hadn't regained consciousness, Annalise decided to try and wake him. He didn't respond. His eyelids didn't flutter. His pulse didn't change.

Dread snaked through her.

She had carefully monitored the amount of chloroform they'd administered, but J.T. wasn't waking up.

From her place beside the bed, Cora looked up. "There's something wrong, isn't there? What is it?"

"He's not waking up from the anaesthetic as quickly as I'd like." Annalise patted the other woman's arm. "He'll come around. It's just taking him a while."

But two hours later, he still hadn't. She hadn't seen chloroform affect anyone this way before. All she knew to do was continue to monitor his pulse and condition.

Cora's features were pinched with worry. "What now?"

"All we can do is wait. I'll stay until he wakes up."

Cora brought another chair into the room and positioned it at the head of the bed for Annalise.

The hours dragged by. Night fell. Annalise continued to reassure her friend. She truly believed J.T. would wake up. But at midnight, when there was still no change, she was hit with full-fledged panic. She had to tell Cora.

She shifted in her chair.

Immediately, Cora straightened, her face full of trepidation.

"I believe he's in a coma," Annalise said gently.

The older woman's eyes filled with tears. "Does that mean he's going to stay that way?"

Annalise refused to consider the possibility. "No. I believe he'll come to."

She was praying with everything in her that he did and she hoped it was before seventy-two hours had passed.

To her knowledge, no one had ever been known to wake up at all after that amount of time.

"What if—" Cora's voice cracked. She didn't ask the question, but it hung there between them anyway.

What if he doesn't wake up?

The Landis brothers were at the front of Matt's mind when he and Russ passed their last barn and rode into the yard just before noon. They'd spent two and a half days chasing those bastards and hadn't caught them. The trail had gone cold on the far side of the Eight of Hearts Ranch. It was as though the outlaws had just disappeared into a hole.

Matt and the others had made the return trip slowly, searching for any sign they might have missed. There was nothing. Matt was still of the opinion that Reuben and Pat Landis were the ones who had ambushed him. It wouldn't surprise him if they turned out to be the rustlers, too. Hell, the whole family had done plenty of thieving—cows and horses—before being thrown in jail this go-round.

Matt was hot and sweaty and seething with frustration. He was also hungry. His breakfast of coffee and biscuits seemed a long time ago. As did the last time he'd seen Annalise. He'd missed her, more than he'd thought he would for the short time he'd been gone.

Though he was anxious to see her, he wanted to check on Pa first, then eat and clean up before he went to Whirlwind. Russ's observation about the morphine-induced lethargy had been playing in Matt's mind since that night around the fire. His brother wanted to check on Pa, too, which was why he had stopped here on his way to Whirlwind.

They rode straight into the barn and dismounted. As

he unsaddled Dove, he spotted Annalise's buggy against the back wall. He smiled. She must've gotten word from the wire Davis Lee had sent, letting everyone know no one was injured and they would all be home today.

Russ brushed down his paint gelding, tilting his head toward the buggy. "Looks like your lady doctor is here."

"Now we can both ask her whatever we want about the surgery."

"Yeah."

Matt finished with Dove and sent the mare out the back door of the barn into the pasture beyond, then he and his brother started for the house.

They stepped up on the wraparound porch, their boots hitting the pine floorboards with a solid thump. The front doorway was tall and wide enough for any one of the Baldwins to step inside without ducking or having to turn to the side. That had come in handy when Pa had ended up in the wheelchair.

Matt opened the heavy wooden door to see Cora hurrying toward them. The pale weariness of her face immediately had him on alert.

Russ, too, Matt realized as his brother moved toward their stepmother, looking apprehensive. "Cora?"

It was Pa. He knew it. Jerking off his hat, he took three steps, gaze skipping past the rock fireplace then the dining table to the left. Annalise stood in the doorway of the downstairs bedroom.

A sick feeling gripped him. "What's happened?"

"Is it Pa?" Russ curved one arm solicitously around Cora's shoulders.

The women exchanged a look that tangled the knot in Matt's gut even tighter. He strode around the kitchen table with Russ right behind him. He tossed his hat onto the table. Annalise stepped back as he reached the doorway and stopped dead.

Pa lay on his stomach, head turned toward them, eyes closed, face lax. A white sheet covered him from the waist down.

Even after being confined to the wheelchair, J.T. Baldwin never took time away from any ranch chores to lie abed. Cold dread slicked down Matt's spine. "What's happened?"

"He had the surgery," Cora said.

Those words were enough to cut his breath. "What? Why? Why would he do that?"

"Especially while we were gone." Russ frowned.

Matt braced his hands on his hips. "*When* did he decide to do it?"

"A day or so before you left with the posse."

"*Before* we left?" Matt asked.

His stepmother nodded.

He noted the shimmer of nerves in her eyes that said she wasn't as calm as she sounded.

His gaze cut to Annalise.

She looked from him to his brother and back. "J.T. sent me a note a couple of days ago saying he wanted me to do the operation. When the two of you joined the posse to hunt the Landis brothers, I thought he would want to wait until you returned, but he didn't."

"So you went ahead and did it," he said in a cold flat voice.

Russ moved into the room and stepped around Matt. "I thought surely he would've heard us and woken up by now."

A sudden tension cut through the room like a knife.

Cora cleared her throat. "He hasn't woken up."

"What do you mean?" Russ looked grim. "He hasn't woken up since you did the surgery?"

"Yes," Annalise answered quietly.

"How long has he been like this?" Matt demanded.

"A little over forty-eight hours."

The bottom of his stomach fell out and he cursed viciously. "Tell us what's going on. Right now."

"I tried to talk him into waiting, but he wouldn't," she began. "He didn't wake up when I thought he would. It made me wonder if the anaesthetic might be affecting him negatively."

"What did you give him? Ether?"

"Chloroform."

A faint sweet scent hovered in the room. Matt stared over her shoulder at his father. "Did you give him too much?"

"I don't believe so. I was very careful."

"Then why isn't he coming to?"

"We're not sure," Cora said.

Matt stared straight at Annalise, a black fury rising inside him. "*You* know why."

"Yes." The dark circles under her eyes testified to hours of worry and a loss of sleep. "He's in a coma."

Coma. The word slammed into him like a bullet. When his brother took a step back, Matt knew it had affected him the same way.

"That means he'll never wake up," Russ said hoarsely.

"No," Annalise assured him quickly, firmly. "It does *not* mean that."

She met Matt's gaze without flinching, which somehow infuriated him even more.

Rage slid like needles under his skin as he fought to control a viciousness he'd never felt.

She had known about this before he'd left and she

hadn't said a word. Not one damn word. Why? Had she been waiting for him to be out of the way? Staring into her clear, earnest eyes, he didn't want to believe it.

A moan came from the big man in the bed.

Everyone spun toward him, but after a long moment when there was nothing more from him, a heaviness descended over the room.

The hope in Cora's eyes died and fear spiked again inside Matt.

His stepmother looked at Annalise. "Does this mean he's not going to regain full consciousness?"

"No. This could as easily be a sign of his mind starting to wake up as a sign that it isn't."

"What do we do if he doesn't wake up?"

"We take care of him," Russ said firmly.

Matt couldn't speak past the knot of dread and anger in his throat.

With sympathy in her eyes, Annalise touched Cora's shoulder. "I'm going to step out for a minute and let the three of you have some time to talk."

Matt's eyes narrowed. Was she trying to dodge him? The thought snapped his last thread of restraint. When Annalise went out the front door, he followed her around to the side of the house.

"You knew before I left that you were going to do this and you didn't tell me. Now Pa might not ever wake up."

She turned, eyeing him warily. "It wouldn't have mattered if I'd told you. The surgery wasn't your decision to make. Or mine."

"You didn't have to do it."

She shook her head. "Why would you want him to carry on like this?"

"I don't!" he yelled, his chest aching. "Russ and I discussed this on the trail. Your point about him having to live on that medicine was good. All I wanted was the chance to talk to you again about the surgery. It's almost like you wanted me to be gone so you could proceed."

"That's ridiculous," she huffed. "I can't believe you even said that. How was I supposed to know you wanted to talk about it again? That you might change your mind about the surgery?"

"It's not that I necessarily think the surgery was wrong—I kind of reached that conclusion on the trail—but I do have a problem with you knowing about it before I left and not telling me."

"That morning at the clinic, I thought you knew. I thought you had come to terms with it, but didn't want to discuss it."

It was true talking hadn't been high on his list. "Why didn't you ask me?"

"Because I thought you already knew!" Her voice rose. "You think I lied? That I deliberately kept this from you?"

He didn't want to think so.

She drew in a sharp breath. "You think I'm lying right now. Why would you think that? What have I done to make you— Oh, no."

His gaze sliced to hers. "What?"

"You still don't believe I told the truth about knowing I was expecting when I left Whirlwind. Did you just pretend to believe me so you could get me back into bed?"

"That's hogwash!"

"Yes, and that's how absurd your accusations are, too."

"How did you get from my pa's surgery to that?" he demanded heatedly, refusing to soften at the stark pain in her eyes. He shoved a hand through his hair. "I thought things between us were going to be different, but evidently that only applies to me. You think *I* have to be different, but you don't."

"That isn't fair. If you really believe I kept this from you deliberately, you haven't changed the way I thought you had." Her voice caught and she bit her lip, her eyes hollow. "Do you really think I lied?"

He hadn't exactly said that, but it was what he meant, wasn't it? "Did you?"

She looked as if she might shatter. "Why should I answer? No matter what I say, you'll think it's a lie." Sadness darkened her eyes. "Have you ever believed me?"

He thought he had. He didn't answer; he couldn't. He thought he had moved on, but right now all he saw were years of distrust, anger, feelings of betrayal.

The blood drained from her face, making her green eyes a stark contrast to her alarming paleness.

Russ called through the open bedroom window. "Pa's moaning again. I think he might be waking up!"

Annalise whirled and rushed back into the house. Matt was right on her heels.

"J.T.!" Cora was kneeling beside the mattress.

"Hello, honey." His words were slurred, his eyes heavy-lidded.

Matt couldn't swallow past the lump in his throat. How he could feel anything past the fury throbbing in his veins was a mystery.

Annalise hurried around him to the foot of the bed and eased the sheet to Pa's thighs then carefully folded back the loose waistband of his drawers, revealing a thick white bandage wrapped around his lower back.

"'Lise?" J.T. lifted his head slightly. He looked groggy and his voice was sluggish, just as it was when he took the morphine.

Annalise checked the bandage. Seemingly satisfied, she moved to his feet. "Can you wiggle your toes for me?"

He did, on both feet.

"Wonderful! Describe any pain you have."

The patient hardly seemed able to keep his eyes open. "My back hurts like blue blazes," he mumbled. "But it's a different pain than before."

"Is it only in one spot?"

"Mmm-hmm." His eyes closed.

Annalise glanced at Cora. "It's the place where I made the incision. That's to be expected."

"You…got it all, 'Lise?" the big man asked in a slurred voice.

"Yes, I got it all."

"Good." His eyes closed and his features went lax with sleep.

Cora gasped.

Annalise put a hand on her friend's arm. "It's all right. This is a natural sleep."

"Thank goodness."

Russ blew out a relieved breath and hugged Annalise. "Pa's going to be okay. You think he'll walk again?"

"It's too early to say, but I'm hopeful. Very hopeful."

He squeezed her hard. "I can't wait to tell Lydia."

"We should let him rest." Annalise gave him and Cora a patently false smile. "I'll be back tomorrow to check on him."

Cora grabbed her in a hug. "Thank you. Thanks so much."

"You're welcome." She gathered her things, gave the older woman some last instructions and started out the door.

Matt was so relieved about Pa, he was almost light-headed as he followed Annalise outside.

"Thanks," he said gruffly. "That doesn't seem adequate for taking away his pain the way you did, maybe helping him walk again."

She didn't respond, didn't turn, just continued walking briskly to the barn.

Replaying the harsh words he'd said to her earlier, Matt grimaced. He'd been a jackass. Just because he had never been so afraid in his life was no call to say what he had to her. "Annalise?"

She didn't pause or stop, just continued on to the barn.

Hell. He'd really pulled the trigger without aiming this time. Catching up with her, he gently snagged her elbow.

"Don't." She whirled, jerking away from him. Color rode high on her cheeks. Her green eyes shot fire at him. "Don't."

"I want to apologize."

"I'm not interested," she said in a cool distant voice he'd never heard then took another step toward the barn.

He moved, planting himself in front of her, panic beginning a slow crawl through his belly. "I'm sorry, dammit. Those things I said were—I know I shouldn't have said them. I panicked. Seeing Pa like that scared the hell out of me."

"It would anyone." She tried to step around him and again he blocked her path.

"If you understand, why won't you let me apologize?"

Angry tears glistened in her eyes. And he saw hurt there, too. Hurt he'd caused. "You just accused me of lying. Again. Your apologies don't hold a lot of water with me right now." Her voice cracked. "We're finished."

"What?" His heart stopped. "You don't mean that."

"I do." Her gaze, bleak with pain, met his. "I'm sick of your distrust. Sick of having to justify myself to you. I've had all I want."

"We can work this out. I was an idiot." A chilling finality filled him. "I'm sorry, Angel. Truly sorry."

"How nice for you." Her face was closed, unyielding as she looked past him. "Henry, could you get my buggy ready to travel, please?"

"Yes, ma'am." The bow-legged man disappeared into the barn.

Matt took a step toward her. "At least let me take you to town."

Her jaw locked tighter than a bear trap. "I'm not going anywhere with you."

"Annalise." Matt wanted to throw her over his shoulder, keep her until she forgave him, but he knew that could be a damn long time. The hell of it was he couldn't blame her. How could he have lost control of his tongue like that? "You can't leave like this."

Behind him, he heard the jingle of harness as the horse and buggy came out of the barn. He tried not to panic. Hell, he was half afraid to say anything else. He sure wished he could take back what he'd said at the side of the house.

"You can't drive back alone."

She didn't spare him a glance. Shoulders rigid, body tight, she waited as Henry led the buggy toward her. When the ranch hand halted a few feet away, she smiled. "Henry, could you please escort me back to Whirlwind?"

"Boss?"

When Matt turned toward the other man, Annalise ducked around him.

Henry looked from her to Matt.

Finally, his jaw clenched tight enough to break teeth, Matt nodded. There was no talking to her right now and that was his fault.

He dragged a hand down his face. "I'll come for you tomorrow."

"Don't. It will be a waste of your time."

"You can't go back and forth without an escort."

She slid her medical bag beneath the buggy seat. "There are plenty of people I can ask to come with me."

"Like who?" he asked hotly. She better not mean Quentin.

"It's none of your business, Matt Baldwin. I said we were finished and I meant it."

Dad-blamed, confoundin' woman! Matt wanted to pull his hair out.

Still looking uncertain, Henry assisted her into the buggy. Without missing a beat, she took the reins and drove out of the yard.

Matt's chest was so tight he couldn't get a full breath.

With one last look back, Henry mounted his bay and followed Annalise.

Matt was about to crawl out of his skin. He knew

he'd hurt her deeply. Apologizing hadn't come close to reaching the pain inside her. She wouldn't talk to him, look at him.

Alarm shot through him. For the first time in his life, Matt had no idea what to do with a woman.

Chapter Fifteen

Annalise was determined to keep thoughts of Matt out of her head. He had all but called her a liar. Nothing had changed.

She'd thought she couldn't hurt any more than she had over his abandonment years ago. She'd been wrong. Blinking back tears, she thought about how unforgiving he'd looked earlier. She was *not* crying over him ever again.

She was mad enough to eat bees and she was going to hold on to it for a good long time.

As she drove into town and thanked Henry for escorting her, her stomach growled. Once she left her buggy and horse at the livery, she went to the Pearl.

After a hearty lunch, she returned to her clinic. She cleaned all her instruments as well as the inhaler tubes and mask. As she replenished the bandages in her medical bag, she glanced at the clock. She'd eaten just over an hour ago and her stomach felt hollow. She was hungry again.

Walking into her kitchen, she opened the cupboard and stared at the stale cloth-wrapped biscuits she'd made on the day she'd been summoned to the Triple B. Remembering that had Matt popping back into her head.

"Stupid man." Angered all over again, she slammed the cupboard door shut. "He isn't even worth shooting."

"Who isn't?"

She gave a little cry and turned to find Quentin in the doorway.

He smiled, which softened the sharp angles of his face. "Didn't mean to startle you. I knocked on the back door, but when you didn't answer, I went ahead and came in that way, as usual. Is that okay?"

"Of course." There was no ramp for her friend's wheelchair at the front door so he used the back stoop, which was level with the ground.

"I came to check on you and from what I just heard, you need it." He tilted his head. "Or maybe it's Matt who needs checking."

"Don't talk about him." In the pantry, she picked up a jar of peach slices. She could make a pie, but that didn't sound good either.

Quentin rolled into the room and parked himself at the corner of the table where he could see her face. "All right. Let's talk about why you're tearing up your kitchen. What are you looking for?"

"Something to eat." She studied the two eggs left in a basket on the lower shelf. "I'm starving."

"Let's go to the Pearl."

She gave him a sheepish look. "I ate just an hour ago."

"Obviously not enough. From what Russ said, you

put in a lot of hours with his pa. Did you eat during that time at all?"

"Yes." Dreading Quentin might say something about Matt, she steeled herself. "What else did Russ say?"

"Come to the Pearl with me and I'll tell you."

They left the clinic, Quentin maneuvering alongside her as they angled across Main Street toward the restaurant. "Russ told everyone you operated on J.T. and may have fixed his leg."

"The surgery was a success." She wasn't sure exactly what Russ had said and she didn't want to give away anything confidential. She hoped J.T.'s hours in that coma hadn't damaged him in any way.

Quentin held the door for her and she walked inside The Pearl. Red-checked-cloth-covered tables were set in neat rows.

Once they were seated, Quentin asked, "Do you think he'll walk again?"

"I'm hopeful."

He was quiet for a moment before his gaze met hers. "Do you think something like that would work for me?"

Annalise smiled. She'd never heard Quentin express an interest in learning more about his condition. "I'd have to examine you before I could say."

"How likely is a coma? Like what happened to J.T.?"

"It's not likely, but there is a risk," she admitted. Russ must indeed have shared a lot of details.

"Okay. I'll think about it."

They turned their attention to the menu. He asked a few more questions about J.T.'s surgery, mostly dealing with the anaesthetic she had used. She knew his worry about that came from J.T.'s experience.

No food on the menu sounded appealing either, but Annalise didn't tell Pearl. There was no reason to hurt the woman's feelings and it would. In the end, she just ordered a glass of lemonade.

As soon as she did, Annalise froze. *Lemonade.* The only time she ever wanted anything to do with lemons—no! She couldn't be pregnant! But nothing else explained why she wanted only that drink. What was she going to do?

Quentin asked her a question and she tried to focus. She didn't want him to suspect anything was wrong, but she needed to get back to her clinic so she could deal with this revelation.

And what about Matt? Her mind whirled as disbelief, joy, apprehension all crowded inside her.

About half an hour later, Quentin escorted her back to the clinic.

With that hollowness still gnawing at her stomach, she paused in front of the mercantile. She had to have some lemons. "I need to stop here for a bit. Do you need anything?"

"Not that I can think of. I'll just wait here until you get inside."

"All right. Thanks for taking me to the Pearl."

"Anytime."

She squeezed his hand then walked inside the store.

Drawn to a corner by the scents of citrus and soap, Annalise finally found a basket of the yellow fruit. After making her purchase, she walked past Cal Doyle's law office to her clinic.

Was she really expecting? Despite her sudden taste for all things lemon, she could hardly take in the situation. Tears threatened.

A man stood on the front porch, knocking on the door.

"May I help you?" she called, hoping whatever he needed could be taken care of quickly. She wasn't in the best frame of mind to deal with a patient.

He turned, rumpled and dusty, leather gloves tucked into the back pocket of his denims. "You the saw-bones?"

"Yes."

"I'm from the Eight of Hearts." He didn't look much older than she was. He jerked off his hat, revealing thinning red hair and a sagging left jaw. The muscle had somehow been destroyed so one side of his face was lower than the other and appeared lopsided. "One of the hands, Frank, is in a bad way. He needs a doctor."

She sighed inwardly. "Let me grab my bag."

He nodded, staying outside, holding his hat. His gaze darted around town. She could tell he was impatient, maybe a little nervous. About his friend? Or perhaps the outlaws still on the loose?

They and the rustlers made everyone nervous. Annalise didn't travel anywhere these days without her derringer. Though she typically didn't carry it in town, she hadn't taken it out of her skirt pocket after returning from the Triple B.

Soon she followed him down the steps. "I'll drive my buggy and follow you, Mr.—"

"You can just call me Sherman. And that'll be fine."

He strode quickly across to the livery with her and helped her harness the mare to the buggy. A few minutes later, they were on their way. He rode alongside her on a red roan gelding.

As they headed toward Mr. Julius's ranch, she noticed the ranch hand frequently looked around. He was definitely jittery.

Annalise glanced at him. "What happened to your friend?"

"He was gut shot. He's bleedin' a lot."

"Perhaps you should've come for me earlier."

"Yes, ma'am, I think so."

He didn't elaborate and Annalise decided he just wasn't much for talking. "How did your friend come to get shot? Does it have anything to do with the Landis brothers?"

The man looked at her sharply. "Why would you ask that?"

"There was a posse after them until today. They lost track of the gang on the other side of the Eight of Hearts ranch. I thought maybe the hands there might've had a run-in with them."

"As a matter of fact, it does have to do with them."

"I'm sorry." Those outlaws had hurt a lot of people. "I'll do everything I can for your friend."

"Thank you, ma'am."

He fell silent after that. Impatient to tend the wounded man so she could get home and sort out what she wanted to do, Annalise found her thoughts on Matt. He could easily have been hurt just like the man she was planning to tend.

Despite being angry and hurt, she was thankful he hadn't been injured. Fool that she was, she loved him. She had never stopped, but he didn't trust her and she didn't know how to change that. She didn't know if there was any way to change it.

She had taken another chance on him, on letting go of the past, but he couldn't do the same. They obviously couldn't make things between them work.

The realization filled her with a mix of sadness and regret, and that just made her angry all over again. She felt as though she would never stop being mad at him. And now there was the baby to consider. She didn't know whether to laugh or cry.

Even though Matt's visits to town didn't happen with any regularity, Annalise knew she wouldn't be able leave their past behind if she had to live with the threat of seeing him hanging over her head.

She couldn't stay here, not in the same town. And now she felt as though she couldn't go. That made her angry, too.

An hour later, Matt, Russ and Cora had finished changing Pa's bandage and sheets then had returned the man to his bed. As they all stood outside his bedroom, Matt was cussing himself. He would never forget the devastation, the raw stark pain on Annalise's face.

How could he have hurt her again like that? Why had he said those things? Especially when he didn't believe them. How could he have doubted her once more?

He was a fool. He could kick his own butt over this. What if he'd killed everything between them? There was no reason to think he hadn't.

With their father fed and now asleep again, Russ scowled at Matt. "You shouldn't have let her leave. Not like that."

Cora peered around Russ.

Matt looked at both of them. "Did you hear everything?"

"All of us did." His stepmother's mouth flattened disapprovingly. "The window was open."

"Then you know I didn't *let* her go."

"Hmm." Cora crossed her arms, scrutinizing him.

Irritation flickered across Russ's features. "You're an idiot."

"You think I don't know that?" Matt snapped.

Cora's hazel eyes softened the tiniest bit. "You better try to do something about it before it's too late."

"Like what?" A bone-deep fear that he'd gone too far settled inside him. "She hates my guts."

"For starters, get your hind end to Whirlwind."

J.T. cleared his throat, announcing he was awake. "Even if Annalise knew you didn't know about the surgery, she wouldn't have told you."

At his father's words, Matt squeezed past Cora and Russ, moving into the bedroom. The other two followed.

J.T.'s eyes met Matt's. "I asked her not to tell either of you and she gave me her word. If you want to be mad at somebody, put it on me."

Pa didn't deserve his anger either. Only one person did.

"No." He squared his shoulders. "I should put it on me. I know Annalise didn't lie, not then, not now."

"Then why did you accuse her of it?" his brother asked.

Because he'd reacted out of fear and panic. Because he'd been ambushed by the memory of their mother dying of a tumor. Matt glared at Russ. "Seeing Pa like that scared me. It scared you, too."

"True, but—"

"It was like I couldn't stop saying those things." Matt's gut twisted into a vicious knot.

Russ moved closer to the bed. "Why would you ask Annalise to keep the surgery from us, Pa?"

J.T. shifted carefully on his stomach. His eyes were alert and focused. His gaze encompassed both of his sons before he sent a pleading look to Cora.

Holding up her hands, she shook her head. "It was your idea, mister. You can explain."

What did that mean? Matt waited expectantly.

"Russ already feels bad enough about me being in this condition. I thought if I took complete responsibility, he wouldn't blame himself if something went wrong."

Knowing how deep his brother's guilt went, Matt shook his head. "I don't think it would work."

"Well, it's neither here nor there now," J.T. said briskly. "What you should be concerned about is Annalise."

"I apologized. Or tried to. Maybe y'all didn't hear her response, but it wasn't forgiving. She doesn't want anything to do with me. Can't say I blame her."

"It's true you have a lot of making up to do," Cora said.

As if Annalise would ever let him close enough to do it. "She said she'd be back tomorrow."

The other three shook their heads in unison.

"You can't wait," J.T. said adamantly.

Cora nodded. "You've got a choice. And it *is* a choice."

"There. I second what Cora said." Pa looked pleased.

Russ nodded. "Yeah, you better git and git now. Don't let pride stand between you."

"Like you almost did with Lydia?"

"Right."

Matt had never learned exactly what had come between his brother and sister-in-law before they'd gotten together, but he did know Russ had suspected her of keeping something from him.

"It's not pride." He dragged a hand down his face. "I really hurt her. Part of me feels like I should respect her wishes and keep my distance."

"If the two of you are really finished, you'll be keeping plenty of distance."

"I don't know."

"Son, do you want to wonder the rest of your life if you should've apologized once more?"

No, he didn't.

She might be done with him after the way he'd ripped into her, the deep hurt he'd inflicted, but his family was right. He couldn't just let her walk out of his life.

"I'm going after her."

"That's my boy."

Before he left, he squeezed his father's shoulder. "Thanks, Pa."

He hugged his stepmother. "You, too, Cora."

"You're welcome." She smacked him on the butt. "Now, go."

Russ rode to Whirlwind with him. Matt pushed his horse hard and his brother kept pace. As they flew across the prairie, he practiced different ways to apologize, trying to choose the one that would work.

He brought his horse to a skidding halt in front of Annalise's clinic, spraying dirt and pebbles. He jumped down from the saddle onto the porch while his brother went on to his hotel.

Matt tried the door, but it was locked. He knocked. It wouldn't surprise him if she was upstairs, ignoring him. Hurting.

He pounded again on the door, but there was still no answer.

He didn't blame her for not wanting to see him, but he wasn't leaving until he'd had his say. Or begged, crawled or whatever she wanted.

He slipped around to the back and easily picked the lock and let himself in.

"Annalise!" He strode quickly through the hall and upstairs, taking the steps three at a time. "Annalise!"

He didn't really expect her to answer. He had never seen her so angry. But he didn't expect the bedroom to be empty either. Walking across the hall, he checked the parlor. She wasn't there.

He rushed down the stairs and to the examination room. Everything was tidy and in its place—cots, cabinet, medicines. No sign of her.

Where was she? He found himself standing in the hallway outside the kitchen. His gaze scanned the room for signs she'd been there.

The cupboard against this wall was open; a cloth-wrapped bundle sat on the table next to a plate of lemons. He checked the stove. Cold. Maybe she hadn't come here at all. Going out the same way he'd come in, Matt walked across to Davis Lee's house, but in answer to his question, Josie said she hadn't seen the doctor today.

Something nagged at him. He walked around to the front of her clinic. If he had to go into every business, knock on every house door, he would. Matt would never forget the deep, sharp pain in her green eyes. Pain he'd put there.

He started down the street, stopping first at Cal Doyle's law practice next door, then at Haskell's. No one had seen her.

Along with the gut-twisting fear that he had ruined everything, he became increasingly uneasy.

"Baldwin?"

Matt turned from where he stood on the mercantile's porch and saw Quentin in the street.

He walked down to meet the man. "Have you seen Annalise?"

"Yes."

"Good."

"I was coming to talk to her."

The flood of relief Matt felt was blocked with the newspaper man's next words. "She's not at the clinic. Where could she be?"

Quentin frowned. "We ate at the Pearl earlier. Or, rather, we went there to eat. She was hungry, but she didn't order any food."

Only half listening, Matt's gaze moved up and down the street. "Mmm."

"All she wanted was lemonade."

Matt's head jerked toward Quentin. "What did you say?"

"She only wanted lemonade. She must've had a gallon of that stuff."

"Lemonade?" The image of those lemons in her kitchen flashed through his mind.

She said she had craved lemons when—

Matt went completely still inside. For a heartbeat, his mind blanked, then questions rushed in.

Was she *pregnant?* If so, why hadn't she told him about the baby? After the way he'd acted, why would she?

He gave himself a mental shake. He could ask all that later. First, he had to find her. The cemetery maybe? he wondered. If she *was* expecting, maybe she had gone to visit their son's marker.

Barely controlling his impatience, he asked, "Where did she go after y'all went to the Pearl?"

The other man shook his head. "I'm not exactly sure. I was coming to talk to her about my legs. Anyway, I saw her drive out of town with some man. Going west."

Matt stiffened.

"Before you get jealous, I think it was someone who needed help. She went freely. Drove her buggy."

"Did you get a look at this guy?"

"Yeah. He was a scrawny fella. Looked like something was wrong with the left side of his face, but I didn't get a close look. His mount was a red roan." He paused, as though remembering something. "A gelding. He had a patch of jagged scars on his left hindquarters. Like he'd gotten tangled in some barbed wire."

Matt cursed, wanting to put his fist through something.

"What?" Alarm streaked across Quentin's features. "Do you know who that man is? Is Annalise in danger?"

"I'm afraid she may be." Matt pivoted and headed for the jail, telling himself to narrow his focus, concentrate on finding her. He wanted to be wrong about who Annalise had left with.

The chair wheels squeaked as the other man sought to keep up. "Where are you going?"

"To tell Davis Lee and gather some men."

"Damn it, you're forming a posse! Tell me what's going on."

Yes, he needed to. Matt slowed, turned. Before he could get out a word, Quentin slammed a fist down on the arm of his wheelchair. "She's in danger and here I sit in this damn chair. I couldn't have helped her even if I'd known she needed it."

"Not true. You're helping her right now. If you weren't in that chair, you wouldn't have been going to see Annalise and you wouldn't have witnessed what happened."

"Exactly what did happen?" Frustration sharpened his voice. "Who did she leave with?"

The thought of Annalise alone with that man was

enough to make Matt want to kill him, but if she was pregnant and something happened to her and the baby…

He couldn't, wouldn't finish the thought.

"Dammit, Baldwin!"

"Sorry." Matt had been trying to deny it since he'd
heard the description of the horse but there was no denying it now.

He met Quentin's grim gaze with his own. "The man's
description doesn't match any of the Landis brothers on
the wanted poster, but he could've shaved. However, that
horse belongs to one of them."

Annalise tried to keep her thoughts on the cowhand
who needed her attention. Hearing he'd likely been shot
by the Landis brothers had made her think of Matt. And
that brought back all her anger. And hurt. Not to mention
thoughts of the baby.

It took effort, but she managed to put all of that out
of her mind and focus on the man who needed her help.
Sherman had led her around Julius's large sprawling
home to the bunkhouse in the back.

The patient, who looked to be barely twenty years old,
was unconscious when she arrived. He was resting on a
bed, his breathing shallow, his face dangerously pale.

Sherman hovered in the doorway. A few other cow-
hands milled around outside. Frank moaned when she
checked his belly wound.

"Doc?" Sherman asked nervously.

Annalise glanced over her shoulder. "The bullet went
out so I don't need to dig around looking for it."

"That's good, right?"

"Yes, but your friend has lost a lot of blood."

He quickly checked around outside then walked to
the other side of the bed.

"Even if I stitch him up, it might be too late to save him."

The boy in the bed reached for Sherman's hand and made a sound. The red-haired man nodded. "Frank wants you to sew him up."

"All right." The man was so weak she was afraid to give him any anaesthetic. The best thing would be for him to pass out until she finished.

She cleaned the wound with her mixture of water and carbolic acid. After threading a needle, she said to Sherman, "You may need to hold him down."

He grimaced, but sat on the bed, keeping Frank in place when he jerked against the pain. After a long moment, his muscles relaxed and she knew he was out.

She stitched as quickly as she could. A dull ache throbbed at the base of her head. Sweat trickled down her spine. Late-afternoon sunlight slanted in the bunkhouse window, falling across the foot of the rough-hewn wooden bed instead of across the middle where it would help the most.

"When did this happen?" she asked.

"A day or two ago."

"There's no sign of infection." She pulled the needle through flesh. "That's encouraging."

She heard the murmur of voices outside the bunkhouse. As she tied off the thread, she caught Sherman's attention on the door again. Why was he so nervous? He had her itching to look over her shoulder every other minute.

Finished with the stitching, Annalise cleaned the wound again then began to bandage it.

"Sherman." The deep masculine voice coming from the door startled Annalise.

Jumping, she glanced back. The ranch manager, Cosgrove, stood there in his shirtsleeves and dark trousers. Nice garments, not work clothes. His dark-brown eyes traveled over her and she thought she saw a flicker of irritation. At her?

But when he spoke, he was pleasant. "Hello, Dr. Fine."

"Cosgrove." She smiled. "I should be finished here in a minute."

"Very good. I need to talk to Sherman. Could you stay with Frank until he returns?"

"Certainly." Was it her imagination or had his voice turned terse?

Looking defiant, the ranch hand walked out with his boss. A sudden uneasiness crept over Annalise, but she couldn't say why.

She managed to wrap the bandage around Frank's belly and waist, covering both the entrance and exit wounds.

She could hear Cosgrove's deep bass and occasionally the desperation in Sherman's higher-pitched voice. Leaving a small amount of laudanum for the patient when he woke, she dribbled a little bit of carbolic acid solution on a cloth and cleaned her needle then returned everything to her satchel.

She closed the bag, easing down into the chair next to the bed and leaning over to check the patient for fever. None so far. His breathing was shallow, his face too pale for her liking, but she had done all she could do.

There were more voices now, the tones low and urgent. It sounded as though more men had joined Cosgrove and Sherman. What were they discussing? Ranch business probably.

She glanced around the bunkhouse. She supposed it

was clean by a man's standards. No clothes were strewn about. Bedrolls sat neatly atop each bunk, but it still smelled like dirt and unwashed bodies and cattle.

A stove squatted in the middle of the room. A rocking chair sat along one wall as well as a small table with checkers and a checker board. In the far corner, she saw a branding iron with the Eight of Hearts brand—a center eight flanked on each side by an outfacing heart. And in the wall, burned into the wood, she noticed the Triple B brand.

At first, she didn't register what she was seeing. Her gaze went back to the Eight of Hearts branding iron and on the floor beside it was a round piece of metal, hollow in the center like a saddle cinch.

A piece that could be heated and used to trace a freehand pattern in a ranch's registered mark resulting in a new brand. It was what cattlemen called a "running iron".

Annalise's gaze slid from there to the burn in the wall. The brand there was a sloppily imprinted pattern of three B's. Two outward facing B's on each side of a center B. The Triple B brand. Matt's brand. And it had been altered to the Eight of Hearts brand.

This was a lousy effort, but no doubt they'd gotten better with practice.

She drew in a sharp breath. Julius's men were rustling cattle. Did he know? Did his manager, Cosgrove?

As casually as possible, she had to get to her buggy and back to town. Once there, she would tell Davis Lee what she'd found. She remembered the fire she'd seen the night she had treated Edward. At the time, she had wondered if it might belong to the rustlers. Now she was convinced it had.

Her nerves were jumping and impatience drove

through her, but she had to be careful not to let on that she knew anything. Outside, the voices lulled. This might be her chance.

She rose and picked up her satchel on the way to the door. Her palms were slick on the leather handle; she tightened her grip. Five men she didn't recognize from her last visit to the ranch stood in a half circle around Cosgrove. Their gazes crawled over her and she shuddered inwardly. All of her senses screamed danger.

She tried not to act affected in any way. "I left some laudanum for Frank. When he wakes up, he'll need it."

With a wary look at his boss, Sherman moved toward her. "Thanks, Doc."

She forced a smile. "You're welcome. I guess I'd best be going."

Looking put out, the ranch manager's attention shifted to Annalise. "I'm afraid you won't be going anywhere, Doctor."

"Why not?" Though her stomach dropped to her knees, she managed to keep her voice steady. "No one else appears to need my help."

Cosgrove narrowed his eyes at Sherman. "I told you no doctors."

"Yeah, I heard you, but Frank's our brother. I ain't gonna just let him die, especially when he got shot because he was stealing cattle for you."

Stealing cattle? Brothers? Frank and Sherman were brothers as well as some of these other men? "Are you all brothers?"

The taller of the five men stepped toward her. Annalise held her place, noticing a ragged scar across the bottom of his chin. "All of us but Cosgrove."

"There are seven of you in total." They were the rustlers and she knew exactly who these men were.

She hadn't recognized Frank, but now she could see Sherman's resemblance to his picture on the wanted poster. If he hadn't shaved his beard, she would have realized sooner. Still, she asked anyway. "So, just who are you?"

"The Landis brothers," the tall one answered.

The fear she'd felt before sharpened to a razor's edge. And now she wasn't only concerned for herself, but also for the baby. Her mind whirled as things fell into place. Frank had been wounded a day or two ago. That's when the posse from Whirlwind had been chasing them. He had likely been shot by one of those men. Maybe even Matt. And here she was, treating the outlaw.

Matt. She'd been painfully clear that she wanted nothing more to do with him. He wouldn't know she was here. Would anyone? Did anyone even know she was gone?

"And now that you know everyone's identity, you aren't going anywhere." Cosgrove clamped a hard hand on her upper arm.

She tried to pull away. If she could get to Mr. Julius, she might have a chance of escaping these men. "What are you going to do?"

"Not sure yet. I'll have to ask Theo."

Well, so much for Mr. Julius. Feeling panic well up, Annalise battled it back. She had to stay calm if she was going to get herself and her baby out of this. And right now it looked as though she was their only chance.

Chapter Sixteen

Annalise. Matt struggled to stay calm as he told his brother that Quentin had seen Annalise drive off with someone who matched the description of Sherman Landis. In less than five minutes, they had a posse formed with the two of them, Davis Lee and Bram.

As they thundered out of town and west across the prairie on their horses, he refused to let himself think about what might be happening to Annalise. And he absolutely couldn't let himself think about the baby she might be carrying. If he did, he wouldn't be rational and that would endanger her and their child.

He needed to be smart and focused. That was the way to help Annalise, but right now fury and fear rode him hard. He didn't know if he could shut down enough emotion to keep him from going in with guns blazing when they finally found her and Landis.

Maybe Sherman had given her a story about needing a doctor. That seemed the most likely scenario, considering she had appeared to leave willingly with him.

As they rode, they kept an eye out for signs that might point them somewhere specific. They stopped at Riley's ranch and when he heard what had happened, he joined them. They covered Baldwin land without incident.

Yesterday, they had lost track of the Landis brothers on the other side of the Eight of Hearts ranch. Matt wanted to tell its owner what was going on, not only so Julius could keep an eye out for Annalise, but also in case he wanted some of his men to join the posse.

The five of them rode into Julius's yard and up to the front porch of his large two-story home.

The businessman stepped outside, his sharp gaze taking them all in. "Trouble?"

Matt kept his seat. "Earlier, Dr. Fine was seen leaving Whirlwind with a man matching Sherman Landis's description."

Julius straightened. "Is she all right?"

"As far as we know. She appeared to go willingly so we think he may have told her that he or someone else needed a doctor. I don't think she had any idea of his identity."

The other man frowned. "That means the rest of them are probably with him, too."

Matt nodded. "We thought you'd want to know. We plan to ride on, but if you'd like to send some men along, you're welcome to. These bastards stole some of your cattle, too."

"I appreciate that. Let me talk to my men and I'll be right back." The man disappeared into the house.

Matt folded his hands over his saddle horn as he listened to Julius's shiny polished shoes tapping on the hardwood floor.

Bram eased his horse over beside Matt, saying in a

low voice, "Somebody in that upstairs window is trying to get your attention."

He looked up and saw Julius's guest, Edward, whom Annalise had treated for a cracked vertebrae. He lifted a hand in greeting as the boy threw open the window.

The kid leaned out, his gaze darting nervously around the yard. "Mr. Baldwin!"

"Hi, Edward."

The boy gave a nervous glance over his shoulder, then said in a hushed voice, "That man you described to Mr. Julius rode in with Dr. Fine, around to the bunkhouse and they're still there."

Everything inside Matt went still. "Is someone hurt? Do they need a doctor?"

"I'm not sure."

Matt said to Russ, "We should warn Julius before he walks into an ambush."

He started to draw his Peacemaker and fire off a shot then halted at the boy's next words.

"No, sir! Don't. Mr. Julius may not know Dr. Fine is here, but he knows those other men are and so does Cosgrove."

Julius and Cosgrove both knew? Anger rose inside him like a molten seething pulse. He narrowed his eyes at Edward. "Why are you helping us?"

"Dr. Fine probably kept me from being a cripple. I'll do whatever I can for her."

Matt gave a curt nod. "Stay inside until one of us comes to get you."

"I will," he said, and stepped back from the window.

Russ's gaze swept over the big house. "Now what?"

The others moved their horses closer to Matt. "Let's

spread out and surprise them. Move quietly so we can find out first what we're dealing with."

In agreement, everyone dismounted. Matt and Russ started stealthily around one side of the house; Davis Lee, Riley and Bram went to the other.

From his previous trips, Matt recalled the barn was about a hundred yards from the house. A bunkhouse sat on a diagonal between the two buildings. A couple of old cedars shaded the near side of the bunkhouse and provided some cover.

Attached to the opposite side of the barn was a corral. Two wooden horse troughs were set on either side of the single gate.

Matt eased up to the corner of the house and peered around. Julius and Cosgrove stood just outside the bunkhouse, talking to a group of six men. Movement in the doorway caught Matt's eye just as Annalise stepped onto the front stoop.

Pushing aside the black fury that threatened to overtake him, Matt forced himself to take stock of the situation. He counted six Landis brothers, plus Cosgrove and Julius. Beyond those men, he caught sight of Davis Lee, Riley and Bram silently making their way to the back of the barn. They would be able to take cover inside as well as defend themselves.

Once they were in place, Matt started to signal Russ. Before he could, Cosgrove pivoted toward them.

"Guns!" The ranch manager dove inside the bunkhouse.

Annalise gave a startled scream when Julius locked an arm around her neck and dragged her inside after him. Matt had only a brief glimpse of her struggling before Julius slammed the door shut. The Landis brothers were left outside. One of them tried to shove the bunkhouse door open to get to cover, but the door wouldn't budge. The others drew and gunfire erupted.

Knowing Annalise was in danger had a cold sweat trickling down Matt's spine.

Gunshots blasted through the air as he and Russ kept up a steady hail of bullets against the outlaws. Davis Lee, Riley and Bram did the same from the other side. The scent of gunpowder burned the air. Bullets whizzed past, dug into the ground around them.

Matt saw George Landis fall, then Pat. Another man went to his knees, but from this angle Matt couldn't tell who. Two more fell.

Abruptly, the shooting ceased. One lone shot rang out from the barn and Matt eased up to the corner, waving to show the others it was all right to stop.

Six of the Landis brothers lay dead, but this fight wasn't over yet.

Suddenly, the door to the bunkhouse swung open. Julius stood in the doorway with Annalise in front of him like a shield, the barrel of a revolver drilled into her temple. One arm was clamped around her neck, his head right against hers. He held her inside the cage of his body, his legs spread wide enough to position his feet on the outside of hers.

Matt focused on her. There was terror in her pale face, but she was calm. "Are you all right?"

"Yes."

Julius tightened his arm around her throat and she clamped one hand on his arm, rising on her tiptoes in an attempt to escape the pressure.

"Let her go." Matt barely managed to keep his voice from shaking. "You'll never make it out of here alive."

"With her, I will."

Out of the corner of his eyes, Matt saw Davis Lee,

Riley and Bram creep out of the barn toward the bunkhouse. None of them had a clear shot at the bastard. Any bullet would hit Annalise.

The thought made Matt sick to his stomach. He didn't know how to get her out without hurting her.

He saw Bram disappear around the side of the bunkhouse then return, shaking his head. That could only mean that Cosgrove was no longer inside. Matt reasoned that since the bastard hadn't come out the front, there must be a back window or door that he'd sneaked out of. But that didn't give anyone a better shot at Julius.

Frustrated, racking his brain, Matt whipped his gaze back to Annalise. She was staring hard at him.

She looked pointedly down at her free hand. She was trying to tell him something.

What was she thinking? Matt didn't know, but emotion swirled in her eyes, asking him to trust her. He gave a barely perceptible nod and kept talking to Julius.

"So how did this work? You paid the Landis brothers to rustle cattle for you?"

"Sounds like you've got it figured out," the man sneered.

"Well, surely *you've* figured out that your partners are all dead now. You're on your own. Surrounded. Put down your weapon and let her go."

"I'm taking the lady and we're walking out of here."

Over his shoulder, Matt murmured to his brother. "Annalise has something in mind. Be ready for an opening of any kind."

Tension frayed his nerves. He didn't know what she planned and he hated the idea that he couldn't protect her, but right now there was no way to do that safely. If she had an idea, he was all for it.

If anything happened to her—

He swallowed hard, tried to keep Julius's attention on him. "If you put one mark on her, you're a dead man."

Something flickered in Julius's eyes. Matt wanted to think it was fear, but he couldn't tell.

He saw Annalise slowly, slowly ease her hand into her skirt pocket and close around something.

Her gun! He'd forgotten that she had been carrying it since her return.

He realized what she meant to do a split second before she did it. Aiming the gun toward the ground, she pulled the trigger, blowing a hole right through her dress and Julius's foot.

The man screamed. In what appeared to be pure reflex, he dropped his arm from around her neck and shoved her away. Matt sprang from his hiding place and rushed toward them.

Stumbling, Annalise darted toward him. Julius raised his weapon. Matt caught Annalise with one arm, firing at Julius at the same instant.

Several shots rang out in rapid succession. Then silence.

The businessman lay on the ground, his eyes open and glassy. Sharp relief ached in Matt's chest. Unsteady at her close call, he closed both arms around Annalise and buried his face in her neck, tears stinging his eyes.

Her mouth dry, her entire body quivering, Annalise held on tight. She had been so relieved to see Matt that her knees had nearly buckled. No matter how things were between them, she knew Matt would die trying to protect her. So would those other men. It was the code they lived by.

She didn't know what she would've done if they hadn't

shown up, but she would have killed Julius herself before she let him hurt her baby. *The baby. Matt's baby.*

Against her chest, his heart hammered as hard and fast as hers. He smoothed a hand down her hair, murmuring soothing words to her, and she let herself be held a little longer.

In the background, she heard Russ say he and the others had found a wagon. They were going to load the outlaws' bodies into it and drive them back to Whirlwind.

Annalise knew that neither Matt nor any of the other men with him had had a clear shot at Julius. She had sensed Matt's frustration, felt it herself, but she'd had an idea. All she'd needed was for him to trust her. And he had!

She didn't know how much weight to give that.

His brother and the others had loaded the wagon and were ready to go. Riley went inside to get Edward.

It was a long moment before she felt she was steady enough to stand on her own. Still trembling, she pulled back to look up at Matt. His face was pale, his eyes filled with emotion. "How did you know?"

"I didn't. Quentin saw you leave town. The description he gave of the man's horse fitted one of the Landis brothers' mounts. We formed a posse. Just stopped here to warn Julius. Edward clued us in that you were here."

Her pulse skipped at the thought of what might have happened to her if fate hadn't been on her side. "Thank you for saving my life."

"You're welcome." With one rock-hard arm wrapped snugly around her, he stroked her hair back from her face.

She stiffened slightly, but he felt it and lowered his hands to her waist. Pain flared in his eyes, reminding her of how they'd left things between them the last time they were together. Had it only been that afternoon?

Turning, she quietly thanked Russ and the others.

Bram's voice came from inside the bunkhouse. "One of the Landis brothers was gut shot and he's dead in here," the rancher said.

"That's Frank," Annalise explained.

"Bram thought he hit one of them during the brief time we saw them a couple of days ago," Matt said.

She nodded. "He'd lost too much blood by the time Sherman came for me."

"Is that how he got you to go with him? Told you his brother needed a doctor?"

"He didn't say his brother, just a friend." Stepping out of Matt's hold, she moved back. He seemed reluctant to let her go. "He said they were both ranch hands at the Eight of Hearts. When I realized Sherman was part of the Landis gang and Cosgrove was involved with them, he said I couldn't leave because I knew who they were and that they'd been rustling cattle. At first, I thought Mr. Julius wasn't involved, but it became clear he was."

Matt's jaw tightened. "When he grabbed you, it scared the hell out of me."

"Me, too."

A corner of his mouth lifted. "And you took care of him. That was something to see, Angel."

She couldn't be angry at him right this minute—the man had saved her life, after all—but she was still hurting over his earlier accusations.

Which was another reason she still couldn't believe he had trusted her enough to let her take charge for that moment, especially in a situation in which he definitely had more experience than she did. He hadn't even hesitated.

Matt's smile faded. "I guess the thefts he and Cosgrove reported to Davis Lee were lies, just to avert sus-
picion, if there was any. Did Julius admit to rustling the
cattle?"

"No, but Cosgrove and the others already had. Plus I
found a running iron in the bunkhouse. There's a section
of wall where they practiced changing brands, among
them the Triple B's."

"I'm glad to have some proof," he said huskily, his
gaze so soft on her face that she felt herself flush.

"Hey, look here!" Davis Lee appeared in the doorway of the bunkhouse, holding up a pair of shoes with
a cow hoof attached to each sole. "Looks like your and
Annalise's theory about this was right. It couldn't have
been easy to imitate the stride of a cow, but they did it.
They strapped these shoes on over their boots on the
nights they stole the cattle. It's pretty ingenious."

Bram and Russ tied their horses to the back of the
wagon loaded with bodies and started toward Whirlwind.
Davis Lee took the cow-hoof shoes and the running iron,
riding off with Riley.

She and Matt were alone. He studied her face. "I'm
going to drive you back."

He wasn't asking permission, Annalise recognized,
yet he was waiting to see what she said. He probably
expected her to protest, but she didn't.

They needed to talk. She didn't yet know whether she
was going to stay in Whirlwind, but she knew she had
to tell Matt about the baby.

As he helped her into the buggy, he replayed that
image of Julius holding her hostage. Matt had felt as
though his heart might never beat again. He could've

lost her. Remembering his last words to her, he realized he still might.

He offered her his canteen of water. After she drank her fill, he slid it beneath the seat and climbed in beside her.

She kept her attention on the prairie stretched out before them. "You said Quentin told you he'd seen me leave Whirlwind. Did he come to the ranch?"

"No. I was in town."

Her gaze searched his, but she didn't ask the question plain in her eyes.

"I was in town for you. It didn't take me long after you left the ranch to figure out I had to find you and apologize."

An uncertain look crossed her face. "Matt."

"Please, let me." He hoped with all he was that she would listen to him, *believe* him. And change her mind about them. "There's no excuse for those things I said to you earlier."

"I just don't understand why you did. I thought we had started fresh."

"So did I." The lingering hurt in her voice made him want to gather her close, but he didn't. "That's what I wanted."

"You have a funny way of showing it," she said sharply.

He winced. "I know. I was a real bastard."

"But why?"

"Fear, for one thing."

She frowned. "Fear?"

"Coming home and finding Pa like that…. He looked as though he was already dead and it brought back memories of my ma."

"Because she died of a tumor?" Annalise's voice softened with understanding.

For the first time, Matt felt a flare of hope. At least she was still listening. "Partly, but more because when she died, Russ and I promised we would take care of him.

"Coming home to find him in a coma scared me out of my wits. Here he'd had a surgery I knew nothing about, and I felt like I let him down, let them both down."

Annalise sat silently with a thoughtful look on her pretty face. Matt realized he'd stopped the buggy at some point and they were stock-still in the middle of Eight of Hearts land.

Looking at the gunshot hole in her skirt, he lightly fingered the fabric. "I love you, Angel. I've never loved anyone but you and I never will."

Her blue eyes were full of anguish and confusion. "That wasn't enough before."

"It was, but I was too much of a fool to know it."

She frowned.

"Earlier, you asked me to leave you be, but I can't. I'm truly sorry for the things I said. I know I busted something we'd only started to put together again. I do trust you. All I want is a chance to prove it."

She studied him for a long moment, the silence scraping across his nerves. "You didn't hesitate when you learned I had an idea about how to get away from Julius. You didn't even blink."

"That's because I knew you wouldn't do anything rash."

"You trusted me even though you didn't know my plan." A soft smile curved her lips. "That told me more right there than a thousand words."

Hope flared. "Does this mean you can forgive me?"

Her green eyes searched his face. Finally, she nodded. "Yes."

"Does this mean you still love me?"

She nodded.

"Are we truly reconciled? For good?"

"Yes."

Emotion tightened his chest. Matt dragged her into his lap and kissed her hard. When he let her up for air, she laid a palm on his chest.

The sober, slightly dazed look on her face had him asking, "What is it?"

"We aren't just talking about us anymore."

"We aren't?" He held his breath. Was she truly pregnant, as he'd suspected when he spotted the lemons in the kitchen?

Taking his hand in hers, she laid both on her stomach. Matt felt tears prick the backs of his eyes.

"We're going to have a baby."

Overwhelmed with joy and fear and gratitude at this second chance, he couldn't speak. He closed his eyes then opened them to find her looking uncertain.

He kissed the end of her nose, unable to keep from smiling.

She drew back to look at him. "You knew," she said in disbelief.

He laughed. "Not for sure. I found lemons in your kitchen and Quentin told me you had only lemonade at the Pearl today."

"Just hours ago, you would've accused me of keeping it from you."

"And I would've been wrong."

"Did you really believe I would tell you?"

"Yes, I did."

"You didn't doubt it once?"

He rubbed his hand across her stomach, feeling the stiff shell of her corset. "When I first realized you might be expecting, I wondered if you had kept the news from me because I was such a jackass earlier."

"That wasn't why."

He grinned. "It was because you didn't know yet."

"That's right. Why were you so sure I'd tell you?"

Lifting her chin, he leveled his gaze into hers. "Because I believe you've never knowingly held anything back from me. Took me a while to figure that out, huh?"

Tears filled her eyes. "I love you."

"I love you, too, Angel. This has been a long time coming." He brushed his lips against her temple. "Whatever happens from now on, I'll be there and you can trust that."

She framed his face in her hands, saying softly, "I do."

Epilogue

Later that evening after washing up, Matt and Annalise stood in the Whirlwind cemetery with their arms around each other. A light breeze drifted around them as the sun set. They stared down at the new grave marker for their son.

Matt reached out and traced the carving in the sandstone memorial. "Hardy Fine Baldwin," he read, his voice gruff. "When did you do this?"

"About a week ago, just after you and I discussed it."

"Do you know how much this means to me?"

"I think so."

Squeezing her waist, he brushed a kiss against her temple. "Thank you."

"You're welcome." She laid her head on his shoulder.

He was getting another chance with her. She was giving him another chance. Matt wasn't going to botch this one. He could've lost her permanently during that shoot-out. He had no intention of wasting any more time.

Reaching over, he laid a hand on her stomach. "I want this baby to have my name. I want *you* to have my name."

She searched his face. He hoped she could see his commitment.

"We'll make it this time, Angel. Whatever happens, we'll face it together. I never want to be without you again." She had to believe him.

A slow smile curved her lips, her green eyes shining up at him. "I feel the same way."

"So...you'll marry me?" He was even more nervous than he'd been the first time he asked her.

She hesitated.

"What is it?"

"Where will we live?"

"We'll work it out."

"You'll need to be at the ranch."

"We can build you a clinic halfway between the Triple B and Whirlwind."

Pleasure warmed her face. "You've given this a lot of thought."

"I'm really hoping you'll say yes."

"Yes," she whispered.

After a long kiss, he murmured against her lips, "What do you think about having four kids?"

"You really have been thinking about this!"

"So? What do you think?"

"Four?" She wrinkled her nose. "That's an awful lot of lemons."

"And I'll be here for every one of them." He pulled her close. "I'll be here, Angel. Always."

She cupped his cheek and said the most important words she'd ever said to him, "I know."

* * * * *

COMING NEXT MONTH FROM

HARLEQUIN®
HISTORICAL

Available January 25, 2011.

- **LADY LAVENDER**
  by **Lynna Banning**
  (Western)

- **SOCIETY'S MOST DISREPUTABLE GENTLEMAN**
  by **Julia Justiss**
  (Regency)

- **MARRIED: THE VIRGIN WIDOW**
  by **Deborah Hale**
  (Regency)
  Gentlemen of Fortune

- **A THOROUGHLY COMPROMISED LADY**
  by **Bronwyn Scott**
  (Regency)

REQUEST YOUR FREE BOOKS!

HARLEQUIN® HISTORICAL:
Where love is timeless

2 FREE NOVELS PLUS 2 FREE GIFTS!

YES! Please send me 2 FREE Harlequin® Historical novels and my 2 FREE gifts (gifts are worth about $10). After receiving them, if I don't wish to receive any more books, I can return the shipping statement marked "cancel." If I don't cancel, I will receive 6 brand-new novels every month and be billed just $4.94 per book in the U.S. or $5.49 per book in Canada. That's a saving of 20% off the cover price! It's quite a bargain! Shipping and handling is just 50¢ per book.* I understand that accepting the 2 free books and gifts places me under no obligation to buy anything. I can always return a shipment and cancel at any time. Even if I never buy another book from Harlequin, the two free books and gifts are mine to keep forever.

246/349 HDN E5L4

Name _____ (PLEASE PRINT)

Address _____ Apt. #

City _____ State/Prov. _____ Zip/Postal Code

Signature (if under 18, a parent or guardian must sign)

Mail to the **Harlequin Reader Service:**
IN U.S.A.: P.O. Box 1867, Buffalo, NY 14240-1867
IN CANADA: P.O. Box 609, Fort Erie, Ontario L2A 5X3
Not valid for current subscribers to Harlequin Historical books.

Want to try two free books from another line?
Call 1-800-873-8635 or visit www.morefreebooks.com.

* Terms and prices subject to change without notice. Prices do not include applicable taxes. N.Y. residents add applicable sales tax. Canadian residents will be charged applicable provincial taxes and GST. Offer not valid in Quebec. This offer is limited to one order per household. All orders subject to approval. Credit or debit balances in a customer's account(s) may be offset by any other outstanding balance owed by or to the customer. Please allow 4 to 6 weeks for delivery. Offer available while quantities last.

Your Privacy: Harlequin Books is committed to protecting your privacy. Our Privacy Policy is available online at www.eHarlequin.com or upon request from the Reader Service. From time to time we make our lists of customers available to reputable third parties who may have a product or service of interest to you. If you would prefer we not share your name and address, please check here. ☐

Help us get it right—We strive for accurate, respectful and relevant communications. To clarify or modify your communication preferences, visit us at www.ReaderService.com/consumerschoice.

HH10R

*Harlequin Romance author Donna Alward is loved
for her gorgeous rancher heroes.*

*Meet Wyatt as he's confronted by both a precious
little pink bundle left on his doorstep and his neighbor Elli
who's going to show him the ropes....*

Introducing
PROUD RANCHER, PRECIOUS BUNDLE

THE SQUAWKING QUIETED as Elli picked the baby up, and
Wyatt turned around, trying hard to ignore the feelings of
inadequacy as Darcy immediately stopped fussing.

"Maybe she's uncomfortable. What do you think, sweet-
heart?" Elli turned her conversation to the baby.

"What do you think is wrong?" Wyatt asked, putting the
coffee pot back on the burner.

A strange look passed over Elli's face, one that looked
like guilt and panic. But it was gone quickly. "I couldn't
say," she replied.

"But you were so good with her this afternoon." Wyatt
put his hands on his hips.

"Lucky, that's all. I just…remembered a few things."
The same strange look flitted over her features once more.

Wyatt took the coffee to the table. "You fooled me. You
looked like you knew exactly what you were doing." So
much so that Wyatt had felt completely inept. A feeling he
despised. He was used to being the one in control.

Elli and Darcy walked the length of the kitchen and
back. After a few moments, she admitted, "I haven't really
cared for a baby before. The things I thought of were simply
things I'd heard about. Not from experience, Mr. Black."

Her chin jutted up, closing the subject but making him

want to ask the questions now pulsing through his mind. But then he remembered the old saying—*Don't look a gift horse in the mouth.* He'd benefit from whatever insight she had and be glad of it.

"I don't really know what babies need," he said. "I fed her, patted her back like you did, walked her to sleep, but every time I put her down…"

Wyatt almost groaned. Of course. He'd forgotten one important thing. He'd been so focused on getting the formula the right temperature that he'd forgotten to check her diaper. Not that he had any clue what to do there either.

Pulling calves and shoveling out stalls was far less intimidating than one tiny newborn.

"She's probably due for a diaper change, isn't she." He tried to sound nonchalant. This was a perfect opportunity. Elli must know how to change a diaper. He could simply watch her so he'd know better for the next time.

Instead, Elli came around the corner of the counter and placed Darcy back in his arms. "Here you go, Uncle Wyatt," she said lightly. "You get diaper duty. I'll fix the coffee. Cream and sugar?"

Oh boy, Wyatt thought, looking down into Darcy's pursed face, his smug plan blown to smithereens. He was in for it now.

Will sparks fly between Elli and Wyatt?

Find out in
PROUD RANCHER, PRECIOUS BUNDLE
Available February 2011 from Harlequin Romance

Try these Healthy and Delicious Spring Rolls!

INGREDIENTS

2 packages rice-paper
spring roll wrappers
(20 wrappers)

1 cup grated carrot

¼ cup bean sprouts

1 cucumber, julienned

1 red bell pepper, without
stem and seeds, julienned

4 green onions
finely chopped—
use only the green part

DIRECTIONS

1. Soak one rice-paper wrapper
   in a large bowl of hot water
   until softened.

2. Place a pinch each of carrots,
   sprouts, cucumber, bell
   pepper and green onion on the
   wrapper toward the bottom
   third of the rice paper.

3. Fold ends in and roll tightly
   to enclose filling.

4. Repeat with remaining
   wrappers. Chill before
   serving.

Find this and many more delectable recipes
including the perfect dipping sauce in

HARLEQUIN *Presents*

USA TODAY bestselling author

Sharon Kendrick

introduces

HIS MAJESTY'S CHILD

The king's baby of shame!

King Casimiro harbors a secret—no one in the kingdom
of Zaffirinthos knows that a devastating accident has left
his memory clouded in darkness. And Casimiro himself
cannot answer why Melissa Maguire, an enigmatic English
rose, stirs such feelings in him…. Questioning his ability
to rule, Casimiro decides he will renounce the throne.
But Melissa has news she knows will rock the palace
to its core—*Casimiro has an heir!*

Law dictates Casimiro cannot abdicate, so he must find a
way to reacquaint himself with Melissa—his new queen!

Available from Harlequin Presents
February 2011

www.eHarlequin.com

HP12972